354440

PB-SL

Slater,

Liar

"Most definitely one of the best psychological thrillers I have ever read."
—*USA Today* bestselling author Angela Marsons

"Wow!! Simply wow!! Each chapter hooked me further... Unputdownable till the end."
—BookReviewsByShalini.com

"From the moment I picked up *Liar*, I was sold."
—BeckieBookworm.com

"Menacing, intense and eerie!"
—WhatsBetterThanBooks.com

"Brilliantly gripping and unputdownably fascinating!"
—ChocolatenWaffles.com

"A gripping page turner...highly recommended for fans of psychological thrillers."
—CompulsiveReaders.com

"A compulsive read...Slater really has a knack for developing wholly unlikable characters that are utterly fascinating...She also does a terrific job at bringing a heavy sense of unease and dread the entire time as she takes the reader down dark paths full of surprises."
—NovelGossip.com

"Deliciously creepy!"
—TheAyalas.com

"Completely blew my mind. This 'shocking twist' definitely lived up to its standards."
—Fuzzable.com

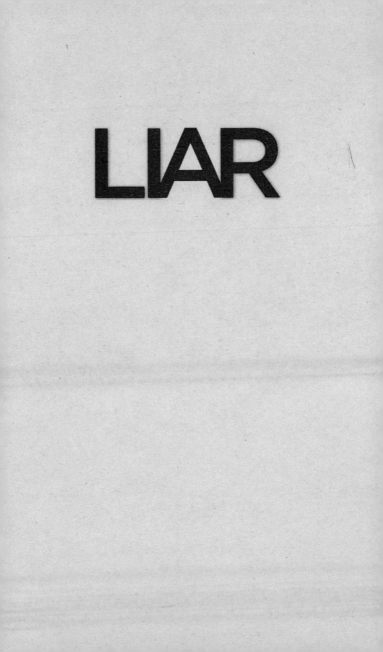

LIAR

ALSO BY K.L. Slater

Safe With Me
Blink

LIAR

K.L. SLATER

Thompson Nicola Regional Library
300 - 465 VICTORIA STREET
KAMLOOPS, BC V2C 2A9

GRAND CENTRAL
PUBLISHING

NEW YORK   BOSTON

This book is a work of fiction. Names, characters, places, and incidents are the product of the author's imagination or are used fictitiously. Any resemblance to actual events, locales, or persons, living or dead, is coincidental.

Copyright © 2017 by K.L. Slater
Excerpt from *Blink* copyright © 2017 by K.L. Slater

Cover photo: Erika Ray / Offset
Cover design by Henry Steadman
Cover copyright © 2019 by Hachette Book Group, Inc.

Hachette Book Group supports the right to free expression and the value of copyright. The purpose of copyright is to encourage writers and artists to produce the creative works that enrich our culture.

The scanning, uploading, and distribution of this book without permission is a theft of the author's intellectual property. If you would like permission to use material from the book (other than for review purposes), please contact permissions@hbgusa.com. Thank you for your support of the author's rights.

Grand Central Publishing
Hachette Book Group
1290 Avenue of the Americas, New York, NY 10104
grandcentralpublishing.com
twitter.com/grandcentralpub

Originally published by Bookouture, an imprint of StoryFire Ltd., 23 Sussex Road, Ickenham, UB10 8PN, United Kingdom.
First Grand Central Publishing mass market edition: July 2019

Grand Central Publishing is a division of Hachette Book Group, Inc. The Grand Central Publishing name and logo is a trademark of Hachette Book Group, Inc.

The publisher is not responsible for websites (or their content) that are not owned by the publisher.

The Hachette Speakers Bureau provides a wide range of authors for speaking events. To find out more, go to www.hachettespeakersbureau.com or call (866) 376-6591.

ISBN: 978-1-5387-4783-4 (mass market)

Printed in the United States of America.

OPM

10 9 8 7 6 5 4 3 2 1

ATTENTION CORPORATIONS AND ORGANIZATIONS:
Most HACHETTE BOOK GROUP books are available
at quantity discounts with bulk purchase for educational,
business, or sales promotional use. For information,
please call or write:

Special Markets Department, Hachette Book Group
1290 Avenue of the Americas, New York, NY 10104
Telephone: 1-800-222-6747 Fax: 1-800-477-5925

3 5444 00415824 1

To my husband, Mac
Thank you for everything...
I couldn't do it without you x

THE END

She stands very still, holding the knife. Her fingers press into the moist, sticky mess that covers the handle and thins to a trickle down her wrist.

The house is quiet and still, as if it's holding its breath. She can hear the ticking of the wall clock and a low rumble now and then as a large vehicle passes by on the road outside.

She stares down at the woman crumpled on the floor before her. They have despised each other for so long, and toward the end there have been times she simply could not bear to look at her. Now, she cannot tear her eyes away. She is transfixed by the blossoming ruby-red halo that seeps from the dying woman's head.

It couldn't continue, this silent war between them. In the end, one of them had to go.

She feels calm inside now, calmer than she has felt for a long, long time. How she has hated this woman. Hated her for so long, and yet now . . . she feels nothing.

The woman's eyes are closed, but there is slight movement in her chest. Every few seconds there is a quick, desperate pulsing underneath the thin fabric of her soaked red breast. A blouse that used to be pure white.

Who killed Cock Robin?
I, said the Sparrow,
With my bow and arrow.
I killed Cock Robin.

She whispers the words of the nursery rhyme and smiles as she remembers how it was one of her own favorites as a child. The boys have a book at home with the rhyme in it, and sometimes she reads it to little Josh.

The boys.

How happy they'll be that finally they are hers alone.

The one thing she has always been certain of is that the boys will be hers.

And the most beautiful thing of all is that now, nobody can ever take them away from her again.

THE BEGINNING

CHAPTER ONE

Present day

Amber

The job and the flat had been sorted for a while, and finally the story of her past was in place. She had rehearsed it all in her head until it had felt real.

The waiting had been hellish, but she knew it was essential that any loose ends were eradicated. That had been completely necessary to ensure the success of this, the final, glorious stage.

The last three years had been tortuous and long. She'd felt so impotent and hopeless, but that was all behind her now. The jagged pieces would start to slide together, slowly and smoothly, like an exquisite jigsaw.

For a time, Amber had considered engineering a situation where she might bump into Ben Jukes as if by accident, but in the end there had been no need for that. She happened to call in at the newsagent's around the corner from work one morning and there he was. Standing on his own, browsing the newspaper shelf.

Slipping behind him in the queue, she'd self-consciously clutched her own tabloid newspaper and a breakfast bar. He'd smelled of soap and sandalwood, pleasant scents to most people, but she'd felt her stomach twist slightly,

Oblivious to her presence, he had continued to stare out of the window as the queue shuffled forward, his jawline stark and pale in the unforgiving morning light. She took a small step to the side so she could see more of his face, watched how his unfocused eyes betrayed that he was lost in his thoughts. Possibly thoughts about his cold, dead wife. She smiled to herself.

The beeping of the card machine and murmur of customer voices had buzzed around her like irritating insects, yet on another level she began to feel like it was just her and Ben standing there.

"Next, please," the sales assistant barked.

Ben had suddenly snapped out of his trancelike state and stepped forward. She realized he wasn't going to glance her way after all and felt the spark of anticipation fizzle out in her chest like a spent match, but she quickly caught herself.

It was just a blip, that was all. They would be together, of that she was certain. It was fate, after all.

Nothing could stop it happening. She simply wouldn't allow anything to stand in her way.

The day after their initial near-meeting, Amber had set the alarm for six, styled her hair and even taken the time to put on makeup before leaving her poky studio flat.

At her low point, she'd had no interest in grooming or her appearance. So, titivating herself before work had made a change from her usual rushing out of the house in a morning with minutes to spare, complete with bare face and damp hair.

She'd been surprised how much difference a little effort made to her appearance. With a mere corner curl of liquid eyeliner and a brief lick of mascara, her unremarkable dull gray eyes were transformed into a sleek almond shape, almost feline.

Once she'd applied a slick of hair gel and a good dousing of inexpensive hairspray, her greasy blond mop quickly morphed into the chic feathered crop the hairdresser had intended it to be.

Food was now an inconvenience to Amber. Her appetite had long been poor, marred by the troubled thoughts that seemed to seep into everything she did. She'd learned to deal with it by simply eating something when her stomach growled in protest.

Likewise, over the years she'd gleaned no pleasure from clothes shopping; it all seemed so futile and shallow. Still, when she opened the wardrobe doors, she saw there were still a couple of outfits there that didn't look *too* tatty, so she selected one of those.

It had taken her a long time to get this close to speaking to Ben Jukes, and now that there was a strong chance she would see him again, she knew that planning was key.

The years spent grappling with a fire inside that all but threatened to consume her, the relentless planning and then the seemingly endless wait for her opportunity...she certainly had no intention of messing things up now.

After that first fortuitous sighting of Ben, Amber made certain to arrive at the newsagent's ten minutes earlier than usual each subsequent morning. People tended to develop a habit of dropping into small shops like that, so she knew it was highly unlikely he'd used it just the once and would never return. Besides, she knew it was the closest shop to his workplace.

So she resolved to stick religiously to her new routine. Sure enough, three mornings later, there he was again. And this time, she vowed silently, she would make it count.

She hovered near the biscuits and crisps, and at the last moment picked up a carton of milk from the small refrigerated section near the door. She moved effortlessly to the counter the exact same time as he did. But just before he joined the short queue, she stumbled slightly in front of him, dropping her car keys near his foot.

"Sorry! I'm so sorry," she stammered. "I'm such a clumsy clot."

She bent forward at just the right angle, knowing full well he couldn't avoid catching a glimpse of her smooth, lightly tanned cleavage.

Up she stood again, fumbling with the carton of milk, her purse and keys. She smiled without quite meeting his eyes. Finally, just as she feared he might turn away without acknowledging her, he spoke.

"Always busy in here, isn't it?" He smiled, and she noticed that his teeth were clean and even. "I keep threatening to call in at the Tesco on Palmer Street instead, but that's probably even worse."

"I work just around the corner," Amber explained, pulling herself up to her full height. "So it suits me to come here."

She stood only a couple of inches short of his own six foot one. Close up, she could see his eyes were a hazel shade. She could smell the sandalwood scent again and she tried to keep her breathing shallow.

"Where is it you work, then?" Ben's forehead creased as he made the connection. There wasn't much else around here, aside from the newsagent's and the housing estate. "The school?"

"The children's center," Amber replied. "We're tucked away just behind the school."

"You're a teacher?"

She laughed, shaking her head. "I'm a family support worker."

"Small world." He grinned and offered her his hand. "Ben Jukes. I teach at the school."

"No way!" She widened her eyes in pleasant surprise as she grasped his fingers. She wanted to laugh. "Small world. I'm Amber Carr."

She'd known for months exactly where Ben worked.

She knew the name of the road he lived on and at which local supermarket he did his weekly food shop.

She knew that his mother came over to do his cleaning on Wednesdays and Fridays.

And most importantly, she knew the names of both his sons.

CHAPTER TWO

Judi

Everything is ready.

The pork is in the oven with the foil off now, and a quick satisfying peek confirms that the crackling will be done to perfection. Just how Ben likes it.

The apple crumble, with my own special oaty topping, sits on the side, and I have a big carton of Marks and Spencer's vanilla custard stowed away in the fridge. I find nobody notices a little cheat, so long as it's just here and there. The trick is not to overdo it.

I've always enjoyed cooking; it's one of the few things I genuinely feel good at. In recent years, I've become engrossed in programs like *Masterchef* and *The Great British Bake Off* and my enthusiasm has grown in direct relation to my family's love of eating my food. My Sunday lunches have become quite the family tradition.

I glance at the clock. Half an hour and my boys will all be here.

The back door opens and Henry's grinning face appears. "Something smells good."

He shuffles into the kitchen, his old leather boots

shedding ridges of freshly mowed grass on to the newly swept kitchen tiles.

"They'll be here in about thirty minutes." I turn away, plunging my hands into a sink full of scalding-hot soapy water. "You were going to show the boys some photographs after lunch, remember?"

"Ah yes, so I was," he says. I hear him kicking off his boots in the utility room. "I'll scoot up to the attic right now. Any chance of a cuppa?"

When I pull my fingers out of the water, I see they are chapped and red. The once tight, smooth skin on the backs of my hands is on the turn: a little crêpey and slower to snap back when pinched. I used to be a stickler for wearing rubber gloves and using hand cream. I can't recall when I stopped doing it.

I close my eyes briefly and endure the steaming water, which continues to sting hard. I suck in air and hold it in for a moment or two.

My heart is racing and my knees feel weak for no apparent reason. It keeps happening at the most inconvenient of times. It's OK, I tell myself. It will soon pass.

It's the thought of everything I've still got to do. Lunch. That's all it is, but the slightest thing just lately feels like there's a mountain to scale.

I always long for everything to be just perfect, but it hardly ever is.

Soon the boys will be here and the house will be transformed into a home once more. Noisy, glorious chaos again, just like when Ben and David were young. Long before the bad decisions and the terrible consequences.

Over a period of ten years, when we were first married, Henry worked his way up to the position of branch manager at the big National Westminster Bank in the center of Nottingham. Some might say we had a staid, predictable life back then, but I'd never longed for the glitz and glamour of London that some of his colleagues had chased, or even, for that matter, a career of my own.

I'd been happiest home-making: baking bread and spending school holidays with the boys, growing vegetables down at the allotment or during the summer at our little holiday cottage in Staithes, where Henry would join us at the weekends. We didn't rent it out; it was for our own use only. Our wonderful little bolthole against the world.

Now, I find it difficult to even think about those times.

Henry appears at my side.

"Penny for them?" He presses a little closer to me, as if he can read my thoughts. I push the image of the cottage from my mind.

Snatching my hands out of the water, I flick off the bubbles.

"Just running through what's left to do for lunch." I grab a tea towel and dab at my scarlet hands. Henry takes a step back.

"I just asked if you wanted me to lay the table before I hunt out those old photos."

"No, that's fine, thanks. I'll do it." I reach for my glass of water and take a sip in a bid to relieve my dry mouth. "I've bought the boys some Thomas the Tank Engine napkins."

Henry begins to shuffle out of the kitchen, then hesitates, turns back. "I thought they were into all that superhero business now, Marvel characters and the like?"

"That stuff is too violent. I don't want to encourage it. Pass me a clean tea towel, will you?"

I strain the potatoes, add butter and full-cream milk and begin to mash.

After a few minutes, I hear Henry scrabbling around in the attic above my head, searching for the photographs.

I heard him telling Noah and Josh, earlier in the week,

about the things their dad and Uncle David got up to at the cottage. Silly stories the boys loved, about hunting dinosaurs and finding rare fossils beneath the cliffs.

Stories that made my heart squeeze in on itself until it felt like a shriveled prune hanging there.

"Found them." He returns to the kitchen a few minutes later, holding a bulging carrier bag aloft like a trophy.

The ghost of a smile flits over my lips, but it's the best I can do.

We both start at the sudden growl of a car engine and a skid of gravel on the driveway.

"They're here." Henry hurries into the hall.

"They're early." I glance at the clock as my heart rate picks up again.

The front door bursts open and the welcome sounds of my grandsons' arrival fill the hallway. Walls are clipped by buzzing light sabers and whirring plastic monsters that morph into elaborate vehicles at the touch of a button.

Shoes are left on; I can hear them clomping across the laminate in the hall.

Louise always shepherded the boys into the house in as orderly a manner as she could, but of course, Ben didn't even notice and I loved him for that. It was just over two years since we'd lost Louise, and he was doing a sterling job of bringing up his sons alone.

I replace the saucepan lid, leaving the potatoes half mashed, and wipe my hands on my apron as I walk to the kitchen door to say hello.

I try to catch Ben's eye, but he is busy unlacing his boots.

It crosses my mind that perhaps he's feeling a little unwell. He is usually singing or humming, and sometimes a combination of both. Today he seems unusually quiet.

Right away my breath quickens. I try to remember what

The Complete Book of Women's Health said, the one that's squirreled away at the back of the wardrobe.

Reach for better thoughts.

Relax your shoulders.

Breathe.

I try.

"Dad's bought us the new Transformers Generation Leader," Noah tells me in one long breathless sentence. He pushes an aggressive-looking white and red foot-high plastic robot toward me. "Look, he's got neutron blasters in his arms, Nanny."

"Wonderful." I prod cautiously at the contraption with a forefinger. "I do hope he likes my cooking; he looks as though he could get quite cross."

Ben finally looks up from unlacing his boots and winks at me.

"Transformers don't *eat*, Nanny." Josh hoots with laughter. "They're *missile robots*."

"Of course they are." I offer my cheek to Ben. "How silly of me."

I grab Josh when he tries to run past and bury my face in his apple-scented hair. Ben has obviously started using the shampoo I bought for them last week, and although I know it's silly, I feel inordinately pleased.

Josh struggles, eager to join his brother in the lounge, and reluctantly I let him go.

I return to the kitchen to finish up the lunch, my step a little lighter, my heart full.

My boys are home.

CHAPTER THREE

Judi

I'm sure that if it could, the big old oak dining table would groan slightly under the weight of the china tureens that brim with roast potatoes, mash, vegetables—including everyone's favorite honeyed parsnips—and a platter of thickly carved slices of roast pork.

The early March sunlight shines weakly through the window behind Ben, lighting up his hair like a halo. Noah and Josh tuck into the food with gusto. I feel my shoulders drop a little and I take the tiniest sip from the small glass of white wine Henry has poured me.

Seeing this table full and the house buzzing with the people I love the most fills my heart up too.

"We love Nanny's dinners, don't we, boys?" Ben watches his sons, eyes crinkling with pride as he turns to me. "We look forward to your Sunday lunch all week, do you know that, Mum?"

"The meat's cooked perfectly again, Jude, well done," Henry remarks.

My cheeks flush with pure pleasure as I reach over for the gravy boat, pouring the rich brown oniony goodness over

Josh's meat and potatoes. Feeding my family feels like the purest kind of love.

I beam at my son. "Our little family, all together like this, it makes me so happy."

"It's what life is all about," Henry adds.

Louise's death hit us all very badly. Two years ago, when Noah was six and Josh just three, she was diagnosed with leukemia. Louise and Ben broke the news to me and Henry during our Sunday walk in Wollaton Park as the boys ran ahead and we paused to admire the new life: tight green buds, snowdrops and crocuses, springing up all around us like scattered confetti.

She died in October of the same year. All very quick and heartbreakingly painful.

All we could do was pull closer together, support each other and keep life as normal as we could for Noah and Josh. Ben turned to us, his parents. He let us into their lives, allowed us to help and support him.

I immediately reduced my hours at the doctor's surgery, and Henry took early retirement and knocked his overnight fishing trips on the head, at least for a while.

Our grandsons became our number one priority. I usually picked them up from school each day and gave them tea at Ben's house in Colwick, staying with them until he got home from his job as a science teacher at Colwick Park Academy.

Far from draining me of energy, I felt years younger.

The gray, endless mornings and drab, eventless evenings were suddenly filled with things to do. I cleaned Ben's house a couple of times a week and did their laundry. It was a labor of love, and Henry had learned a long time ago to keep his mild disapproval to himself.

I've been trying to convince Ben to move closer to us for some time. Lady Bay, not far from our house in West

Bridgford, is a more desirable area and the schools there are preferable for the boys.

Up to now he has seemed reluctant, but with the neat new estate just five minutes' walk away from our house nearing completion, it really is the perfect time for them to up sticks.

A few months ago saw the second anniversary of Louise's death. We decided to mark it with a visit to our local church and a celebration dinner back at ours, dedicated to Louise's life. Ben made a touching collage of photographs and we talked to the boys about Louise and how much their mummy had loved them.

It was difficult but apt. Very apt, I thought.

I catch Henry looking expectantly at me and I shake my head surreptitiously. It would be just like him to blab out our surprise before time, and I want to wait until after lunch, so there are no distractions and we can enjoy the full reaction of Ben and the boys.

After the last scrap of homemade apple crumble and vanilla custard has been wolfed down by my ever-hungry grandsons, Henry helps me clear the table while Ben plays with Noah and Josh and their new robot contraptions in the living room.

"I'll take the photos through in a moment, shall I?" Henry whispers as he scrapes the plates.

"Yes." I nod eagerly. "I can't wait to see their faces."

I carry through a tray of coffee and Henry follows with the photographs. Within minutes, precious images of Ben and his older brother, David, are scattered all around the floor. I move away and stand near the door.

"Gosh, I remember this day," Ben exclaims, picking up a print of him and his brother. He turns it slightly so the boys can see. "Two minutes after Grandad took this photo, your uncle David wouldn't let me have a turn with his new cricket

bat, so I took it off him and cracked him on the shins with it."
He pulls an exaggerated sad face at his sons. "My backside
was stinging for hours after your grandad spanked me."

Noah and Josh collapse in fits of laughter.

"You can't say you didn't deserve it, though," Henry
chuckles. "Shame parents aren't allowed to discipline their
kids anymore. The odd slap never did you and your brother
any harm."

"Why did Uncle David die, Daddy?" Josh asks, his clear
voice cutting through the dense air like a scalpel.

Old enough now to understand the taboo subject, Noah
frowns and administers a sharp nudge to his younger
brother. Ben clears his throat.

"He had an accident, Josh." He glances at me. "But we
don't want to think about such sad things right now."

The absence of David fills the room like an impenetrable
fog for a second or two.

"We never get smacked, Grandad," Noah says solemnly,
breaking the spell. "Because we're never naughty."

Ben pretends to choke on his coffee. "What about last
week, when you didn't put newspaper down despite being
told to a thousand times, and got paint splatters all over your
bedroom carpet?"

"It was an *art* accident," Noah protests, a wounded
expression settling over his face.

The next day, when the boys were at school and Ben was
at work, it had taken me three goes with the Vanish stain
remover before the marks came out.

"Oh yes, and when Noah swung on the wardrobe door
dressed in his Batman outfit." Ben tries to look stern and fails.
"Busted all the hinges, he did. Was that an accident too?"

The boys see through his attempt to show a strict
demeanor and grin at each other.

"Enough talk of naughtiness, I think." I smile meaningfully at Henry. "There's a reason we wanted to remind you of the lovely times we had on holiday when your daddy and uncle were young."

Ben frowns.

"I traced the new owners of our old holiday cottage," Henry says. "Turns out they're renting it selectively to friends and family. So I asked them if it was available..."

"*Our* cottage?" I say faintly. "We've discussed renting somewhere, but I didn't know you were thinking of—"

"Yes, our cottage, the very same. And I'm going to rent it for two weeks in the summer," Henry blurts out, obviously unable to wait a moment longer. "We're all going on holiday together. Our treat!"

Noah and Josh begin jumping up and down on the spot, repeatedly chanting: "We're. Going. On. Holiday!"

Henry laughs and hastily snatches the photographs out from under their trampling feet as they chase each other from the room.

But Ben...Ben doesn't say a word.

"You and the boys haven't had a holiday since...well, for three years," I say lightly, pushing thoughts of the cottage away. "We thought this would be the ideal break for you all."

It was neither the time nor the place to take issue with Henry's unexpected plans. But later, I had every intention of doing so.

"I...It's really kind of you, Mum, Dad," Ben stammers, a maroon flush blooming on both cheeks. "I'm grateful to you both. It's just that..."

"It's just that what?" Henry interjects, taking in my expression. "Don't tell me you've got something else on, Ben. You never go *anywhere*."

"That might be changing," Ben says, his cheeks on fire

now. "I was going to tell you when I first got here, but I wanted to wait for the right moment. I mean, it's nothing massively serious yet, but..."

"Spit it out then, man." Henry rolls his eyes.

"It happened a couple of months ago. Entirely unexpected, but these things often are, I suppose." He takes a breath. "It's just that I... well, I've met someone."

"Met someone?" I hear myself echo.

"Yes, Mum." Ben reaches for my hand. "I've met someone special. Her name is Amber."

CHAPTER FOUR

Amber

When Ben had been served at the counter, he turned and smiled at Amber as he walked past her to the door of the newsagent.

She fought the urge to watch him go, stepped forward to the counter to pay for the milk she didn't want.

"Can I get this, please?" The idiot sales assistant was faffing around under the counter. Meanwhile, Amber watched as Ben walked past the shop window, away down the street. He was getting farther away from her again.

"Be there in a sec, love," the assistant mumbled. "Dropped my blooming pen down here somewhere."

"Oh, just forget it." Amber slammed the milk down on the counter. The carton split and a pool of thick white liquid began to seep out. She turned and stalked toward the door, ignoring the disapproving gawps of the customers who were standing right behind her.

"Hey!" she heard the miffed assistant call out. "You'll need to pay for this."

She didn't turn back and she didn't answer. Her head filled with the dismal fog that drifted in now and again and made everything around her sound far away.

But as soon as she stepped outside, the dark clouds lifted. He was waiting for her a little way down the street. As she drew closer, she slowed her pace right down and pretended to search in her handbag for something.

Out of the corner of her eye, she saw him approach.

"Amber. That's a really nice name." His shoulders were broad, his arms powerful, but his cheeks were schoolboy red. "I don't suppose you'd...I..."

She waited. Watched him squirm.

"What I mean is, would you like to maybe go for a coffee or something?" He tapped his rolled-up newspaper against his thigh. "I mean, if you're not in a relationship or anything. I don't want to..."

"I'm not," Amber said. "And thanks, I'd love to go for a coffee with you."

"Oh!" For a split second, he looked astonished. "Thanks. I mean, that's great. Really great."

Despite four o'clock being far earlier than most people finished work, Amber was dismayed to find there were hardly any free tables in the café they'd agreed on.

She'd arrived a little early to grab a table, but the entire place was stuffed to the brim with young mothers, sniveling tots in their designer pushchairs and a few leery teenagers who barely looked up from their mobile phones even when talking to each other.

She scanned the place and spotted a small round table at the back that was free. She headed straight over and saw that it was sandwiched between the wall and a businessman sitting in front of an open laptop and talking animatedly on his phone.

She grabbed an abandoned tray, propped up against the wall, and stacked it with the empty coffee cups and cake wrappers that were scattered across the table. She didn't want to lose the table, so she left the tray there and sat on the bench seat facing the door. Glancing at her watch, she saw there were still five minutes to go until their designated meeting time.

Her hands felt clammy and she could feel her heart rate was up a little, but overall she felt good. It was early days, but everything seemed to be dropping into place just as she'd planned.

The businessman, still on his call, let out a ridiculously loud, theatrical laugh.

"Are you serious? That's just not going to cut it, mate, it's a week after the date we agreed. Yeah, I get that, but the answer is still no. Got it?"

Out of the corner of her eye, Amber saw him glance at her, as if he were trying to gauge whether she was impressed by his managerial confidence.

She ignored him and stared ahead. Directly in front of her sat a table full of yummy mummies with their waist-length hair extensions and slug-like brows. Their designer-dressed toddlers pulled and pinched at them until the women finally stopped whatever nonsense they were chirping on about and remembered they had kids, handing them a biscuit or a beaker of frothy babyccino before turning away again.

Amber felt sure that Ben wouldn't find this set of airheads remotely attractive, but all the same, she was relieved she'd bothered to make a bit of an effort with her appearance. She ran her fingers through tufty hair and pressed her lips together so that the pink lip gloss remained evenly distributed.

The businessman stood up and grinned down at her. "Mind watching my stuff for a sec, love? Just while I get another coffee."

His jacket was shiny at the elbows and the fabric had a nasty, cheap sheen to it.

"Look after your own stuff," she said. "You tosser."

"Hey, what did you just say?"

The yummy mummies looked up at the sound of a raised voice, their thick black eyelashes batting furiously like speared spiders.

"Don't cause a scene," Amber said quietly. "Or I'll tell the management you're harassing me."

"Huh?" he huffed, looking wildly around with his palms up, trying to gather support from other customers. But in the hubbub of the coffee shop, nobody had heard Amber's threat. "What're you talking about, you crazy bitch?"

Amber looked down at her hands and began twisting her fingers.

"Are you OK?" A staff member looked up from wiping a nearby table and called over to her.

"Is *she* OK? What about me?" the businessman retorted.

Amber kept her poker face but wanted to smile. People were so gullible; it wasn't difficult, as an attractive woman, to manipulate a situation to suit your own ends.

The coffee shop door opened and Ben appeared, looking around, trying to spot her.

She raised a shaky hand and he smiled and began walking across.

"Is he your boyfriend?" The businessman began snatching up his things, zipping his laptop into its padded case.

Ben arrived at the table.

"Good luck to you, mate, that's all I can say." With a prolonged glare at her, the man stomped out of the shop.

"What's wrong?" Ben frowned after him. "Are you OK?"

"I'm fine," Amber said quietly.

"Everything all right?" the staff member asked as he picked up the loaded tray of dirty cups from her table.

"Yes. Thank you for stepping in." She gave him a little smile.

"No problem," he replied and turned away.

"I'll get our coffees in a moment." Ben sat down beside her and touched her lightly on the arm. "Did you have some kind of argument with that man?"

Amber looked up to find the other customers had thankfully already lost interest.

"He asked me out on a date," she said. "Just like that, out of the blue. And when I said no, he started kicking off, calling me a bitch. It was ... awful."

"Blimey." Ben's eyes widened and he shook his head. "The cheeky git. Some blokes, honestly."

"It happens a lot." Amber shrugged. "Some men seem to think that when a woman is alone, she's easy pickings. And I ... well, I've been on my own for a while now."

She saw him take in the fact that there was no one else on the scene. His expression softened.

"Well, you're not on your own now," he said manfully, standing up. "What's it to be, latte or cappuccino?"

"Thank you, Ben," she said, flushing a little. "I'll have a skinny latte, please."

She watched him walk to the counter, a sudden swell of warmth filling her chest. She felt calm and in control, as if she'd just made an important first move in a game of chess.

This was a game she was going to enjoy. She would play it perfectly and she would win.

There was no doubt at all in her mind about that.

CHAPTER FIVE

Judi

More than anything in the world, I want Ben to be happy. So I'm disappointed when a familiar dull thud begins in my temples, heralding one of my headaches, as Henry always refers to them in a disapproving tone.

"Someone special?" I make a real effort to keep my voice light, and even manage to smile at Ben. "Well, you've kept that quiet."

Of course, I've always known that Ben would meet someone eventually. But this soon...and so out of the blue? I confess I didn't see it coming.

"I just wanted to be sure, Mum." He shrugs and smiles, and as he turns to look at his father, he looks just like David. "Before I said anything to you both, I mean. We've been seeing each other for a couple of months now."

"A couple of months! He's a dark horse, isn't he, Jude?" Henry chips in.

I take a breath. "Ben, it's barely been two years since Louise passed away. Don't you think...?"

"It's well over two years, and that's a long time, Mum." He presses his lips together. "To be honest, I knew Amber was special the moment I met her, but I've waited to make sure of my feelings."

"He's old enough to know what he's doing, love," Henry says, beaming at Ben.

"And you're *this* sure, after just a month or two?" I try to pretend I'm feeling light-hearted about it, but the way Ben's looking at me, I'm not sure I've managed to pull it off.

"Like Dad says, I'm not sixteen anymore, Mum," he sighs. "I know my own mind."

"Of course you do." I reach for his hand. "And I'm pleased for you. Have the boys met...Amber yet?"

"A couple of times," he says with a nod. "We've just told them she's Daddy's friend from work. For the time being."

Noah and Josh's innocent faces spring into my mind and I bite back tears. I'm being ridiculous; I don't know what's wrong with me.

"Are you OK, Mum?"

"Of course I am!" I feign an over-the-top smile. "If you've met someone deserving of you, then that's wonderful news."

"Nobody is *ever* going to be deserving of you, son." Henry winks at him. "You do know that?"

"Louise was," I say tightly, standing up. "Louise was perfect."

The strange sensation starts deep in my solar plexus.

I know I haven't got much time, so I pull on my cardigan and step out of the kitchen doors into the garden. I shiver in the cool air, but it feels good. The sun was deceptive; it is cold enough for a coat. Not that I'll be needing one in a second or two.

I breathe in a chilly lungful of crisp air, but it does nothing to dissipate the wave of heat that is now flooding my lower abdomen and rapidly rising into my chest, neck and head.

In the beginning, the hot flushes were confined just to the nighttime. It was fairly easy to creep from the bed without disturbing Henry, who has always been a deep sleeper, and spread a couple of towels on the soaked sheet. I then changed the bed in the morning once he'd gone out into the garden. He was a man of routine and I could rely on it.

I didn't want him to see the evidence that my body was changing. I was late starting, compared to the average age of fifty-one, I'd already started to feel it was like waiting to be shot and now I was having trouble coming to terms with the dreaded "M" word myself, without suffering the indignity of my husband seeing the awful signs.

Henry has always been a bit squeamish about women's problems, as he labels anything remotely connected to the female reproductive system. The thought of his wife negotiating the menopause would probably take him over the edge.

But this last month or so, the flushes have graduated from nighttime only and made an appearance unexpectedly at the surgery, and sometimes at home during the day. And it's happening again, right this minute.

It isn't something I can hide by fanning my face discreetly like a Victorian lady. Right now there are rivulets of sweat streaming down my cheeks and neck, collecting in my clavicle and in the hollow at the bottom of my back. My blouse is soaked through both front and back; without doubt I'll need to change it when I get back inside. All this in around four minutes.

It reminds me of a documentary I once watched about mountain climbers. There's this phenomenon where delirious climbers in below-freezing conditions suffer a brain malfunction that tells their bodies they are overheating, and so, on top of a mountain at minus forty degrees, they strip off all their clothing, ensuring certain death.

It seemed a great exaggeration to me back then, but I totally understand it now. Far from standing outside in my garden in the chilly English springtime, my body makes me feel like I'm trapped in forty-degree heat on a Dubai beach. Not nearly as idyllic as it might sound.

Behind me, the kitchen door opens. Josh comes barreling out and runs past me, down to the bottom of our sizable garden. My shoulders relax, and in spite of the sweltering heat within, I smile. Josh wouldn't notice if my hair was on fire.

He disappears behind the short row of conifers Henry planted ten years ago to afford us extra privacy from the neighbors. Josh endearingly calls it a wood.

Thirty seconds later I hear a whoop of delight.

"Nanny, look!" Josh runs back up the garden and gingerly holds out his hand as if it contains something utterly precious.

A small white feather nestles in his palm. Somehow it has escaped the mud that now covers his jeans and boots.

"It's beautiful," he breathes, nipping the hollow shaft and holding it up to the air. He turns it slowly in the arrows of weak spring sunshine that slip through the pale-green new leaves. Through Josh, I see the magic too.

The feather is small, but dry and perfect. The sleek, sturdy strands soften into white fluff at the bottom. Delicate and yet so strong.

"It really is." I lay my hand on his small shoulder. "It's a miracle."

We stand for a few moments, lost together in the beauty of this tiny piece of nature. A soothing balm to the ever-present guilt and blame that I silently torture myself with every day. The horror I can't discuss with anyone else.

Spending time with my grandsons acts as a welcome distraction from the tablets Dr. Fern prescribed to help me sleep, which I've hidden from Henry at the back of my bedside drawer. I haven't taken any yet; I've been trying to manage without them.

When I think back to when my own sons were young, there always seemed to be so much to *do*. Stuff that seemed important at the time but that I now know really wasn't.

"But you've still got stuff to do now," my colleague Maura said when I tried explaining the joys of being a grandparent to her. "You work, you keep that whole enormous house shipshape with zero help. I don't know how you find the time to look after the boys as much as you do."

I knew what she was getting at, and she was right that Henry didn't lift a finger in the house, but she was missing the point. The laundry, housework and cooking—none of it mattered.

My grandsons had taught me that if it didn't get done, then so what? The house didn't blow up. We didn't starve.

"Think about your own life, Maura," I said. "Imagine if someone took away all the chores and pressure and worries and replaced them with the sweetest joy that filled your heart and left you wanting nothing. If you can imagine that, then you start to come close to feeling what a grandparent feels."

"Blimey." She grinned. "You *are* smitten; you're going all soppy on me. There's no hope for you, my friend. You're destined to babysit and play Lego for the rest of your days."

"I can't think of anything better," I said with a smile. "Sounds like a dream, to me at least."

Of course, I didn't know back then that there would be no such dream. Instead, there would be only the worst nightmare.

CHAPTER SIX

Judi

When the flush has abated somewhat, I lead Josh back inside. He plonks himself on his grandad's knee.

"What have we got here, then?" Henry says, looking down at Josh's hand.

I can feel Ben watching me, trying to get a handle on whether I'm upset or not, but I avoid his eyes and pull my thin cardigan closer in the hope that he won't spot the wet patches.

Josh slowly unfurls his fingers to show Henry, and Noah sidles up to see too.

"I found it in the wood," he says softly. "Nanny says it's a miracle."

"It is rather impressive, champ."

"It's just a feather." Noah is dismissive.

"I think it *is* a miracle," I say from the doorway. "Just look at it."

Nobody says anything.

"What kind of bird do you think it came from?" Henry jostles his knees.

"Maybe a pigeon?" Josh suggests without hesitation, squirming to stay balanced.

"I think you might be right," Henry murmurs. "Pigeons like woodland. I suppose it could've been a dove, though. They're all white, aren't they?"

"Hmm," Josh says distractedly, peering closer at his feather. "Grandad, look, the top of the feather is smooth and the bottom is fluffy."

"Well spotted," Henry says, gently prodding the edge of it. "See the sleek strands? They're called barbs, and the fluffy bit at the bottom near the shaft is called the after-feather. Bet you didn't know that, did you?"

"No." Josh looks up at him. "You're smart, Grandad. You know everything about everything."

"Try telling that to your nanny, son."

I stick my head back round the door and Henry grins that same cheeky grin he flashed me outside the Savoy cinema in Nottingham thirty-five years ago as I stood waiting for the bus with my friend Ann.

"Fancy a lift, ladies?" he quipped as he sauntered by. "I'm parked around the back and I can assure you that my intentions are completely honorable." Then he gave me that grin.

Two years later, we were married, and a year after that, David was born.

But I don't feel strong enough to start thinking about David and what happened. Not right now.

I'm scraping the plates in the kitchen when behind me someone clears their throat.

"You OK, Mum?" I turn to see my son, his forehead lined with concern.

"I'm fine," I say a little too brightly, putting down the dirty plate and wiping my hands on a tea towel. "I'm so glad you all enjoyed lunch."

Ben walks slowly toward me.

"You've been saying for a while now that it's time for me to start again. You meant it's maybe time for me to meet someone, Mum."

"Yes, I know." I put the tea towel down and hold on to the worktop behind my back. "It's just that... well, I suppose I didn't expect it to happen *now*. As quickly as this."

"I know you're just being a mum and worrying about me, but she's really nice, you know. Amber." He swallows, his Adam's apple bobbing powerfully underneath the slightly whiskered skin of his neck. "I wondered if you and Dad would like to meet her? Only if you want to..."

I clasp my hands together and smile. "Oh, Ben, of course we'd love to meet her. You must bring her over." I think for a moment. "What about next Sunday, for lunch?"

"Really?" His face brightens and the furrows above his brow instantly fall away. "That'd be brilliant. I mean, if you're sure."

He wraps his arms around me and rests his chin on the top of my head. It doesn't seem that long ago that he only came up to my chest and I used to do the same to him. I bury my face in his chest and squeeze my eyes shut so my tears don't spoil the moment.

I'm pleased for him, I really am. It's just these silly, ill-timed emotions getting in the way again.

"Gosh, you feel all hot and damp, Mum." Ben takes a step back and looks at me. "Are you feeling all right?"

"I'm fine." I waft at my cheeks with one hand and clutch my cardi closed with the other. "It gets really warm in here with the oven on; that's why I stepped outside for a few minutes."

"I can't wait to tell Amber about lunch," he beams. "She's dying to meet you and Dad."

"Well, it's all arranged now," I say, patting his arm. "And if she's nervous, tell her the day will be very informal. We won't bite."

"No need for that." Ben laughs and turns back to me as he walks out of the kitchen. "Amber doesn't get nervous about *anything*. In fact, she's got more confidence than anyone I know."

CHAPTER SEVEN

Judi

When Ben and the boys have gone home, I take Henry his customary afternoon coffee and biscuits.

Despite his diabetes, Henry eats far too much sugar, but my concern has always fallen on deaf ears, so I say nothing now.

"Heavens, Jude, haven't you fed me enough?" He pats his stout belly and I see that the buttons of his shirt are straining. "I keep telling you I'm trying to cut down. In fact, like I told you the other day, I've been thinking about joining that new gym in town. They've got some good opening offers on."

"Did you?" I can't remember him saying so, but my mind has been like a sieve lately. I turn to carry the tray back into the kitchen.

"You might as well leave it here now," he says. "No sense in a perfectly good cup of coffee going to waste. Or the biscuits, for that matter."

I put the tray down on the side table by his maroon leather armchair and stand staring through the window, up at the gray sky, blotchy with heavy clouds.

He takes a slurp of the steaming liquid and frowns. "What's the matter, love? You look harassed."

"You didn't mention it was *our* cottage you were renting," I say slowly. "The surprise for Ben. It was...so unexpected."

Henry laughs. "Surprises often *are* unexpected, or hadn't you noticed?"

"Yes, but..."

"But nothing. It won't do you any harm to face the place again, Judi. I don't know why I haven't thought of it before." He shifts in his seat. "David didn't perish *in* the cottage; he fell off the cliff. You need to remember that, or else it'll soil all our lovely memories of the place. There's something to be said for facing one's fears. It might get the blasted thing out of your head once and for all, after all this time."

His words cut through me like a knife through butter. To Henry's logical brain, enough years have now passed to put the family tragedy firmly behind us, but for me, that will always remain an impossibility.

"Ben won't go now he's met this new girl," I say, perching on the edge of the sofa. "Amber."

"He didn't say no outright, though, did he? He might even want her to come with us." He took another slurp of his coffee. "If you don't frighten him off, that is."

"What do you mean?"

"I mean, your face when he said he'd met someone. Running off into the garden like that. It was...awkward, to say the least."

"I was just hot and a bit flustered, that's all. All that cooking." I pause to think of the right words. "I'm pleased he's met someone. I really am."

Henry dismisses my excuse with a cursory wave of his hand.

"Your face said it all," he says smugly. "You can't keep the lad chained to you all your life, you know. He must be more than ready to get his leg over; it's been a long time since—"

"Henry, please!"

"Oh, stop being so bloody prim and proper. Used to like it yourself once, remember?"

I stand up and brush down my skirt.

"I'm going to finish off in the kitchen." I turn and walk out of the room, silently praying my legs will support me.

"Yes, you do that," he shouts after me. "Beats talking about your own hang-ups, doesn't it?"

In some ways, a long marriage is a bit like embarking on a journey. There's a point at which you might realize the journey isn't really for you anymore. But every time you get a chance to change paths, you just stay put because it's easier. You end up trudging along the same old way and watching as life happens to other people as you pass by.

Then one day you just stop looking around you... and well, here we are.

I load the cutlery into the dishwasher and push the gravy-stained tablecloth and napkins into the washing machine. After that, I wipe down the worktops and use a small brush and dustpan to sweep the floor tiles of the errant crumbs of our feast.

Then, when I think I've given it enough time, I pad softly down the hallway and peer through the crack in the living room door. As expected, Henry has dozed off in the chair.

My shoulders drop a little and I head for the stairs. Kicking off my soft shoes at the bottom, I climb slowly, enjoying the framed photographs that are staggered across the walls, all the way up to the landing. Happy family photographs of the four of us, but also, many pictures of the boys together at various ages, right up to David reaching fourteen.

There are no more photographs together after that, of course.

I sigh and stop in front of my very favorite picture. Both

boys are crouched down in the garden. Ben is petting next
door's puppy and David is smiling and watching him, one
hand resting on his brother's shoulder. You can't tell from
the photograph, but Ben was slightly taller and broader than
David, despite being two years younger. Still, David was
protective toward his brother, always looking out for him,
particularly at school.

They didn't look that much alike, with David's very dark
hair and Ben's sun-kissed brown locks, but you could still
tell they were brothers from their mannerisms and certain
facial expressions.

I close my eyes and rock on the spot as a swell of hopelessness fills my chest. It's a relief to let it happen, away
from Henry's critical gaze. I turn away from the photograph
and grip the banister tightly, concentrating on my stinging
palms.

My sadness is like a living thing that helps fill the gaping
space David left inside me when he died. Sadness brings its
own sort of comfort. A reassurance that it will never leave, it
belongs to me alone.

After a few moments, I take in a gulp of air and then
another. I wish I could throw back my head and howl like an
animal, but instead I loosen my fingers and prize my shaking hands from the stair rail.

I look back at the photo and allow my fingertips to touch
David's face over the glass. My boy. My poor dead boy.

He'd bolted down breakfast and run out of the cottage just
like any other day at the coast. I'd called for him to take his
fleece and he'd ignored me, of course. The last time I'd see
my boy and that was as much notice as I'd taken.

The next time I saw him, he was cold and broken at the
bottom of Cowbar Cliff.

It often feels as if everything and everybody has moved

on completely. That nobody misses David James Jukes...
that mostly nobody even remembers him. Perhaps it's unfair
of me to think that. Perhaps people do think about him and
just don't show it. We're not a very *showing* sort of family.
Henry doesn't really agree with that sort of thing.

"It's not healthy to dwell in the past," he reminds me
whenever he catches me staring into space or looking at
David's photograph. I begged him to let me keep David's
room as it was the day he died, and he grudgingly agreed,
but he now disapproves of me spending any time in there.

I tear myself away from the photographs and continue
up the stairs. When I get to the top, I take a long stride to
avoid the creaking floorboards and tiptoe down to David's
bedroom.

I reach out and grasp the brass handle. It feels cool on my
heated palm and I grip it without applying any pressure for a
moment. I purposely haven't cleaned the handle since David
died. The other door handles cast their dull, brassy glow into
the dim hallway, but David's no longer shines.

There are still minuscule traces of him on this handle. It
doesn't matter that I can't see them; I can *feel* them. I can feel
them right now on the tips of my fingers and it comforts me.

I step inside the room, and because the latch has a loud click,
I push it behind me rather than fully closing it. And then I smile
and stretch my arms out to the sides, breathing freely.

"Hello, son," I whisper out loud. "I miss you."

I have only ever lightly dusted in here, using a soft cloth
with no cleaning products on it. I never open the window. I
don't want fresh, clean air sullying a magical space that still
holds traces of David's breath.

I crouch down and reach under the bed and slide out the
box. Perching on the edge of the bed, I open it, taking out
one of the small cardboard boxes within.

I take care to unfurl the tissue paper without tearing it, its crisp transparency gathering around my hands. I run my fingertips over the chalky flat plane of an outsized beige beach pebble. When I inspect my hands, I see they are patterned with traces of chalk.

If I close my eyes, I can almost hear the seagulls, the way their distant screeches fractured the damp, salty air. The feel of the wind in my hair and the sound of the gushing waves as they hurled themselves against the rocky shoreline.

A couple of times a year—usually, I've noticed, when his father is out—Ben comes up to David's room to look over the Staithes stones. That's what we've always called them, because the boys would both collect them diligently on Staithes beach. But they were really David's stones; he was the true collector.

Unlike Ben, who would hastily gather the first stones he spotted, David was very particular about which ones made his final collection, and would categorize each one in his notebook.

Whenever I washed David's shorts or jeans, more often than not I would have to remove a stone or two from his pockets before laundering them.

The tension that has gripped my neck and shoulders all day has finally begun to ease. I sit, my fingers tracing the surface of the stone, and allow the happy memories to run free in my mind.

"Judi?" Henry stands in the doorway, his hair a bit wild from sleep.

I jump up off the bed and David's stones rattle in the box, whispering their secrets.

"What on earth are you doing stuck up here on your own?" His frown settles on the pebble box. "Ah, I see. Torturing yourself again."

"Not torturing myself, Henry." I push down the lid of the box. "Just remembering our son."

"Same thing." His eyes dart around the room. "It's not right that part of our home is still a shrine, Judi. It's not..."

"Healthy." I finish the sentence for him and fix him with a gaze. "It's not healthy to bury my feelings, to bite back the tears and push away David's memory, either. But I do all that on a daily basis to please *you*."

His eyes widen, and for a moment he looks as if he might say something. But he doesn't. Instead, his eyebrows knit together.

"David died, Judi," he says softly, as if he's speaking to a small child. "He died and it was a very sad thing for us all. Very sad." He takes a breath and I just know the *smart lad* speech is coming. I know all the speeches, word for word. "What happened that day, it was nobody's fault. David was a smart lad, he was fourteen years old. He knew what he was doing. Am I right?"

"I know, but I wish I'd taken more notice. I wish I could have just—"

"Let's not go there." He coughs. "It's not worth the upset, love. You're not...well, just lately, you've not seemed yourself."

I open my mouth to defend myself, but what can I say? To be perfectly honest, I'm astonished he's noticed the change in me, but he is right.

I'm not myself at all. There are times I feel like I don't know who I am anymore.

CHAPTER EIGHT

Amber

Ben swung the car into a narrow road and pulled up outside a dull brick-built Victorian-style terraced house.

"Well, this is it," he announced as he turned off the ignition. "This is home."

He wasn't to know that Amber had seen the house many times before. She'd walked past in all weathers and at varying times of the day. At dusk, from across the road, she'd watched the boys diving around in the living room, climbing and bouncing on the furniture like caged monkeys, with the curtains open and the lights on.

Hood pulled down and umbrella up, she had imagined, many times, the day she'd get to finally step inside.

They had been dating a good while now. They'd been to the cinema, the bowling alley, out for a couple of meals and a few quiet drinks. She had cooked two meals for him at her own flat, but he'd been unable to stay over because of his sons.

She'd held out on sleeping with him for the first two weeks as a matter of principle. She wasn't going to give up the candy right away for someone who seemed to be protecting his children from her; it had always been the plan to proceed cautiously in that area.

Playing the damaged, wary character she had so carefully created didn't fit well with jumping into bed with him on their first date.

Finally, they had taken the boys swimming after school one evening. He'd told them Amber was a work colleague, but it was progress of sorts. And then he'd really surprised her when he announced that he'd finally told his parents of her existence.

"Mum's invited you for lunch this coming Sunday," he said, teasing her with a nudge. "You should feel honored; it's usually a strictly family-only invitation."

"That's so nice of her," Amber said sweetly, kissing him on the cheek.

She was looking forward to meeting the interfering old battle-ax around whom Ben constantly trod on eggshells. This was a woman who still insisted on doing her son's cleaning and laundry, and who even filled his fridge once a week with home-cooked meals.

He was thirty-three, not thirteen, for God's sake. The fact that he had to consider his mother in everything he did was a source of irritation for her. It had got to the point where she had wondered if he was ever going to invite her back to his house at all. But now, here they were.

"It looks . . . lovely," she said as she climbed out of the car.

"Nothing to shout about, I know, but it's home." He smiled, coming to stand next to her and staring at the house, a strange look on his face. "I've been thinking, actually, about maybe buying something a bit newer. There's a new-build just completing at Lady Bay, close to where my parents live."

She'd seen his parents' nice detached property in West

Bridgford and it looked big enough to house Ben and the two boys as well as his parents. Judging by how he lived in their pockets already, it surprised her that he hadn't moved in there after his wife died. Still, she was grateful that hadn't happened; it would have made her plans a great deal more difficult to implement.

"Come on." Ben draped his arm around her shoulders. "Let's go inside and I'll put the kettle on."

Inside, the house was predictably plain and lacking any real style.

Seeing as his wife had only been dead two years, Amber decided the woman had either possessed zero taste, or Ben had managed to let things slip in a monumental way. This wasn't a comfortable home, merely a functional shell.

The plain cream-painted living room walls were a hotch-potch of family photographs, nearly all of them featuring the aforementioned dead wife: Louise, or *Lou*, as Ben sometimes annoyingly referred to her.

Two God-awful oversized black leather couches had somehow been shoehorned into the small space, leaving no room for a dining table or chairs. Amber counted four pairs of assorted-sized trainers scattered about the place. Even worse, brightly colored toys and boxed games spilled out from behind various pieces of furniture. She guessed this stuff had simply piled up over time, with nobody caring enough to tidy it away.

"Sorry it's a bit of a mess," Ben said behind her. "Mum doesn't do her main clean until Friday."

"It's homely." She turned round to face him. "And home should always feel comfortable."

"I agree." He grinned and kissed her on the cheek. "Has

anyone ever told you, Amber Carr, that you're perfect in every way?"

"Oh, lots of people." She sighed theatrically. "But you get a bit fed up of hearing it after a while."

He laughed and squeezed her closer.

"I mean it." His face was serious. "You're perfect for me. Every day I thank God I met you."

"Fancy a great big fella like you having such a soft center. How incredibly sweet."

He narrowed his eyes and began to tickle her midriff.

"OK, I give in," she squealed, laughing wildly. "I'm sorry. I'm sorry!"

He grabbed her and kissed her on the mouth, his soft lips lingering on hers.

"I'll let you off this time," he growled. "But next time you might not be so lucky."

"Promises, promises," Amber murmured, and pressed in closer against him. She liked it when he played a little rough with her. If things were different, she might even fancy him.

His body felt strong and hard. He wanted her so badly.

In her wildest dreams, she wouldn't have dared hope that things would go this well.

CHAPTER NINE

Judi

Sunday comes around all too quickly. I leave Henry snoring in bed and slide out from the covers just before six a.m.

The heating switches itself on at five for two hours, so at least it's nice and warm downstairs in the kitchen. As always, my first job is to make a cup of tea and sit at the worn oak table, savoring the peace.

I take my seat at what used to be David's place. We had specific places for mealtimes when the boys were growing up. Henry was always a stickler for order at the table. David sat at this very place setting for his whole fourteen years. Even after so much time has elapsed, I think we all still think of it as his. I know I do.

I put down my cup and run my finger over what looks like a thick black smear in front of me. My fingernail dips into the slight hollow I know so well. It's a burn mark. David always seemed entranced by fire, and this particular day, before dinner, he was messing about with a candle at the table. He set a piece of paper alight to impress Ben, and when it burned down to his fingers, he let it fall. It scorched the table quite badly.

I tried to stop Ben running out of the room, but he easily dodged my attempts to intercept him and went straight to his father. We were always a close family, but during arguments, we sometimes fell into two camps: myself and David, and Ben and Henry.

This was one of those times, and there was no stopping Henry. Once he got something into his head, there was to be no reasoning with him. And that day, when Ben ratted on his brother, Henry decided that David must be punished.

I inhale deeply, hold it there for a few seconds and then let it out slowly. Sipping my tea, I close my eyes against the steam. I need to loosen up a little, I can't afford to get lost in the past today.

The house is far from dirty, but I need to just spritz round with the duster and vacuum and then prepare the Sunday lunch of all lunches. Because today is the day we are to meet Ben's new friend, Amber.

The girl who has somehow managed to turn my grieving son's head in record time.

I'd always imagined Ben would wait until the boys were a little older before getting himself involved in another relationship. He's never said as much; I suppose it's just something I've grown to assume, even though I often encourage him to think about the future and making a new life for himself.

When Louise died, he made a point of repeatedly saying, "Mum, the boys are my only priority. My job's important, but losing Lou put everything into perspective, and that's all my teaching will ever be now. A job."

Ben is a good, effective teacher. His school's recent Ofsted inspection and the comments of the inspectors proved that. Every day he turns up, carries out his job to the best of his ability and then collects his paycheck at the end

of the month. But there is no ambition there anymore, no
striving to take on extra responsibilities at work nor setting
his sights on a deputy head's position as he once did.

He works his contracted hours, including the planning
and the marking, and the rest of his time goes to his sons.

Despite Ben's world being torn apart, leaving him with
the almost insurmountable grief and trauma, I am so proud
that my son has always showed a quiet dignity.

So I really don't mean to appear disapproving or churlish
that he's met someone.

I've just been taken by surprise. That's all it is.

At twelve o'clock, I take the meat out of the oven to rest. All
the veg are prepared and sitting in cold salted water ready for
when I fire up the hob. The house has been polished and swept.

Everything is almost ready. I've left the final half hour
to spruce myself up a bit for introductions. Then I hear the
telltale sound of gravel shifting under wheels at the front of
the house.

"They're here," Henry calls and appears at the kitchen
door. "They're quite early, I know, but don't look so star-
tled. I'll put the kettle on and get the teapot warming while
you…" His eyes take in my appearance. "While you get
yourself sorted."

I dash to the front room and stand behind the curtain, peek-
ing through the nets. Ben gets out of the car first and walks
around to the passenger side. He opens the door and holds out
his hand to a tall, slim girl with short-cropped blond hair and
smooth tanned skin. I'm astonished at this previously hidden
chivalry. I never saw him do such a thing for Louise.

A wave of heat rolls up into my already ruddy face. I
don't know how time has run away with me like this. I'm

usually so organized, and yet I have to admit that just lately I've often found myself ill-prepared and rushing out to work. Now I find myself clad in old leggings that have rips on the inside thighs and a baggy gray T-shirt that I rescued from Henry's designated dustbin pile of clothes following his recent wardrobe clear-out.

I rush back to the kitchen, ignoring Henry's questioning look. As I hastily cover up the meat, I knock the roasting dish, causing hot fat to spatter my skin. I cry out, but I haven't time to run my arm under the cold tap because I hear voices in the hall.

It's too late to redeem the situation. I've allowed myself too much time wallowing in thoughts instead of keeping a close eye on the clock.

I can't even escape upstairs. It would be so rude to just rush past them without stopping.

"Judi? Come and say hello," Henry calls, and I catch the slight impatience in his voice.

My heart thuds and I can feel the heat gathering inside me again.

I have to face facts. I look a dreadful mess and there is absolutely nothing I can do about it. This will be Amber's first impression of her new boyfriend's mother. Ridiculously, I feel my eyes prickling.

"Coming," I call.

I run my hands under the cold tap and pat them on to my burning face before dabbing it dry with a tea towel. Then I stride out of the kitchen trying my best to look confident.

The hallway is a hive of activity. Henry slouches at the living room door clutching the newspaper at his side and watching proceedings with an amused look on his face.

Ben and the chattering boys bustle near the door, taking off shoes and coats, and I catch sight of a figure moving behind Ben. She hangs a silver-gray mac on the coat stand and then bends down to unzip long boots from slender jean-clad legs.

"Hello!" I say brightly.

The boys rush up, their hands full of monstrous-looking robots, eager to explain what each one morphs into.

"Hi, Mum." A slight frown knits Ben's brows as he takes in my disheveled appearance. "This is Amber. Amber, meet my mum."

He stands aside and the young woman straightens herself up and turns to look at me.

I'm struck again by how tall she is: nearly as tall as Ben, and boyishly slim. She has elfin-short ash-blond hair, which I can see has been expensively highlighted with three different shades.

"Hello, I'm Judi." I stretch out a hand. "I'm pleased to meet you, Amber. So sorry I'm a mess; I'm afraid the time quite ran away with me this morning."

Cool eyes sweep disapprovingly up from my feet to my face and hair and back down again. It happens so quickly, I wonder for a moment if I've imagined it.

"Pleased to meet you too, Judi." She smiles, but her eyes remain cold. "Ben's been telling me all about your legendary Sunday lunches for weeks now."

"Nonsense." I grin, waving away her compliment. "Don't listen to him, Amber, he's biased."

"Mum's being modest." Ben laughs. "She's always bragging she makes the best Yorkshire puddings in the whole of Nottinghamshire."

I tut and he dodges my jokey raised hand.

"Would you excuse me, Amber, just for a few minutes?" I run a hand through my hair. "As you can see, I've yet to get myself cleaned up."

"Oh, don't disappear now, Mum," Ben protests. "You look fine, and Amber's been dying to meet you."

Amber looks at him and smiles. She slides her hand neatly into his and turns back to me, regarding me warmly. Me and my silly imagination; she seems perfectly friendly now.

She has large, full lips and almond-shaped gray eyes. Her makeup is immaculate.

"Honestly, I'll only be a few minutes." I take a step away, filled with an urge to remedy my slovenly appearance.

"No, no . . . you can't just disappear now everyone's here, dear," Henry says firmly. "You look perfectly fine. Let's all have a drink and find out more about this delightful young lady."

Amber giggles coyly and they all move into the living room, and suddenly there I am, standing out in the hallway alone.

CHAPTER TEN

Judi

By the time we sit down to lunch, I've forgotten I look a mess. I'm hot and tired and frankly, not hungry in the slightest.

Henry opens a bottle of chilled Sauvignon Blanc, and once everyone is seated, I busy myself helping the boys get food on to their plates.

"My favorite estate for grapes, the Marlborough," Henry says, pouring Amber a large glass. "Crisp and aromatic. See what you think to it, Amber."

Amber sniffs the contents of her glass and takes a dainty sip. "Mmm, this is really lovely," she declares.

"It's from New Zealand," Henry adds.

"You seem to be very knowledgeable about wine." Amber takes another sip. "I wouldn't know where to start with all the different types. Hopefully I can learn from you."

"Just stuff I've picked up over the years." Henry shrugs, but it's obvious he's pleased with the compliment.

I watch out of the corner of my eye as Ben fusses over Amber. Would she like a little of this, or that? Perhaps another slice of beef? Even Henry is passing tureens of steaming potatoes and vegetables to her before helping himself. It's unheard of.

Once the boys are happily eating, I put a little of everything on my own plate, but not much. Nobody notices.

Soon Amber and I are looking at the tops of four heads as the plates of food begin to be demolished.

"So, Amber, tell us a bit about yourself," I say. "Are you from—"

"Oh, Mum. You're not seriously going to use *that* corny line, are you?" Ben looks up, grinning, but there's a meaningful look behind his smile. "It's not a job interview, you know."

"It's fine, Ben." Amber reaches for a tureen of vegetables and gives me a little nod. "Go on, Judi, please."

"I was just going to ask where you live," I say reluctantly. I'm only trying to show willing, to show an interest for Ben's sake. "Close by here?"

"I live in an apartment now, near the city center," she replies, prodding at the buttered carrots.

"And your family," I continue. "Do they live in Nottingham too?"

Amber drops the carrot batons she's spooning all over the tablecloth. "Oh! I'm so sorry. How clumsy of me."

"It's Mum's interrogation technique," Ben laughs. "It's enough to turn anyone into a bag of nerves."

"The cloth will wash, don't worry," I say, spearing a piece of broccoli on my fork. I want to repeat my question about her family, but somehow it feels difficult to do so now.

"Ben says you work with children?" I say instead.

"That's right, at the children's center. It's actually attached to Ben's school." She dabs at the buttery orange stain with her napkin. "I'm the lead parent support worker there."

"That's a fancy title," Henry remarks with his mouth full. "What does a *lead parent support worker* do, then?"

"Well, one of my main roles is to help disadvantaged families access the services available to them," Amber says levelly, taking a sip of her wine. "And a big part of the job is providing practical and emotional support to families with young children. It's very rewarding."

"I see," Henry says, looking a bit baffled.

"It's a really important facility for the local community," Ben says, and Amber looks at him gratefully, squeezing his hand.

"Are you a teacher, like Daddy?" Noah asks her.

"Don't speak while you're chewing please, champ," Ben remarks.

"No, I'm not a teacher, Noah." Amber smiles. She's pushing the food around on her plate, but I'm not sure anything has reached her glossy mouth yet.

"Nanny says that the only people who are really important in school are the teachers," Noah states, shoveling a heap of creamy mashed potato on to his fork. "It's because you have to go to university to be a teacher, but anyone can do the other jobs."

"Oh, Noah, I'm sure I didn't say anything of the sort," I splutter, laughing off my embarrassment. "Everyone's job is important in school."

"But, Nanny, you said—"

"Well, I confess I haven't been to university, so that'll be a black mark for me," Amber says.

For a second or two the air is thick with an awkward silence. Then she laughs. And Ben and Henry join in.

"Honestly, the way little ones get things muddled up." I laugh myself, relieved. Still smiling, I reach for my glass of wine and glance over at Amber.

She has stopped laughing now, and she blinks and holds my stare until I look away again.

* * *

Once the table is cleared and we move to the living room, everything feels a little more relaxed.

"Tea, coffee, anyone?" I offer.

Henry opts for a coffee, but Ben pours Amber another glass of wine. Her third, I think.

"Will you excuse me? I need to use the bathroom." She stands up.

Ben directs her upstairs and then comes through to the kitchen while I'm making the hot drinks.

"So, what do you think?" he whispers.

"She seems very nice," I say, spooning ground coffee into the cafetière. "I do hope she enjoyed her lunch." She didn't comment on the food once. I saw her prodding at her meal quite a bit, but I'm not sure she actually consumed anything.

"She gets a bit stressed out—" Ben glances nervously at the doorway "—talking about her family. There was a tragedy... Her parents and sister were all killed in a car accident. Amber had stayed home with a neighbor. Awful business."

"Oh no, I'm sorry to hear that," I say, pouring boiling water over the grounds. "That's really awful. I hope I didn't upset the poor girl. But I was only making conversation, darling. You should have warned me if there were subjects that were off-limits."

"Yeah, I know. You like her, though?"

I look at him a moment, his face so open and hopeful. What will he do, I wonder, if I tell him I'm not massively impressed with Amber? Will it make a difference? He seems smitten by her.

"She seems lovely," I say, and he smiles.

CHAPTER ELEVEN

Judi

I put the cups and saucers and the cafetière on a tray. I pour single cream into the Royal Albert china jug that used to be my mother's and load a plate with after-dinner mints. Then I carry it all through to the lounge.

As I enter the hallway, Amber appears at the bottom of the stairs. She seems to have been up there quite a while; I assumed she'd come back down ages ago.

"It's a very nice house you have here," she says, waiting for me to pass her with the tray. "Lots of space."

"Yes, I suppose it has," I say, not wanting to sound too boastful. "You get used to it after a while, of course. Sometimes, when Ben and the boys are over, it feels like we could do with somewhere even bigger." I give a conspiratorial laugh.

"But then I suppose if it's just the two of you in the future," she says, "you'll be rattling around in this place."

It's a strange thing to say, I think, and I fall silent as we walk into the lounge.

Noah and Josh pounce on the foil-wrapped chocolates as soon as I place the tray down on the coffee table.

"No more than two each or there'll not be enough for everyone." I wink at them and they grin, knowing they always get to eat lots more.

I leave Henry to serve coffee while I pop up to the bathroom. But as soon as I get to the top of the stairs, I freeze. David's bedroom door is slightly ajar.

I always make a point of keeping it closed because it's a sacred space to me. Cut off and preserved from the rest of the house.

Henry never goes in there on principle, and although Ben has been known to do so very occasionally, he always asks me first if it's OK.

I've walked past this room several times already this morning and I know that the door was most definitely closed.

The only person who has been up here alone since then is Amber.

I pad softly down the corridor and push the door open a little further. I step inside and take a quick look around. Everything seems exactly as it was, but still, my stomach churns.

I'd like a lock put on the door to keep the room totally private. But if I asked Henry to install one, I know he'd either laugh at the suggestion or lose his temper about the fact that I still keep the room as a shrine.

I step back out of the room and click the door closed. I hate the thought that a stranger's hand might have touched David's door handle, Ben's new girlfriend or not.

And how terribly rude of her to go nosing around uninvited.

When I get back downstairs, I glance over at Amber. *Have you had a look around upstairs?* is not the sort of thing I can ask her outright. She looks straight back at me but doesn't smile, simply runs a manicured hand nonchalantly through her cropped hair.

The room is strangely silent, and then Ben rushes in with the kitchen roll.

"I'm so sorry, Judi," Amber blurts out, suddenly distressed when Ben appears. "I just don't know how I could've been so clumsy."

Ben tears off a long strip of kitchen roll and begins dabbing at the wooden flooring. I walk over and peer around the coffee table. My mother's china jug lies in two pieces on the floor, cream flooding around it.

"Oh no!" My hand flies to my mouth.

"I'm so sorry. Ben was just telling me how precious the jug is to you and..." Her voice falters, and Ben lays his hand on her arm—*her* arm!—as if to offer support. "I picked it up to take a closer look and it just slipped from my hand. I'll try and get you another, I promise."

Don't. It won't be the same. I'm working hard to keep the simmering resentment from exploding out of my mouth. *Only* this *jug belonged to my mother.*

"Well, all's not lost. Looks like a clean break, at least." Henry holds up the two pieces. "I'll have a go at gluing them in the morning," He says it as if that should be the end of it all.

I don't answer. It feels like insects are burrowing under my skin, traveling down my arms and into my fingers. I shiver, even though the room is warm, and hug the tops of my arms.

"Sit down, Mum," Ben says kindly when he's finished mopping up the cream. I look down and see that the large area of polished wood is now dull and smeared, and although he's done his best, the cream has surreptitiously seeped in between the boards where it might never be reached. "Mum?"

I blink and see that everyone is watching me, even the

two boys, with some concern. Ben nudges Noah, who moves to my side and gently pulls at my hand until I sit down.

Amber looks down at her knotted fingers. She looks genuinely distressed.

Ben hands me a cup of strong coffee and I take a sip, thinking how I'd have felt if I'd broken something of sentimental value belonging to Henry's mother on our first meeting. I decide I'd have hoped she'd have looked on me kindly and given me the benefit of the doubt.

"I'm sorry, Judi," Amber says again in a small voice, and I look up and meet her eyes.

"Apology accepted," I reply, and smile at her.

Henry winks at me and Ben's face brightens as he throws me a grateful look.

It's as if everyone unfreezes, takes a collective breath of relief, and we're off again.

"You mentioned that you live in an apartment," Henry says to Amber, and she breaks eye contact with me and turns to face him. "Never fancied it myself. Must feel as if you're cooped up like a battery hen, with having no garden."

"Dad!" Ben rolls his eyes.

"I suppose it might feel like that to some people, but I really like apartment living." Amber smiles, taking a swig of her wine. "There's minimum maintenance to worry about and I feel far more secure there than living alone in a house. I've got one or two pots on the balcony, so there is a tiny garden of sorts, but I haven't been there long enough to make my mark."

"Where did you live before that?" I ask her.

"Oh, another apartment in a different area."

"Tell them what you did. Before you left the last flat." Ben grins.

"Ben, no!" Her cheeks flush with color. "I can't believe you've brought that up."

"Oh go on." He bursts out laughing. "It's hilarious, they'll love it."

"We're all ears." I pour more coffee and notice that Amber's wineglass is almost empty again. I suppose I ought to be glad she feels able to relax so quickly after the jug drama.

"Well…my landlord at the last place was an absolute pig," she begins. Her words are starting to sound just a touch fuzzy around the edges. "And when I say pig, I mean a *real* pig. He used to come round to my flat on the pretense of checking the meters and he'd 'accidentally' touch me up as he walked by. You know the sort, right? It just kept happening."

Henry arches an eyebrow and I glance at Noah and Josh, who fortunately are absorbed in a game of Buckaroo, oblivious to the rather inappropriate conversation.

"To cut a long story very short, when I worked up the courage to finally tell him where to get off, he gave me six days' notice to leave. He said he wanted to sell the flat and he didn't want me there when prospective buyers came over to view it."

"That's not on." Henry shakes his head. "He sounds a bit of a rogue to me."

"Cut to the interesting bit." Ben beams, nudging her.

"This is so embarrassing." She buries her face in his shoulder.

"Trust me, it's brilliant," Ben tells us.

Amber looks up again. "Obviously I had to get my own back. So once I'd packed everything up, and while I waited for the removal firm to arrive, I hid fresh prawns all over the flat."

"Prawns?" I repeat, puzzled.

"Have you ever whiffed rotting prawns, Judi? I tucked them under the edges of the carpets and in the folds of the

Roman blinds, and then I poked a couple of holes in the cushions and pushed them into the foam filling."

"She even stuck some into the air vents." Ben laughs and slaps his knee. "Brilliant!"

"I bet the old perv is still searching for where the smell is coming from." Amber grins, draining her glass.

"Heavens," I say faintly.

"Well!" Henry manages a little chuckle, but I can tell he's rather taken aback. "You certainly found an inventive way of exacting your revenge, Amber my dear."

"Told you they'd love it," Ben tells her, squeezing her thigh. "Good story, eh, Mum?"

They both look at me, amused.

"Indeed," I say, taking a sip of my rapidly cooling coffee. "Just remind me never to get on the wrong side of you, Amber."

She throws back her pretty head and laughs, and everyone joins in.

CHAPTER TWELVE

Judi

"Sooo," Maura says, the next morning at work. "How did it go?" She carefully places a mug of coffee down on the reception desk in front of me.

"Fine," I say lightly, taking a tiny sip and grimacing as the almost boiling liquid scalds my lips. "It was fine."

"Oh no, don't think for one second you're getting away with that." Maura grins and perches her trim derrière on the edge of the desk. She's lost a bit of weight recently and looks better for it. "Come on now, how did it really go?"

"It was...OK." I sigh, inhaling the irresistible smell of coffee. "She seems a nice girl and I suppose I've just turned into a cynical old crone."

Maura laughs. "Hey, less of the old crone; at forty-nine, I'm only six years behind you. You didn't like her, I take it?"

"No! I mean, yes, I did like her. She seemed nice. Honestly."

"Judi." Maura lowers her chin and looks at me like a school teacher. "How long have we been friends?"

"Oh gosh, I don't know. Twenty years or more?"

I first met Maura when David started comprehensive school. She was the school secretary at the time. I offered to help out at the Christmas fair she was organizing and we just sort of bonded. Years later, when she became the business manager at the local GPs' surgery, she encouraged me to apply for the admin assistant position.

"I'd say we've known each other at least twenty-five years. So I kind of know when you're saying something that doesn't agree with what you're really thinking. Got it?"

"Yes." I flash her a sheepish grin.

"OK," she sighs. "So let's start again. You didn't like her?"

"She seemed quite a nice girl, but... I don't know, there was just *something*."

"Something like... ?"

"She was very confident," I say, deciding to start with something positive. "And she had Ben and Henry eating out of her hand right from the off."

Maura picks up her mug and waits.

"But she broke my mother's jug, a little Royal Albert one she used to cherish." I explain what happened.

"How awful," Maura sympathizes. "Such a shame. I'd imagine the poor girl was mortified."

"Well, that's just it, she wasn't really. Not overly," I say. "I mean, she showed remorse at first, but then she seemed to just forget about it."

"That could've been just embarrassment." Maura shrugs. "She was probably so keen to put it behind her that she just pushed it completely out of her mind."

I'm slightly peeved that Maura's sympathies appear to lie so completely with Amber. So I tell her the landlord story.

"Well, at least she didn't boil any bunnies." Maura laughs and then sees my face. "Oh, come on, Judi. You've got to admire the girl's imagination. It sounds like that landlord needed taking down a peg or two."

"I agree, but the boys were there listening and she'd only

just met us. She was a bit forward, and frankly, I found it all a little odd."

Maura shrugs and drinks her coffee. "Does she get on with the boys?"

Taken aback, I think for a moment. "You know, she didn't seem to really notice them."

"She's probably just playing it cool," Maura suggests. "Not wanting to be too overbearing at your first meeting. I'd say that's a good thing."

"Hmm, maybe."

It hadn't struck me before now, but I can only remember Amber speaking to Noah once, about my disastrous school jobs comment, which I didn't intend sharing with Maura. I don't think she actually spoke to Josh at all the whole time they were there.

"And how do Amber and Ben seem to get on?"

"Oh, he seems totally smitten." I smile. "He's kept his gentleman's manners quite well hidden up until now, but they were on full glorious display yesterday."

When they left ours, around four o'clock, I clocked that Ben helped Amber on with her coat and opened the car door for her again.

"Not being picky, but she didn't thank us either. I remember when I first met Henry's parents, I so desperately wanted them to like me. I tried to say all the right things and offered to help clear up and thanked his mother profusely for the lovely meal she'd prepared. But Amber just said 'Nice to meet you' when she left, and that was it."

"I wouldn't take it to heart," Maura says, standing up and smoothing out the creases in her skirt. "Young people are so different nowadays. Far more confident than we ever were, and they expect the good things in life. It's maybe not such a bad thing."

I nod in agreement and she touches my arm lightly.

"Ben doesn't need protecting anymore, you know, Judi. He'll be fine. Maybe you should give this girl a chance."

I feel a faint prickle behind my eyes. Maura was a good friend to me after David died. She knows what I went through and how it still affects me . . . will always affect me.

"I know," I whisper, and squeeze her hand. "You look lovely, by the way."

She's taken to wearing a little makeup to work. Nothing overbearing, just a lick of mascara and a pretty lipstick. She's got this sort of glow about her.

"Amazing what a bit of lippy can do." She grins and pats me on the hand before walking through the reception area to unlock the doors early for the first patients, already waiting outside in the drizzle.

Maura's right. Young women seem far more sure of themselves now. Ben is a good judge of character and he seems sold on Amber. I'm sure she's a perfectly nice girl.

I silently resolve that I'm not going to let old insecurities get in the way of getting to know her.

CHAPTER THIRTEEN

Judi

We're an hour into the morning appointments when I hear Maura's sharp intake of breath.

"Uh-oh, Fiona Bonser's here. That's all we need," she murmurs and begins to leaf busily through the patient prescriptions. "Your turn this time, I'm afraid, Judi."

I watch as an impoverished-looking woman in her early twenties struggles through the automatic doors with a baby in a pushchair and her two older children trailing behind. A couple of Aldi bags dangle from the buggy handlebars and the wire tray underneath the seat is packed with bottles of fizzy pop.

Fiona's over-bleached yellow hair hangs in ropy strands, matted like candy floss and damp from the inclement weather. She has small, delicate features under slug-like blackened brows and heavy, dark eyeshadow that frames otherwise very pretty green eyes.

Despite her application of a thick makeup base and garish lipstick, old acne scars are still visible, chiseled deep into her pale complexion.

No matter what the weather, she always wears the same

short skirt, exposing bare mottled legs in high-heeled court shoes that for some bizarre reason always make me think of Minnie Mouse. Although her three children often look scruffy and unkempt, I've never seen them without coats and trousers whenever the weather is colder.

"Do that again and I'll brain you," she snarls as they pile into the reception area. The eldest boy—Harrison, if I recall—steps warily away from his mother's raised hand.

She looks up suddenly and sees me watching. And she hesitates. For a moment, I think she's going to turn around and walk back out. But it's just wishful thinking on my part, because of course, she doesn't. She keeps on coming.

"Morning, Fiona," I say brightly as she approaches the curved reception desk. "How are you today?"

"I need to see the doctor," she mutters, avoiding my eyes.

"Have you got an appointment?"

She stares at me then and I brace myself for the inevitable explosion. We've seen them many times before, here at the surgery.

"No. I haven't got an appointment. Can I sit and wait?" Her reasonable tone gets a surprised glance from Maura.

I survey the collection of patients we have in that morning. Most of them are alone and quite old, or else very young with their own small children. There are lots of the same faces we see week on week.

Of course, they are all taking an interest in this interaction. Fiona's reputation precedes her in this small and often unforgiving community.

I'll need to choose my words carefully. If we're seen to give preferential treatment, the place will be in an uproar. The injustice will spread like wildfire on the surrounding housing estates.

"I can make you an appointment for early next week,"

I say, scrolling down the computer screen. My heart sinks when I see the already oversubscribed schedules for our three GPs. "That is, unless it's an emergency."

Fiona nods to her brood. "Do you think I'd drag this lot out and traipse all the way down here unless it was an emergency?" she snaps.

I watch as Harrison slyly snatches a mangled fruit chew out of the hand of his baby brother in the pushchair. A wail rises and fills the surgery. People shake their heads and roll their eyes at each other.

Fiona reaches into her pocket and wordlessly hands another chew to the baby. The noise stops.

"No, I don't suppose you would," I reply.

"There is no sit-and-wait at the surgery on a Monday morning, Fiona," Maura intervenes from behind me. "I know you're aware of that."

"Yeah, but *you're* not aware of what's up with me, are you? Interfering old—"

"Careful," Maura warns. "Otherwise I'll have to ask you to leave. Again."

Fiona presses her lips together and leans on the counter, wincing slightly as she does so.

I glance at her eldest child, Kylie, a skinny, quiet girl of eight who has her mum's facial features and seems to stare constantly at her own feet. Five-year-old Harrison stands chewing his stolen sweet, glaring at me with Fiona's eyes. It occurs to me that both should surely be at school at nine forty-five on a Monday morning.

"It's one of those inset days, if you were wondering." Fiona shoots me a sarcastic smile as if she's just read my mind. "So am I going to get to see a doctor this morning or what?"

"Make an appointment like the rest of us have to," calls a

flabby, rather unpleasant man who seems to be at the surgery all the time.

"Fuck off, fatso," Fiona says smartly over her shoulder, without looking at him.

It isn't at all appropriate, but something in me wants to laugh.

"Watch your language, Fiona." Maura frowns. She lowers her voice. "You can sit and wait this once, but don't ask for special treatment again."

Fiona gives a single nod, throws me a hard look and sits down gingerly in the front row of seats, her children clustered around her like hungry chicks.

CHAPTER FOURTEEN

Amber

Amber sat in her tiny flat, cradling a cup of lukewarm coffee and listening to the booming bass beat and heavy footfalls that emanated through the ceiling from the apartment above.

Since the day she'd moved in here—nearly six months ago now—she'd tried everything to get those inconsiderate bastards to quieten down. She'd pushed a note through the door. Then she had politely knocked and asked them to turn down the volume. But the guy had simply stood there looking through her, as if she were speaking in a foreign tongue. His stare had been unfocused as a zombie's, with the bass beat pulsing through his body like an electric shock.

She wasn't sure exactly who the registered tenant was upstairs, as there seemed to be a motley collection of ragged males, all of them skeleton-thin and spaced out, constantly coming and going at virtually all hours of the day.

The property was a three-story detached Victorian villa that at one time must've been quite a grand residence, but in recent years it had been converted into six minuscule flats. The conversion had obviously been completed on a shoestring, as, with the original wooden floors and no soundproofing, every creak or boom beat could be heard.

Amber had emailed the property company who were responsible for maintaining the building and, in a moment of frustration a few weeks ago, had even complained to the antisocial-behavior department at the local council. Needless to say, she hadn't received a response from either party, and precisely nothing had changed.

It was hardly worth getting het up over, though. If things went to plan—which it seemed, even at this early stage, they would—then she wouldn't be stuck in this rancid hole much longer, at the mercy of the crackheads upstairs.

The flat was situated on the edge of Forest Fields—certainly not the most desirable place to live in Nottingham. Amber had initially spotted it on Rightmove because the monthly rental amount was one of the lowest she could find close to the city. But it was only an eight-minute tram ride into the Old Market Square and it sat just at the edge of the main park-and-ride bus route. For these benefits, Amber had to pay nearly five hundred pounds a month for what amounted to little more than a soulless shoebox with a cooker and a toilet.

It was hard making ends meet, paying all the bills herself from the crappy salary she got at the children's center. She paid the rent from the modest sum of money she'd received from the sale of her mother's house, and it was fast disappearing.

The solicitor had told her eight months ago that most of the capital from the small stone-fronted terrace had been swallowed up by her mother's debts—debts Amber had known nothing about and that hadn't become apparent until it was time for her mother to sell up and move into the care home.

It was yet another reason for her to stick unswervingly to her plan and to get out of here as soon as possible.

She shifted on the cramped two-seater settee decorated with cigarette burns, pulling down her skirt to stop her thighs sticking to the cheap leather-look cushions.

When she'd first moved here, she had worked out early on that if she sat in a certain position in a certain place in the room, she could see just sky out of the window. The dirty brickwork across the road and the broken-down vehicles disappeared and there were no more hooded youths lingering on corners. Just sky and clouds.

It reminded her of when she and her sister were kids. They'd lie on their backs in the fields near home like fine-weather snow angels and identify shapes in the clouds.

Amber had been pretending she was somewhere else ever since.

She laid her hand on top of the A4 envelope full of photographs that was usually kept carefully hidden, clipped inside her old waxed outdoor jacket inside the wardrobe.

The envelope contained precious images that triggered a deluge of emotions. Happiness, sadness, regret and fury. She didn't feel strong enough to look at them again right now. She would be driving over to Ben's in just over an hour and she'd have to ensure her mask was firmly in place.

She pushed the envelope away, thinking how she'd spent most of her life dreaming about a future where she might be happy and content, free from the wretched thoughts that plagued her from dawn until dusk.

Perhaps that time was finally drawing near.

She sipped at her coffee, grimacing as the cool, bitter beverage coated her tongue. She set the mug aside and her mind drifted back to Sunday at the Jukeses' house. She didn't know quite how she'd managed to get through what she considered to be a three-hour ordeal, rather than the pleasant family meal Ben had promised.

When they'd first arrived at his parents' house and she'd met Judi, Ben's mum, Amber had had to practically pick her jaw up off the floor.

She'd looked just like a bag woman, wearing torn old clothing that clearly should have been binned long ago.

Granted, they'd arrived a little early and it was pretty obvious that Judi had been caught unawares. In fact, it was clear that the woman was mortified. Amber might've felt sorry for her if it had been anyone else.

"Mum and Dad don't have many visitors," Ben whispered behind his hand as his mum stood staring into space, looking a bit vague. "You should be flattered."

The look of failure on Judi's face spoke volumes, and Amber realized that the woman had probably seen the day as a rare chance to show off her wonderful home, picture-perfect family, and Cordon-Bleu cooking skills.

She sensed that Ben was a bit embarrassed by his mother's appearance, but he just laughed it off and Amber herself pretended not to notice.

It didn't take long for Amber's brief sympathy to evaporate.

From the second she arrived, Judi's eyes were on her at every moment: judging, evaluating, quite obviously *hating* that her husband and son were so distracted by her.

When they eventually all sat down, Amber found it nigh on impossible to relax, because the meal was so ruddy formal.

After listening to Ben's father bore on for far too long about wine, she couldn't wait to pour the stuff down her throat. She knew drinking was risky, in terms of saying something she shouldn't, but she promised herself she wouldn't have more than a glass or two. If she was honest, it felt essential to get her through the ordeal.

It was clear to Amber from the outset that Ben's mother

had planned to the nth degree, including a table setting featuring so much china, silver and glass it resembled a Michelin-starred restaurant. Ben constantly cooed and complimented his mother over the meal, but to Amber's disappointment, the food was distinctly average, dripping with fat and too many bland and unimaginative flavors.

Noah and Josh had been little demons as usual, *so* badly behaved. Yet nobody else seemed to notice. They constantly interrupted the adults' conversations, and gobbled down their food like it might get up and run away at any moment. The older boy, Noah, even belched loudly after his meal without a single challenge from anyone.

Amber witnessed how Ben's parents overindulged the children, and frankly, Judi treated Ben as if he wasn't much older than his own sons.

And then Amber had broken the precious jug, of course. That hadn't gone down too well; the atmosphere had turned decidedly icy for a short time. Judi had looked at her incisively for several minutes, as if she was trying to make her mind up whether Amber had done it on purpose or not.

Still, she didn't regret going. It had been more than a worthwhile exercise. She'd been able to see how the family dynamics worked, and that would come in very handy in the future.

Amber stood up from the couch and picked up the mug of now-cold coffee to take through to the kitchenette, smiling to herself.

Soon, a less-than-perfect Sunday lunch would be the very least of Judi Jukes's worries.

CHAPTER FIFTEEN

Judi

I get home early afternoon, and predictably, Henry is out. He often meets other retired colleagues from the bank on Mondays, down at the local snooker hall. At least that's what he tells me.

There have been, shall we say, some *inconsistencies* over the years in terms of Henry's whereabouts. There have been other women in the past; one I knew about—a colleague at the bank—others I suspected. I always sat it out, dropped hints and waited for Henry to come to his senses about how much he'd got to lose. Which he always did, in time.

The woman at the bank, Helena, she contacted me. Knocked on the door one day, if you can believe it. Told me my husband was in love with her and that I should do the right thing and let him go, let him "be happy."

I remember she was small and pale and blond, looked as if she needed someone to protect her. That sort. And she had her big blue eyes set on my Henry.

I didn't let her in; I shut the door in her face before she could say any more. I didn't want to hear it, you see.

That night, Henry came home from work to find his bags packed and me and the boys ready and waiting in the hallway to wave him off. That certainly brought him to his senses sharply enough. He put paid to his silly little fling and I never heard another thing about it.

Of course, I had my suspicions that there were others in the years that followed: the faintest whiff of a floral scent on his collar, him taking a shower before bed when he arrived home exhausted after a late meeting, a slight hesitation when asked which hotel he'd be staying at, should I need to contact him at yet another overnight conference... But you can't dwell on such things. Not if you want to keep your sanity.

That was all years ago now, and it's best forgotten. But you know, old habits die hard, and every time Henry tells me he's off out somewhere, that old, sick feeling stirs still in the pit of my stomach.

I sit down with a cup of tea and a sandwich and leaf lazily through a magazine but find my mind keeps wandering back to yesterday.

After lunch, when Ben, Amber and the boys left, I raised her landlord story with Henry.

"If I'm honest, I found it a little inappropriate," I said. "And don't look at me like that; I could tell you were taken aback by how candidly she spoke in front of us."

"Oh, don't be such a stick-in-the-mud, Judi." He rustled his newspaper in annoyance. "I thought she was a lovely girl and she'll be good for Ben. Get him out of the house a bit on a weekend."

"So long as she realizes it's Noah and Josh she's taking on too." I ignored the insult he'd aimed at me. "They come as a package and the boys have suffered enough without feeling pushed out by their daddy's new girlfriend. I have to say, Amber didn't seem particularly child-friendly to me."

"She works with children, for goodness' sake! We all

know that nobody will ever be good enough for Ben in your eyes. Can't you at least give the poor girl a chance? It's very early days to be getting this uptight."

I take my plate and cup back into the kitchen, standing for a moment to stare out at the grass, which is going to need its first cut soon. Maybe Maura was right and I am being a bit unfair. I acknowledge it's early days to be forming a complete opinion of someone, but there's also something to be said for first impressions.

At two o'clock prompt, I pull together a few cleaning materials and the new tea towels I bought last weekend that I know will match Ben's red and white kitchen color scheme perfectly. I pack everything into a canvas shopping bag, pick up my car keys and handbag and make the ten-minute journey over to Ben's house.

I pull up outside and turn off the engine, and for a few moments I look at the terraced house like a stranger might. There is no front garden to speak of, the front door leading out, as it does, over the tiniest patch of grass and straight onto the pavement. The fascia bricks are weathered and worn and the big Victorian sills in dire need of a repaint. I make a mental note to mention this to Henry for his list of spring jobs.

As soon as it's open, I must find a way to get Ben and the boys to take a look round the show home of the new two-bedroom eco-houses that are being built just around the corner from us. A nice new property would be so much more suitable and low maintenance, and I know Henry would agree to us helping Ben out with a deposit.

I'd always thought it would be lovely when the boys were a little older for them to be able to wander around to ours when the mood took them. In the summer, they could make full use of our much larger, south-facing garden. And

I wouldn't mind a bit if Ben wanted to come for his tea every night after finishing work.

But the planning for all this has to start now, and in my humble opinion, this is the ideal time for Ben and the boys to relocate nearer to us. The boys are at an ideal age to start at the new school in the autumn term, and Ben will surely appreciate our continuing advice and guidance for many months before Amber gets a say in proceedings.

I make up my mind to speak to Henry about it later.

I grab the canvas bag and get out of the car. I don't do a lot at Ben's house early in the week: just whizz round with the vacuum, give the kitchen a good wipe down and freshen up the main bathroom. I tend to do the laundry midweek and then give the place a thorough clean on a Friday, so it looks nice for them at the start of the weekend.

I go round to the back of the house and let myself in through the kitchen door. I put the canvas bag down on the worktop and walk toward the lounge, then stop dead in my tracks in the doorway.

The black leather suite that I helped Ben choose last year has been switched around. The three-seater is now opposite the fireplace and the two-seater is positioned against the long wall. It would've been much better left as it was because now the room looks more cramped and it's going to be far harder to get around with the vacuum.

It occurs to me I could just move it back again, but knowing Ben, there'll be a reason for it. Usually he doesn't do anything in the house without asking my opinion, and I like to think I add a woman's touch here and there, to make the place a little cozier for them.

But that's when I notice that the two Lilliput Lane cottages that stood in pride of place on the mantelpiece above the coal-effect gas fire are gone. The boys love looking at my collection at home, and a few months ago I let them each choose a favorite one to take home. They spent ages comparing all twenty cottages, collected over five years or more, and selecting the ones they liked the very best to display at home.

I scan the room to see if they've simply been moved, but the ornaments are nowhere to be seen.

I shrug and move back to the kitchen. I'm sure there's a perfectly logical explanation. I'll just need to ask Ben about it later when he picks the boys up.

I stand at the window and look out on to the narrow lawn as I wash up the breakfast dishes in the sink. It makes more sense to do this than leaving them crusting up in the dishwasher all day and the stuff I find tedious to do at home is a pleasure here.

I'll have to get Henry round to tidy up the lawn and sink a few bedding plants into the bare borders. I know the boys like to spend more time outside once the weather gets better.

It gives me a warm feeling, keeping the house neat and organized for them. Holding down a full-time job, Ben hasn't got time to be faffing around cleaning and ironing, and I feel like I'm performing an important practical duty in supporting my son and the children.

Louise was never a particularly house-proud woman, bless her, and she was the first to admit it.

"Your house is always pristine, Judi," she'd say every time she visited us. "I wish I had your eye for soft furnishings."

She'd always ask my advice when it came to decorating and organizing the house, and of course, I was always more than happy to help out. She fitted into our family like one of our own, and I felt pure happiness the day Ben married her. Louise was the daughter I never had. I still miss her every day. We all do.

I spray and wipe down the kitchen tops and sweep up a few crumbs from the floor. I hang one of the new red-checked tea towels over the oven handle and then neatly fold the other two. When I open the deep drawer to stow them away, I see that the two missing ornaments from the mantelpiece have been tossed carelessly in here.

I pick up Josh's snow-covered cottage and hold it up to the window, and it's immediately clear that the chimney has been chipped clean off.

CHAPTER SIXTEEN

Judi

Later, I pick Noah and Josh up from school and, as Ben has a meeting after school, take them back to ours for tea.

I decide not to quiz them about the broken ornament. It's highly possible one of them has broken it and has been too worried to tell me. Instead, we get out their reading folders and talk about what they've done at school today.

"We did numbers, Nanny," Josh tells me. "Really hard adding-up."

"Pfft!" Noah sniggers. "That's just stupid easy-peasy stuff for babies."

"Noah, that's not very nice," I say gently as Josh's face falls. "Don't forget you had to start with that exact same work when you were in Year One."

Noah snatches up his reading book and uses it as a shield against us, holding it far too close to his face to be able to read. I decide the best option is to ignore his behavior.

"So, hands up who wants Nanny's homemade meat and potato pie for tea?"

"Yes please!" Josh springs up and jumps up and down, one arm stretching toward the ceiling.

"Noah?"

"Please," he mutters morosely. He puts his book down and reaches for the television remote control.

"Two plates of pie coming up." I smile before leaving the room.

I feel a little uneasy about Noah's outburst. I've never heard him sniping at his brother like that before. Certainly they bicker regularly over their choice of television program and who gets the last chocolate biscuit from the barrel. But Noah is usually supportive of his younger brother when it comes to schoolwork. Recently, he willingly spent hours helping Josh make a papier-mâché rocket for his outer-space art project at school.

Later, Ben arrives.

Henry is still not home but he's texted me to say they've decided to go out for a curry, and I don't mind one bit because it will give me time to talk to my son without more accusations that I'm being unfair and judgmental ringing in my ears.

I make Ben a plate of pie and peas and take it through for him on a tray, together with cups of tea for both of us. Noah barely looks up from the television.

"What a day," Ben sighs. "We had a teacher off, so they split the class and I ended up with—"

"Daddy! Hands up or I'll blow your head off." Josh jumps in between us and aims the remote control like a gun at Ben.

Ben puts down his cutlery with a clatter. "Josh, what have you been told? I'm talking to Nanny."

"He's just happy to see you, Ben," I say lightly.

Josh attaches himself to Ben's leg, gripping on to it like a koala bear.

"Daddy," he whines.

"Amber thinks the boys interrupt too much, Mum." Ben

scowls, trying to gently shake Josh off. "And I'm beginning to think she might be right."

"Nonsense," I say, ruffling Josh's hair. "It's just because he hasn't seen you all day."

Ben nods. "Come on, champ. Let Daddy have his tea, eh?"

Josh lets go and sits down, a little dejected, leaving Ben to eat his food in peace.

"I was at the house earlier," I say casually, taking a sip of my tea. "I notice you've had a bit of a change-round of furniture in the living room."

"Oh yeah." Ben gives me a coy smile as he chews. "That's Amber. She's into this whole feng shui thing, so she's moved things round to improve the energies, apparently."

"Ah, I see." I smile to cover up my irritation. "Don't understand that kind of thing myself, but I've heard people say there's definitely something in it."

"Amber loves all that hocus-pocus stuff." Ben takes a sip of his tea. "Crystals, energies, she's even been to psychic readers."

"Blimey." I sense an opportunity to delve a bit deeper. "That was quite a story she told us yesterday, about her landlord. She doesn't pull any punches, that's for sure." I smile to soften my words.

"Ha! I know, she's so funny." Ben grins, loading his fork with pie. "She's straight-talking, is Amber. No messing about or putting on an act like some girls do. I love that about her, that what you see is what you get, you know?"

"Indeed." I take another sip of tea.

"This pie is spot-on, Mum," he says, closing his eyes briefly as he savors it.

"I'm glad you're enjoying it, love." I touch his arm. "How does Amber get on with the boys?"

"Oh, she's brilliant with them," Ben replies quickly,

"She's so good with kids. It's because of her job, see. Although like she says, she's wasted there, really. I reckon she ought to get into teaching."

"She'd need a degree for that, though," I remind him.

"Yeah, but she's only just turned thirty, Mum. I told her last night, she could be qualified by the time she's thirty-four, thirty-five. I'd love to support her in doing that."

I swallow and stay quiet. That sounds like a pretty heavy-duty commitment to even be thinking about when you've only just met someone.

I decide to change the subject. "We should really have shown her around the house properly yesterday, Ben. I hope she didn't think us rude."

"'Course not. She said she could see it was a big place when she went upstairs to the loo."

So she *did* manage to have a little look around.

"Before I forget, I noticed you've taken the cottages off the mantelpiece, which is absolutely fine, of course. But if you'll let me have them back, I'll return them to my cabinet collection."

"Oh." Ben frowns. "I hadn't noticed they'd gone. Amber must've moved them; she doesn't like clutter."

"They're limited-edition ornaments, Ben, hardly clutter." I bristle. "The boys really like them. Do you know where they are?"

"No, but don't worry, Amber will have put them somewhere safe. I'll ask her."

A sharp spike jabs me in the guts when I think about the broken chimney to add to my mother's broken jug. But I don't want Ben to think I've been snooping around at his house, so I'm forced to stay quiet.

"She seems to have made herself at home very quickly." I say it without thinking and he looks up sharply. "What I mean is, it's nice that she feels so comfortable around you and the boys."

"I know." His features relax again and he puts down his fork to consider his thoughts. After a few seconds, he smiles and looks at me. "I just can't believe my luck, Mum. I really think Amber might be the one."

CHAPTER SEVENTEEN

Judi

After Louise died, Maura was a very good friend to me. She found an excellent bereavement counselor for Ben, who in turn organized some short sessions for the boys. They didn't stay in therapy for long, but Ben said it had certainly helped, during those initial devastating weeks.

Maura lost her husband to cancer when she was in her early thirties and she's never remarried and doesn't have any children. Even though I don't see her socially, I know she has a strong network of friends and keeps herself busy as an active member of various local societies.

She is also a fantastic boss and agreed immediately that I could go down to working mornings only at the surgery, finishing at one o'clock each day. That left me plenty of time to pick Noah and Josh up after school and help Ben out around the house.

She then recruited Carole Jeffers to work the afternoon shift on reception.

"I really don't want to lose you, Judi," Maura said at the time. "You're good at your job as well as a good friend and

I'm here to help you in any way I can. You'd be bored stiff at home all day, we both know that."

I felt both valued and supported when it mattered the most, and I still feel grateful now that her flexibility afforded me the time to help Ben and the boys.

As I drive toward Ben's house now, I can see that, annoyingly, there is a car already parked directly outside his residents' bay. A small cream-colored Fiat sits in the place I usually park. It doesn't matter, because I'm able to get a spot just behind it. But I can't help wondering whose car it is... Amber's, perhaps?

I get out of the car and walk around to the boot to lift out the laundry basket full of clean, folded clothes. I often do the boys' washing at my house and then bring it back to Ben's to iron it. That way, it doesn't get all crumpled on the journey over here.

I lock the car, hook my handbag over my shoulder and pick up the basket before walking to the front door, Ben's key already in my hand.

I slide in the key and push the door open with my hip, swinging round with the basket.

I let out an involuntary little yelp as a figure appears in the kitchen doorway.

"Oh! Amber." I place the basket down in the small hallway and press my hand to my chest. "You gave me a start. Ben didn't say you'd be here."

"No, I didn't decide until this morning that I'd be working from home."

Home?

"It's a staff training day, you see."

She takes another step into the hallway. She is wearing bleached jeans with gaping, frayed rips at both knees and a very pretty pink sparkly top that doesn't quite meet the waistband of her trousers, revealing an inch of firm, tanned flesh.

"It's nice to see you again." I push the door closed behind me. "How are you?"

"I'm good, thanks," she replies, folding her trim arms. "You?"

"Yes, I'm very well. Thank you for asking."

My stomach begins to roil. I feel as if I've inconvenienced her somehow, disturbed her at home, which is ridiculous. This is Ben's house and he's only known her for five minutes. So why am I standing here like a lemon, waiting for an invite to go through?

I pick up the laundry basket and walk toward her.

"I'll just put this in the kitchen, and then I can get on with the ironing."

"Oh, leave it in the hall, I'll drop it off at Y-Iron on my way into work," she says. "They turn it round in a day, and I'm sure you've got enough on without skivvying over here all afternoon for Ben and the lads."

I feel my jaw stiffen.

"It's no trouble at all," I say smoothly. "I've done Ben's laundry for the last two years and I'm quite used to it."

"But I'm around now." She smiles sweetly and runs pearly pink nails through her hair. "So you see, there really is no need."

"Well, now I'm here, I might as well stay." I walk into the kitchen, my heart drumming a panicky beat. Our shoulders brush slightly as she steps aside. I put the laundry basket on the worktop and open the tall cupboard next to the fridge. "It won't take me long to run over these few bits with the iron."

I wish she'd just go and leave me to it, but she stands proprietarily in the kitchen doorway and watches as I scan the contents of the cupboard.

"Where the devil is it?" I murmur to myself.

"If you're looking for the iron, it's upstairs. At the back of the airing cupboard."

"Why on earth has Ben moved it up there?" I tut. "It's lived in this cupboard for as long as I've been coming here."

"I moved it."

I look at her and she smiles, displaying small, sharp teeth.

"Oh."

"It's just that I thought we wouldn't need it, and I hate clutter, even when you can't see it. I also told Ben I'd drop the ironing off and pick it up each week." She plucks a piece of cotton from the hem of her top and lets it fall to the floor. "And he's fine with that."

A channel of heat shoots up into my face.

"That reminds me. I see that my cottage ornaments are no longer wanted in the living room," I say curtly. "If you can let me have them back, I'll return them to my collection."

"You actually *collect* those dust magnets?" Her nose wrinkles. "I think they're in a drawer somewhere. I'll find them for you and Ben will bring them over."

I bite down hard on my tongue and taste a faint metallic tang.

"I'll just leave this here then, shall I?" I nod to the laundry basket and shut the cupboard door a little more forcibly than I intended. "No sense in me carrying on today if I'm not needed."

She unfolds her arms and the smirk slides from her face. "Judi, I hope you're not offended. I…I'm just thinking of you. I'm sure you've got enough to do at home."

I can't say anything for fear of bursting into tears. My knees feel like jelly as I walk past her. Part of me wants to throttle her for changing everything I know and love, while the other part longs to reach out to the person my son is replacing me with and explain how I am feeling. But I know instinctively that would be a mistake. Louise she is not, and I'll just sound like a sad, paranoid woman.

"I'm not offended," I manage, forcing myself to breathe. I reach into my handbag and pull out the car keys. "If you want to sort out the ironing yourself from now on, that's absolutely fine. I'll pick the boys up from school as usual today and take them back to mine."

There is no way I'm coming back here with Noah and Josh like I usually do, to feel like an intruder in my own son's home.

"Well, if you're sure," she says when I get to the door. "Then that's perfect."

I don't turn around and look at her again. I just let myself out and make sure I close the door softly behind me.

Once I'm safely in the car, I drive away immediately, in case she's watching out of the window. But once I'm round the corner, I pull over and sit there, just for a few minutes, until I get my breath back.

I try to swallow down the unpleasant sensation—I can only describe it as a sort of *unease*—that's lurking in my bones. An unnerving background buzz that makes me feel like I'm teetering on the edge of panic.

The normality I have gathered around me like a fortress is beginning to slowly crumble, and there's not a thing I can do but hold on tight and hope for the best.

CHAPTER EIGHTEEN

Amber

Amber watched Judi leave in that huffy way she had.

When the car disappeared off down the street, she popped back upstairs to finish putting a few bits into her handbag for the journey she had in front of her.

A smile played on her mouth as she reached for her cardigan. The look on Judi's face when she'd found her here was one of pure shock and indignation. The older woman was clearly outraged that Amber was riding roughshod over her nice, organized little family life.

She'd only just got back in the house when Judi arrived. She'd been into town nice and early to buy some clothes and one or two other interesting bits that made her smile.

She hadn't expected to see Henry, but as it turned out, it had been more than a stroke of luck.

Amber realized that moving the iron without prior permission was obviously pure genius on her part. At one stage during the altercation that ensued, she'd honestly thought Judi was going to burst into tears.

She'd had no idea that such small acts of militancy would

have such a powerful effect, but she intended to capitalize on it from now on.

Fifteen minutes later, she was driving through the city toward Junction 26 of the M1, which would eventually take her up north to the care home she so hated visiting.

She dreamed of the time she wouldn't have to travel up there anymore. That distant day when she would reach her long-awaited goal of finally putting the past to rest and enjoying a fresh start somewhere else with her new family.

But there was a hell of a lot of work to be done before then.

Everything was coming together nicely, and without even realizing it, Henry Jukes had just given her a little extra boost.

There had been an accident on the motorway and one of the lanes was closed, so the journey to Stocksbridge had stretched close to two hours by the time Amber pulled into the small graveled car park of Sunbeam Lodge.

She got out of the car and stood for a moment looking at the crumbling facade of the building, the rotten, splintering window frames and the gaps in the roof tiles like missing teeth. This place was the polar opposite of a sunbeam, she thought wryly.

She signed the visitor book in the porch and tapped the four-digit number into the security keypad. The door clicked open and she stepped into the building, holding her breath as long as she could before she was forced to inhale the dreaded smell of boiled cabbage and pee.

She walked quickly, nodding to a member of staff she'd seen a few times previously but never spoken to as she made her way down the corridor to her mother's room.

She could hear someone crying out repeatedly somewhere

in the distance, and she passed an old man, oblivious to her presence, who was having an animated conversation with an invisible friend.

Familiar feelings of doom and hopelessness filled her. Was this all there was? All that life added up to in the end?

Her mother hadn't been lucky. She'd suffered a lot of heartache, choosing a husband who turned out to be nothing but a no-good bastard. That, on top of the tragedy that had blighted all their lives and almost finished her off ... and now here she was, half mad and stuck in Sunbeam Lodge until the end of her days.

Except if Amber's plans came to fruition, she wouldn't be stuck here indefinitely. Amber would ensure she found a better place for her mother to live out her days, somewhere closer to home. It was the least she could do, despite her mother's ambivalence toward her.

The door was ajar and Amber pushed it open to find the old woman sitting in the single straight-backed chair by the window, looking out over the car park.

"Hello, Mum." She left the door slightly open for air and walked over, bending to give her mother a kiss on her cheek.

"Kathryn?" whispered the old woman as she turned, her face lighting up.

"No, it's me, Mum. Amber."

"I knew you'd come." Her mother smiled and laid a cool, crinkled hand on Amber's cheek. "Don't send your sister here again, she's up to no good. I can tell just by looking at her. Amber's not a good girl like you are."

Amber stared out at the gray clouds while her mother mumbled on, waiting until she fell quiet again before speaking.

"Shall I read to you, Mum?"

"That would be lovely, Kathryn. Thank you."

She opened the book and went back to Chapter One. She only ever read Chapter One, because her mother was beyond remembering enough for her to carry on any further.

"Which book is it?" her mother asked.

"Your favorite, of course." Amber smiled. "*Oliver Twist*."

"Charles Dickens," her mother whispered in awe, her eyes growing vague. "London. Can we go one day soon, Kathryn? To London?"

"One day we will, Mum." Amber nodded. "Soon you'll be away from this place and you'll have your very own little boy, just like Oliver. I'll bring him soon, a boy to keep you company on my visits."

CHAPTER NINETEEN

Judi

Next morning, I'm the first to arrive at work, so I turn on the heaters, open the blinds and make the coffee. I hear the back door open and Maura bustles into the little kitchenette behind reception.

"Horrible drizzly weather." She shivers, shrugging off her damp mac and hanging it on the back of the door. "Supposed to be spring, too. Bring the coffees through, Jude, I've got some goss."

I turn to the fridge to get the milk and secretly roll my eyes. Maura is a kind, generous woman, but she is also a terrible gossip. Sadly, not the best attribute for someone who works in a GPs' surgery.

I take our drinks through and we sit together at the front desk. I can see a cluster of our early patients already outside the main door canopy, but we've another fifteen minutes before the surgery opens.

"You'll never guess what's wrong with Fiona Bonser." Maura's eyes widen. "No wonder she was so desperate to see a doctor yesterday."

"Oh, Maura, you haven't been snooping again, have you?" I shake my head.

"Are you kidding? Nosing at the patient records is what gets me through the day." She pauses to take a tentative sip of her hot coffee. "Do you want to know, or not?"

I throw her a disapproving look.

"Don't you look at me like that," she scolds. "It's worth it, I promise."

When I sigh, exasperated, Maura leans forward.

"She had lacerations on her inner thighs and internal bruising," she hisses. "Work that one out."

"Sounds awful." I frown. "I wonder what—"

"Rough sex, of course!" She sits back again, pressing her lips together in disapproval. "Come on, it hardly takes Hercule Poirot to figure out what caused it."

"What?"

"What are you, a nun?" She glances round to make sure none of the doctors are lurking. "There's only one way to get those kinds of injuries. The dirty cow."

"Maura!"

"What? If you don't believe me, I can show you Dr. Fielder's notes." She flicks on the computer monitor.

"No, I do believe you," I say hastily. "I just mean it sounds awful. Painful. But we don't know how it happened, so we shouldn't judge her."

Maura shakes her head slowly. "There really is no hope for you, Judi. Naïve isn't a strong enough word."

"I'm not stupid," I say, biting down on my back teeth. "I know *how* it must've happened. What I mean is, the poor girl seemed pretty desperate to see the doctor yesterday, so she was probably in pain. She could've been attacked or anything, we just don't know."

"Hmm, I suppose so. I didn't think of that." Maura

presses a few buttons on the keyboard and peers at the screen. "Dr. Fielder has written here, 'Patient reluctant to discuss injuries.'"

I stand up and pick up the coffee cups.

"She could be reluctant to discuss them for a number of reasons, I'm sure. Not an easy subject to broach with your family doctor."

Maura presses another button and Fiona's records disappear from the screen.

"You're no fun, Judi Jukes, do you know that?" she grumbles, sliding back her chair. "I'm going to sort through some of those old archived records in the back office this morning. Will you be OK out here on your own for a bit?"

"'Course," I say, taking the cups back into the kitchen.

"Just give me a shout if you need anything," Maura says. "I'll open the doors now, let the sick in to be healed."

I smile to myself. It's a good job I know Maura's heart is in the right place, despite some of the unethical things she says and does.

The morning progresses as usual. I check patients in, issue repeat prescriptions and answer the phone, mainly to inform callers that, regrettably, there are no free appointments now until Friday afternoon.

My heart sinks when the famously cantankerous Mr. Lewis appears in front of me.

"I need to see the doctor sharpish, duck."

"I'm sorry, Mr. Lewis. We've no appointments left this morning, but there's a sit-and-wait surgery on between four and six this afternoon if you'd like to come back then."

My breath feels a little jagged in my chest as I silently urge Mr. Lewis to accept my suggestion.

"I can't wait till then." He leans forward as if he's going to speak in confidence, but he doesn't lower his voice. "That fungal infection between my toes, it's back."

Unfortunately, I know all about the fungal infection thanks to Maura reading out the doctor's description of the symptoms after Mr. Lewis's last appointment. Several patients are staring, evidently waiting for my reaction. I feel a ridiculous urge to run away into the back office.

"I'm sorry, as I say, there are no—"

"It's gone all crusty and yellow pus is oozing out. It's agony to walk on." Nearby patients grimace at each other as he begins to stoop down. "If I can just get this sock off, I can show you how bad it—"

"No!" I raise my hand in a stop sign. "Not out here, Mr. Lewis, thank you. Wait here a moment, please."

I walk over to the back office door and tap. When there's no answer, I push open the door and peer round. Maura is in there, knee deep in old patient files.

"Maura?"

"Whatever's wrong?" She looks alarmed. "Gosh, you're sweating buckets, Jude."

"Sorry to interrupt, but I've got Mr. Lewis and his fungal infection in reception." I pause to take a breath, fanning my face with a hand. "I've told him there are no appointments, but he's threatening to get his foot out to show me how bad it is."

Maura grins. "Is that all? You shouldn't get yourself all het up over that old goat. Don't worry, I'll sort it." She disappears down the short corridor leading to the nurse's treatment room.

I stand for a moment relishing the quiet privacy of this small room, away from all the prying eyes in recception. It feels like I'm going crazy. On one level I know I've completely overreacted, but on another, thanks to the reading list Dr. Fern gave me, I recognize it's just a symptom; a flash of anxiety that will soon pass.

When I feel ready, I return to my desk and ask Mr. Lewis to take a seat while I deal with the short queue of patients that has already formed behind him.

Two minutes later Maura is back, and thankfully I'm feeling slightly more in control.

"Nurse is going to take a quick look at you, Mr. Lewis," she says briskly. "But if you want to see the doctor then I'm afraid you'll have to come back later and wait like everyone else."

Mr. Lewis shuffles to the nurse appointment chairs and I turn to Maura.

"Sorry about that," I say. "I just had one of my moments."

She smiles and pats me lightly on the shoulder.

"No worries, Jude. Mr. Lewis is enough to give anyone a funny turn."

A funny turn? It's an accurate description but a worrying one. I don't want Maura thinking I'm not up to the job anymore. She can't have people having funny turns on the surgery reception desk, can she?

My job is important to me and I need to buck my ideas up. Enough is changing in my life without it affecting work. I feel needed here. Valued.

I don't like the sense I've had just lately that the ground underneath me is starting to shift.

CHAPTER TWENTY

Judi

When I next glance up at the wall clock, I'm shocked to see it's already noon. That's the thing I love about this job: no two days are the same and you never know what's coming through the door. Sometimes it can be challenging, but generally, time flies and it's never boring.

I find myself wondering what the boys are doing at school today. They break for lunch at twelve fifteen, so right now they'll be just finishing off their last lesson of the morning.

Ben has a staff meeting every Wednesday, so he'll be picking Noah and Josh up from our house a little later than usual. It's much nicer now that I bring them straight here, rather than risking another unpleasant altercation with Amber.

If the weather clears up, we can go to the park before tea, and if Henry is around he'll take a football and the three of them will have a kickabout on the grass next to the play area.

In no time at all, it's time to go. I do a brief handover with Carole, the afternoon receptionist, and after saying goodbye to Maura, I leave work.

The surgery is a thirty-five-minute walk from home, so

I often use that opportunity to get a bit of exercise in rather than use the car. I've never been terribly overweight; food has always been something I enjoy vicariously through others rather than for myself. A combination of eating sensibly and keeping fairly active has kept me just a few pounds above my fighting weight.

But the last few years has seen a persistent and unwelcome padding settle around my middle, which I've so far been completely unable to shift through diet or by stepping up my exercise. Another joy of middle age; the fun just keeps on coming.

This morning I got the bus into work, as I'd checked the weather and knew it was forecast to brighten up later, enabling me to walk home. In my coat and scarf, I'm perfectly comfortable and the drizzle has thankfully stopped now so I find I don't need my umbrella after all.

The sun is making a valiant attempt to break through the thick cloud cover, but it hasn't quite managed it yet. Nevertheless, it's quite a bit brighter than when I stepped out of the house first thing this morning.

I take the slightly longer way home, past Broxtowe Park, where I might bring the boys later. There's a short lull in the stream of cars passing me, and for a minute or two I can actually enjoy the birdsong in nearby trees. But then my ears twitch suddenly as I hear another noise. A sort of strange mewing sound.

I stop walking and look cautiously around me, fearful of seeing a poor injured cat at the side of the busy road, but there is nothing like that. I resume my walk and catch the noise again. A sob, a pitiful moaning.

I peer over the low hedge and into the park, and that's when I see her. Fiona Bonser. Sitting alone on a bench, sobbing her heart out.

I pick up my pace and walk a little further down to the park entrance. The play area is deserted, with most older children being at school and younger children probably kept in because of the earlier spell of rain. The rain-spotted play equipment glistens, its primary colors incongruous against the dull gray clouds and concrete.

Over the other side of the wide expanse of grass I can see a couple of dog walkers, sticking to the narrow path and dodging the drips from overhanging leafy branches. Apart from them, there's just Fiona here. And now, me.

She fumbles in the pocket of her thin coat and pulls out a tissue. As she blows her nose, she looks up with red, swollen eyes and sees me approaching. I watch as she visibly stiffens, sitting up straighter and pressing her knees together. Her bare, mottled legs must be freezing cold. I think about the lacerations on her inner thighs and feel incredibly guilty that I'm party to such personal information.

She sniffs loudly and juts out her chin, her challenging eyes fixed on me.

"Hello, Fiona." I smile as I reach her. "I was just walking by and I couldn't help noticing you seem a little upset."

She looks at me.

"I mean, you're obviously very upset," I clarify.

"Yes," she says quietly, looking away. "But don't worry yourself. I'll be fine."

I sit down on the bench, angling toward her.

"Not very often you see it this quiet," I say, nodding to the desolate play area. "Have you come here to get a bit of peace?"

"The kids are at school, little one is at the free crèche." She shrugs. "I just had to get out of that shitty flat for a bit, before it sends me stir crazy."

"I know what you mean." I smile. "I often come out for a stroll if I'm feeling—"

"Don't pretend we're the same, 'cos we're not," Fiona snaps, staring straight ahead over the marshy grass to the scattering of trees beyond.

"That's not what I meant."

"Yeah? Well, you and me, we couldn't be more different. There's no way you can begin to understand how I feel, trust me on that one."

"I wasn't trying to say I understand exactly how you feel." I can hardly confide in her that I know the reason she saw Dr. Fielder. "And I don't mean to upset you any more than you already are. I stopped by because I just wanted to make sure you're OK. That's all. See if there's anything I can do to help."

She whips her head round, eyes sparking.

"The answer is no, I'm not. I'm far from being fucking OK. Satisfied? So what is it exactly you're going to do for me? You with your nice easy life and your little part-time job at the doctors' surgery?"

"Well, I . . . I meant, if there's anything I *could* do to help, then I'd be happy to."

Fiona lets out a bitter laugh.

"*You* help *me*? That'd be hilarious if it wasn't so fucking sad."

A knot of heat pushes up into my throat and plugs any more platitudes I might think of wasting on her. I understand life must be very difficult for this young woman, but there's no need for her to be so rude and hostile when I'm only trying to help. I stand up and take a step away from the bench.

"I'm sorry if I've disturbed you, Fiona. I certainly didn't mean to make you angry."

"I know you didn't." She shrugs, black eyeliner smudged beneath her eyes, giving a ghoulish look to her pale, pock-marked face. "But trust me, you don't want to listen to my problems."

"Look," I say gently, "I know we lead very different lives. But I'm not easily shocked. I see a lot of things working at the surgery. I'm fully aware that people have to cope with some pretty awful stuff."

She looks up at me, and I hope I haven't gone too far, been too pushy.

"I..." She hesitates, like she wants to say something. "I'd like to tell you, but I can't." Her tone grows firmer. "I just can't."

"I promise I won't breathe a word to anyone," I say, suddenly hopeful that I'm on the cusp of a breakthrough. "I give you my word."

"You say that now, but you'd think differently if I told you the truth."

"I wouldn't, I—"

"Just leave it, will you?" she snaps, and waves me away. "Just leave me alone."

She turns her back on me, and I sigh and walk away. Just before I leave the park, I turn around and look at her again. A pathetically thin and woeful figure, slumped on the bench.

"If you change your mind, you know where I am," I call.

But she doesn't reply. I might as well be invisible.

CHAPTER TWENTY-ONE

Judi

Ben texts me from work while I'm walking home.

Hi, Mum. No need to do ironing today, Amber will sort it. x

I push the phone back into my pocket without replying and allow myself a wry smile. There's no more ironing to do yet, but how very kind of Amber to offer; she's all heart, she really is. Worrying herself constantly that I'm doing too much.

I feel a sort of smog settle around me, spoiling the crispness of the air. I push it away and decide I'll take some time for myself instead of going round to Ben's. Maybe I'll take a long bath, read a magazine or watch something on TV catch-up. I can't remember the last time I did that. I don't like sitting still if I can help it.

It's just an invitation for the past to come flooding back again.

On Friday, I decide to drive to work and I don't mention to Maura that I saw Fiona Bonser at the park.

I'm pretty sure her curiosity will be instantly reignited if

I describe how inconsolable Fiona was, and I don't want to encourage her to delve further into her confidential patient records.

Midway through the morning, when I make us a coffee, I fish out my mobile from my handbag and turn it off. If Ben has any intention of texting to cancel my big weekly clean at the house today, then I will truthfully be able to say that I didn't get the message.

The last two evenings, he has raced into the house to pick the boys up and raced back out again.

"Sorry, Mum, can't stop, loads of marking to do," he said the first evening; then "Got to dash, expecting a call on the landline."

This is unusual behavior from my son. He's always had time for at least a cup of tea and a biscuit when he collects the boys, often staying for a hot meal.

So I haven't had a chance to broach the topic of his relationship with Amber. Things like how quickly it's progressing and, crucially, bearing in mind she referred to Ben's house as "home" the other day, whether they've discussed her moving in.

In my view, it's ridiculously early to be thinking about those things, but then it seems that Amber herself just dropped on us out of the blue.

Yes, my son is in his early thirties. Yes, he's got every right to do as he wishes with his life without consulting me.

However, there are two very innocent and vulnerable parties in all of this, in the shape of Noah and Josh.

I'm loath to admit that Ben seems totally besotted by Amber even at this early stage, and it goes without saying that when widowed men become besotted, they don't always make the right decisions for themselves *or* their children. I've been around long enough to know that much.

And that's why I fully intend to keep a discreet but watchful eye on the situation.

When I finish at the surgery, I drive straight over to Ben's rather than going home first. If Amber is there for some reason, I've already decided I'm not going to get drawn into an awkward situation like earlier in the week, when we all but came to blows over the ironing.

If she's "working from home" again, I shall simply keep my head down and carry on doing what I've done for the last two years before she appeared on the scene. I'm determined to continue to help my son with domestic duties until Ben himself tells me he wants me to stop.

As far as I'm concerned, what Amber wants doesn't really count.

Thankfully, in the event, Amber isn't at Ben's. The house is empty. My heartbeat slows a little.

I leave my handbag and the basket of cleaning products I've bought to replenish the stock I keep here in the hallway and make my way through to the kitchen.

While I'm filling the kettle, I glance around. All seems to be in fairly good order in here. As usual, the breakfast dishes are piled in the sink, and I'm gratified to see there are only three bowls, three spoons and three glasses with orange juice sediment at the bottom.

The kitchen tops are littered with crumbs and the odd smear of butter. It's the typical scenario that greets me when three males are let loose to get their own breakfast.

While the kettle is boiling, I give in to the feeling that's been niggling at me since I walked in here. Sliding open the deep drawer, I root around a bit and see that my ornaments are still in there but have been shoved carelessly toward the back, underneath the clean tea towels and numerous appliance manuals.

I take the cottages out and put them on the worktop, ready to take with me when I go. Then I wander out into the hallway and push open the living room door.

I gasp, rooted to the spot for a moment.

The chimney breast has been papered in the most awful black and ruby striped wallpaper. The numerous photographs of Ben, Louise and the boys are gone from the walls. In their place are now what can only be described as lurid monochrome canvases depicting half-naked women, and two large framed photographs of Ben and Amber. Eventually I spot last year's school portrait of the boys lying flat on a lamp table, on top of a pile of celebrity magazines.

The black leather suite I helped Ben choose for its clean, simple lines is now swamped with gaudy mismatched blankets and shawls, many of them decorated with sequins and glittery threads. The place looks like a boudoir. And *what* is that smell?

My question is answered when I walk over to the windowsill. Piles of ash and the burned-out ends of incense sticks are littered there. It's the same story over at the mantelpiece.

This is not the sort of decoration I can imagine Ben finding attractive or restful to come home to at the end of a busy day. Gone are the practical furnishings and the marks of a loving family home.

It's when I see that the box of toys and games in the corner behind the sofa has disappeared that the slightly irritated feeling gives way to a tightness in my chest.

How *dare* she walk into my family's lives and stamp such brutal assertiveness on it? More to the point, how could Ben let her do such a thing?

The boys should have been eased into this new situation, their daddy meeting someone new. Any big change in their circumstances needs to be properly managed, not just dropped on them with little or no notice. Noah's recent snappiness with his brother and the way Josh clung to his daddy's leg cross my mind. It's probably no coincidence that their behavior is changing.

They might not have said anything, but their actions speak volumes, if you know what to look for.

I leave the sitting room, and before I make my way upstairs, I make sure to double-lock the front door from the inside. My breathing is becoming shallow and rather rapid, but I reassure myself that I'm not doing anything too awful in taking a look around. I'd normally go into all the rooms, making sure things are tidy.

It's just that now, for some reason, it feels like I'm intruding.

CHAPTER TWENTY-TWO

Judi

I stand in the doorway of my grandsons' bedroom.

Gone are the tangled piles of discarded clothes, the Lego structures, the ominous-looking robots, some of which they've hand-built over many hours with Ben. There are Blu Tack marks on the walls where the posters of their favorite footballers and Transformer films and drawings they'd done themselves were displayed. It has now all been removed.

I can actually see the carpet, which is usually swamped with toys and clothes and left like that until I come to tidy up. It is also a great deal dimmer in here, and I realize that a blackout blind has been fitted to the window and hasn't been fully opened. I find the effect unsettling, as I do the thought that the boys are being conditioned to stay in bed longer, probably at weekends.

The corner of something white grabs my attention. I reach down under the bottom bunk and pull out the large plastic box. It contains the toys and games that have been relocated from the sitting room.

The beds are made and the quilts tucked in too tightly, under both mattresses. I reach up to the top bunk and lay my hand on Noah's pillow. Impulsively I pick it up and pull it toward me, burying my face in it to inhale the scent of my grandson.

I close my eyes against the sting of the tears that gather there. I can't let them out; if I do, I fear I'll never stop crying. I don't even know why I'm feeling so vulnerable, but I need to get a grip.

Pulling my face away, I turn to replace the pillow. My eyes widen and I swallow hard when I see what has been hidden underneath it. A silver-framed photograph of Louise, the one that used to have pride of place on the coffee table. I pick it up and turn it to the light.

I remember Ben taking this photograph in our garden. It was a beautiful sunny day in mid July. Ben, Louise and the boys had come over for lunch, and instead of suffering a stifling hot kitchen, I suggested we have an impromptu barbecue.

Henry had dashed to the supermarket to grab meat and salad and I'd made coleslaw and fresh bread rolls.

The boys loved it, helping Henry fetch and carry the meat, prodding at the burgers and kebabs with the impressive new steel implements he had picked up that day.

Louise and I sat drinking white wine spritzers while the men drank beer around the sizzling barbecue. We were watching the boys chasing each other with water guns when Ben suddenly appeared in front of us.

"You look beautiful," he told his lovely young wife, holding up a phone. "Smile."

"Oh, Ben, no," she objected, always genuinely modest. "I hate having my photograph taken."

But when he insisted, she acquiesced and smiled, and when Ben showed me the shot later, I saw he'd captured her natural beauty and her calm, gentle nature. Like the sunlight that highlighted her hair against the deep green leafy trees behind us, somehow the essence of her shone through in that photo.

And now she is gone. *Gone.* Her essence is lost forever, and we have somehow reached a stage where my eight-year-old grandson feels the need to rescue and then hide his mother's photograph under his pillow.

It seems to me to be a desperate act as all traces of her are systematically removed from their home.

Surely it can't be right. It's all too much, too soon. Someone has to make Ben see sense.

I chew the inside of my cheek as I inwardly fume. It feels as if my heartbeat has relocated itself in my head. I close the boys' bedroom door behind me and stand at the top of the stairs, listening for a moment. The road outside is quiet; the house is utterly silent and seems to echo my troubled thoughts right back at me.

What is she up to?

I walk toward Ben's bedroom, hesitating at the door. I visit this room regularly and never think anything of it. My task is usually to gather any laundry or put away my son's newly ironed work shirts and trousers. It isn't unknown for there to be a dirty mug or a crumbed plate to take back downstairs, either.

Today, though, it feels sneaky to be up here, yet as soon as I think the words, I immediately rail against them. Why am I questioning my own motives? I silently remind myself that I don't care what Amber might say or think; I only care about Ben and the boys.

My hand hovers over the door handle and I stand for a moment watching as the dust motes dance to my left, caught in the slender shaft of sunlight that streams through from the small window on the landing.

Every week, I stand in this same place just for a split

second, the center of a universe that previously consisted of only me, my husband, my son and two grandsons. Now there is a new, powerful addition that has forced itself into the very center of that universe, and it seems that I am the only person who has a problem with her.

I slowly press down on the cool beaded handle and push until the door swings open. I don't step inside the room; I just stand for a moment and look at the new bedding.

A black satin quilt cover is neatly edged by a shimmering silver throw studded with tiny diamanté stones. The new tasseled bedside lamps are the exact same shade as the throw, and the black and silver cushions, placed strategically on the pillows, are in assorted shapes and styles, with more glittery embellishments.

Ben's balled-up dirty socks and used crockery are glaring by their omission. I've never walked into this room before, even when Louise was here, and seen it looking so pristine.

Everything is in its place. Not only that, it looks like someone else entirely new lives here. There's no evidence of Ben's disordered pile of cycling magazines by the side of his bed. Nor the rare Matchbox car collection he's displayed on various windowsills since he was a boy.

I open a wardrobe door. As expected, I find Ben's work shirts, formal jackets and trousers. I close that door and open the next one. Here hangs his casual clothing: T-shirts and jeans mostly, with his Lycra cycling gear folded on the shelf above. It's behind the third door that I find three dresses, two pairs of jeans and a fluffy onesie with bunny ears.

I did expect to find something; after all, Amber has already exerted an enormous influence over the house. But I am relieved that, judging by the meager collection of clothing here in Ben's wardrobe, she hasn't yet moved in completely.

Perhaps I'm worrying needlessly that it will happen overnight.

I close the wardrobe, ensuring that all three doors are shut properly and there is nothing to give away the fact that I've been...well, snooping, I suppose.

Next I move to the mirrored chest of drawers. I pull open the top drawer, careful not to leave fingerprint smudges on the glass.

Ben's clean socks and undies are in here, just like I would expect. No surprises in his second and third drawers, either. These contain his pajamas and other miscellaneous items, including a dozen or so magazines that are obviously now barred from his bedside.

But when I crouch down and open the bottom drawer, I wish I hadn't. It contains lingerie. Not your regular, everyday bras and pants, but flimsy dressing-up-type outfits that look no more substantial than bits of colored lace. I don't touch this stuff, but I can see what looks like a maid's tiny frilly apron, a nurse's blue and white uniform and a set of cheerleading pom-poms.

A buried memory surfaces, threads slowly through my mind like a silky ribbon. Not long after Henry and I were married, I went to one of those silly sexy undies parties that a friend was throwing in her home. I bought a pale pink lacy confection to wear to bed, the least naughty thing I could find. When I wore it, it drove Henry wild.

Henry...*wild*! I have to smile at that. Those were the days, when my waist was slim, my stomach firm. Somehow, looking at this stuff makes me ache for what I was back then, and even more, for what we had in our marriage. Where did the sense of excitement go? The longing for each other's touch, the wanting?

Over time, our marriage has faded, like a vibrant painting

left in strong sunlight for too many years. Time has slipped through our fingers like melting snow. We thought we had so much of it, but suddenly it's just cold water, trickling away fast.

We're middle-aged but not over the hill yet. There are potentially many years to come when life could be better—improved. A sense of opportunity floods briefly through me, then just as quickly it is gone.

I've never tried to talk to Henry about how we used to be and how we are together now. He's not the sort of man to want to get entangled with old memories. In fact, we talk about very little together anymore.

I shake my head to disperse the gloomy thoughts and close the drawer promptly, feeling a little sick now.

Straightening up, I turn to look at the two bedside tables. Ben has always slept on the left of the bed, and I spot his exercise wristband next to the lamp and his small, square alarm clock.

I move to the right-hand side. There is nothing on this bedside table apart from the new tasseled light.

Swallowing down a gristly lump that seems to have lodged itself in the back of my throat, I slide open the bedside drawer. My hand flies to my mouth and I step quickly back. I can feel my cheeks burning. I'm half ashamed of myself, half outraged by the contents.

I close the drawer quickly and leave the room, dizzy with the sense that my trusting son is in jeopardy and there's nothing I can do about it.

CHAPTER
TWENTY-THREE

Judi

I head straight back downstairs, dashing into the kitchen to pick up my ornaments, then back to the hallway, where I hastily grab my handbag, leaving the cleaning products where I dropped them. I can't wait to get away from this house; it's a place I no longer recognize.

It's not until I'm halfway home in the car that my throat starts to burn as badly as if I've swallowed acid.

The house—Ben and the boys' home—feels like it belongs to someone else. What on earth was he thinking, allowing someone he's only just met to put her stamp on everything so quickly, stripping its familiarity away?

How dare she take over this space and make decisions that Ben would never dream of making on his own?

My hand moves to my throat, trying to massage away the burning sensation. I open the car window slightly to clear the fuzz in my head, and very quickly, the obvious answer to all my questions emerges.

Thanks to my spot of snooping around, I've discovered some of the methods Amber is employing to ingratiate herself with Ben. It's not something I feel I could ever raise with him, and I feel a heat in my cheeks again just thinking about it.

I like to think I'm far from being a prude, despite the fact that sex between me and Henry has always been what some people would describe as *vanilla* and hasn't happened between us for the best part of a year, but...I admit I'm shocked.

The lingerie, well, that's a bit of fun, I suppose, and some of it was quite pretty. But those things in the drawer? Hard-core sex toys, the uses for which I don't want to even hazard a guess. Several items looked like torture implements to my rather innocent eye. Give me unadventurous and conventional any day.

I shudder, and shake my head to get rid of the unpleasant images.

I've never had my son down as being so weak, so gullible. Where is the man who puts his sons first in everything.... Where has his conviction gone? Has it really come down to a bit of lace and a sex toy flaunted in his face and he starts acting as if he's been lobotomized?

Even worse, what if Noah or Josh venture into his room looking for something and inadvertently open that drawer? Those sorts of items should be locked away, somewhere inaccessible to children.

I feel sick just thinking about it, but I'm unable to share my fears with Ben without admitting I've been up there, nosing about.

I have no choice but to put it all out of my head.

For now, at least.

Later, Ben calls to pick up Noah and Josh and asks if it's OK if they all come round for lunch on Sunday.

"It'll be the three of us and Amber too, if that's OK," he says, calling to the boys. "I can't stop today because Amber's on her way; she's bringing us a Chinese takeaway."

I don't mention the ragu sauce I made for him earlier—one of his favorites—or the fact that Ben has always disliked takeaway food, particularly Chinese dishes, because—to quote his own words—"They're full of awful additives such as monosodium glutamate."

But I can't deny it: I'm very pleased and relieved they're coming on Sunday. Even if I have to put up with Amber too. It's always been a given that Ben and the boys will be here, but I wasn't sure what to expect now, and whether Sunday lunch arrangements might change.

"Of course." I paste a smile on my face. "It'll be lovely to have you all here."

Ben hasn't been home yet, so I know I'll have to tell him I went over earlier.

"I took some cleaning stuff to the house this afternoon."

"Oh!" A look of panic flits across his face.

"I've always done my main clean on a Friday, if you remember, Ben."

"Yes, but...didn't you get my text?"

My phone. I completely forgot to turn it back on.

He frowns. "I sent you a text this morning saying not to bother with the clean today."

"I didn't see it, I'm sorry," I say, feeling slightly ashamed that I turned it off on purpose. "I remembered that Amber is going to sort the ironing out now and I wasn't sure about the cleaning, so I just left the stuff in the hallway. I didn't stop."

"Oh, that's fine." He seems to relax, perhaps thinking I haven't seen the transformation of the house. A sharp intake of breath and the words tumble out in one go. "In fact, Amber and I have discussed it and we're going to sort out all the cleaning and the washing from now on."

"OK, if that's what you've decided. That's fine," I say, swallowing. "Perfectly fine."

He peers at me, his brow furrowing. "You're not upset, are you, Mum?"

" 'Course not." I manage a smile, but I can feel an unwelcome flush of heat rising from my lower abdomen.

"It's Amber's idea," he says brightly. "She's worried we're taking advantage of you. She's really good like that, she's always thinking of others."

"Right," I say, as the boys tumble noisily into the hall from the garden. "Well, we'll see you on Sunday, then." I fan uselessly at my face with my hand.

"We're all looking forward to it." Ben hovers uncertainly and then plants a big kiss on the top of my head. "Sure you're OK with the cleaning thing, Mum? Only you look a bit stressed out."

"I'm just hot," I say, jutting out my bottom lip and blowing air on my face. "You know me. I'm always rushing around, doing too much."

"Exactly." Ben's face lights up again. "That's precisely what Amber said last night. She reckons you should be slowing down at your age, not running around after us."

At your age. I'm in my mid-fifties, not bloody eighty. Nobody ever questions Henry's ability to do things, and he's sixty-three.

I smile but don't reply. I kiss them all goodbye and wave from the door as they drive away.

So, the lovely Amber reckons I should be slowing down, does she? Enabling her to fully take over the reins in the house, no doubt. Neatly cutting me out of my son and grandsons' lives in the process.

Amber and I don't know each other very well at all, but one thing I'm absolutely certain of is this: if she thinks she can manipulate me as easily as she seems to have bewitched my son and my husband, she is sadly mistaken.

It would be a mistake for her to underestimate me.

CHAPTER TWENTY-FOUR

Amber

If there was one single thing that had surprised Amber, it was the affable character of Ben Jukes.

She knew some people might say he was a bit of a wuss, a mummy's boy, and if she was honest, that was probably a fair estimation. But despite it grating on her to admit, there was something quite endearing about him too.

She wasn't developing feelings for him, of course not... How could she? Yet in spite of that, she'd found him surprisingly easy to be with and almost grateful, after being on his own with two small boys, to have someone who was happy to take over and make some decisions.

One of those key decisions had been to give the house a bit of an overhaul. It had been part of her plan from the beginning, not least when she realized it had the potential to seriously irk Judi. And to her surprise, Ben had been all for it.

"I go along with Mum's choices most of the time, but it's all looking a bit too middle-aged in here for my liking," he admitted as they sat talking over a glass of wine one evening.

So she'd spruced things up, given the color scheme a bit of a face lift. She'd chosen wallpaper for the chimney breast that she actually disliked herself, together with some mildly erotic framed prints, simply because she knew it would get to Judi.

And of course it had been immediately evident to Amber that a surefire way to rub old Mrs. Jukes up the wrong way was to introduce some structure to the two spoiled brats' infinite toy box that seemed to currently include the whole damn house.

Amber had been pleasantly surprised at how readily Ben deferred to her in matters of what was best practice for the boys. She had discovered that quoting some nonsense from an old childcare manual she had kicking around usually impressed him.

Apparently Judi had told Ben that she hadn't looked around the house today; she'd told him that she had just left the cleaning stuff in the hallway. But that was an outright lie. Amber was very good at setting traps: bits of cotton sandwiched in drawers and doors that got released when things were opened, for instance.

She could see that Judi had indeed had a good scout around as expected and discovered some of the unsavory things that Amber had purchased from town the other morning and had deliberately planted for her to see... things Ben didn't know even existed. What fun *that* had been.

She was getting very good at second-guessing the stuff that would hurt Judi the most. It reminded her of when they were kids and Kathryn would hold a magnifying glass to some hapless insect in the sunlight and they'd watch it squirm. It was no fun killing the thing right away; watching it suffer was much more entertaining.

She couldn't wait to see the nosy old bag's face on Sunday.

CHAPTER TWENTY-FIVE

Judi

On Sunday, everyone arrives just before one o'clock, and this time I keep an eye on the clock and make certain I'm presentable and ready.

The boys, boisterous as ever, fill the hallway with their laughter and strange robot contraptions.

"Boys!" Amber says sharply, taking me aback. Immediately they both fall silent and look at her with wide eyes as she presses her index finger to her lips. "Sssh! No need for that racket."

"Come on, let's take our stuff in here," I hear Josh whisper to his brother, and they disappear into the living room.

I'm shocked to see her so openly reprimand my grandsons, and I'm also stunned that they actually listened to her. They rarely take any notice of my attempts to get them to quieten down once they're in this sort of excited state.

I look at her, but she seems to be making a concerted effort to avoid my eyes.

Henry and Ben slap each other on the back by way of saying hello and begin loudly debating last night's televised football match, seemingly oblivious to what just happened.

Gathering myself, I walk over to the porch, where Amber is now slipping off her black suede over-the-knee boots.

"How nice to see you again, Amber." I smile. I can't bring myself to kiss her on the cheek, but I don't want her to know how badly she's getting to me.

"Likewise," she replies coolly.

She's wearing a flirty little summery dress, and when she bends over to straighten her boots, I catch a glimpse of the backs of her smooth, toned thighs. Not a dimple in sight.

The contents of her bedside drawer slide into my mind's eye and I push it away.

Amber turns, and I see that the dress is even shorter than I first thought and her lightly tanned legs are completely bare. I hear a shuffle behind me and spin round to catch Henry openly ogling her.

He coughs and swiftly disappears into the other room. I grit my teeth, shocked and hurt. I thought my husband was... well, I suppose, past all that. He certainly never shows the slightest interest in me anymore.

"Will you be warm enough?" I ask Amber when she notices me staring. "I'm afraid we haven't got the heating on today and it might be a bit on the cool side for bare legs, but I have a blanket you can borrow if you'd like?"

"I'll be fine," she smirks. "Ben likes me in skirts, the shorter the better. If I get chilly, I'll just have to cuddle up a bit closer to him."

I smile and hope she doesn't notice my cheeks flushing. I do feel a little guilty that I saw things I shouldn't at the house. Private things.

"I'm impressed you got the boys to quieten down so readily there," I say, suddenly wanting to instigate friendlier conversation. "I often think about putting earplugs in when they first arrive."

"Yes To be honest, I think they've been allowed to get away with some questionable behavior." A slight scowl settles over her unlined brow. "But hopefully it's not too late for me to pull it back."

I open my mouth and close it again. How can disciplining the boys suddenly figure in *her* realm of concern? She's a virtual stranger to them. Yet somehow it doesn't seem my place to say so. Not when Ben is here to defend his sons.

"Oh, by the way, I found my ornaments at the house, just so you know." I smile pleasantly at her. "Someone had shoved them in the back of a drawer. I'm hoping I might be able to repair the damage."

I turn away without waiting for an answer.

I'll need to speak to Ben about what she just said about the boys. And soon.

After drinks, I finally manage to round everyone up and get them seated at the table.

I was hoping Ben might come and see me in the kitchen so I could speak to him about Amber reprimanding Noah and Josh, but I decide my time will come when he calls to pick them up after school tomorrow. I fully intend to raise the subject then.

"Just two slices of meat and some veg for me, thanks, Mum," Ben says when I pick up the dish of roast potatoes.

I frown at him, not understanding. "But I roasted these in duck fat, just the way you like them."

Amber peers at the contents of the dish and wrinkles her nose.

"That's the problem, Mum." He grins and pats his stomach. "Amber's put me on a diet. No more duck fat for me."

"It's just that I've noticed that Ben eats far too much saturated fat, Judi," Amber explains in an apologetic tone whilst her eyes scan the table critically. "Too much of this lovely food could be very bad for his cholesterol."

Henry stops loading cauliflower cheese on to his plate and surveys the numerous china tureens with a perplexed expression.

"But I thought you had a takeaway in the week? Nothing worse than that." I direct my remark to Ben, but it's Amber who answers.

"That was a one-off; we won't be making a habit of it. If you like, I could show you some healthier cooking methods." She beams at Ben and then looks back at me. "You'd be surprised, Judi. You can make big differences just through small changes...Let me know and we can arrange a time. I really don't mind at all."

I say nothing.

"It's very kind of Amber to offer, dear," Henry pipes up, and I catch the nanosecond meaningful glance between him and Ben. "Always useful to learn something new, I think."

I spoon two beautifully crisp, duck-fat-drenched roast potatoes on to my own plate and put down the tureen.

"I've served Sunday lunch to my family now for nearly four decades," I say slowly, smiling in turn at each person sitting at the table. "And as far as I know, there have never been any complaints. Until today."

Amber puts down her knife and fork and leans sideways, slightly toward Ben.

"Judi, I'm mortified if I've upset you. I didn't mean—"

I hold up my hand. "Please, don't apologize, Amber. You're quite entitled to your opinions and I'm always interested to hear them. I was probably the same at your age, swallowing everything the so-called health gurus tell us. Actually, it was Henry who made me see sense."

"I did?" Henry stops chewing and stares at me, clearly astonished that I'm giving him some credit.

Amber's face is steadily reddening and I feel a perverse flush of pleasure.

"You did, dear. You said that the best approach to have in most things is moderation. That's the key to life, really. But there's no shame in trying these things, Amber, if that's what you want to do."

"True, that. Very true." Henry looks inordinately pleased with himself.

Amber opens her mouth to speak, but Ben gets there first.

"You know, I think Mum might be right, sweetheart. One day the so-called experts are saying all fats are bad for us, the next they're saying that the right kind of fats are good — in moderation. We don't know whether we're coming or going."

Amber holds the back of her hand to her forehead.

"You know, I'm not feeling so good," she says faintly, pushing away her plate.

"Oh dear," I say softly.

"I think I'll just go and freshen up." She rises from her seat.

Ben pushes his own chair back and begins to stand.

"No, Ben, you stay here." She smiles weakly. "Enjoy your lunch and your roasted potatoes."

Then she slips quietly out of the room.

"Oh dear," Ben says forlornly as we hear her stomping upstairs to the bathroom. "I think we might've upset her."

"I don't see how," I say, forking slices of succulent beef onto my plate. "Amber is fond of airing her views; surely she doesn't mind others doing the same."

I can barely keep the smile from my face. Today's score: Judi 1; Amber 0.

CHAPTER TWENTY-SIX

Josh

"Is it my go yet?" Josh asked his older brother.

He was sick of watching Noah build the Minecraft stadium. The rules were that they *alternated*. Daddy had said it again before they all left the house that morning. They were supposed to take turns on building duties because Daddy hadn't yet found a way they could both play using the same computer server.

Noah had been assembling the final rows of tiered seats for *ages*. He'd definitely had more than his fair share of turns.

Josh's heart sank as he watched the seat rows slowly growing wider and higher. Soon the whole thing would be finished and Noah would have done it all himself, and that wasn't fair because it didn't feel as good as when you'd both done it together.

It wasn't how you were supposed to *play nicely*.

"Is it my go yet?" he asked again.

But Noah wouldn't answer; he was pretending he hadn't heard. Josh recognized the tightening of his brother's lips and his false determined staring at the computer monitor. He knew that Noah had heard every word and that he was going to finish the stadium seating all on his own anyway.

Even worse, Josh knew there was nothing he could do about it, because Daddy was always busy with Amber now and Nanny didn't understand the first thing about Minecraft so it was no good telling her either.

Noah never used to act like this. Yes, he had always been the one with all the good ideas, but Josh had had a say in stuff too, even though he was only little. And they'd always made important Minecraft decisions together. It had made Josh feel quite grown up.

Lately Noah had taken to acting like he was the one in charge, and Josh didn't like it. He didn't like it one bit.

He glanced over at his daddy, in the faint hope that he might have noticed Noah's bad behavior, but of course Daddy had been sitting for ages on the settee, whispering with Amber. Josh noticed they did this a lot, and Amber always giggled at the things Daddy said, and yet when he wasn't around, she hardly ever even smiled.

Daddy and Amber spent a lot of time staring into each other's eyes, as if they might find something interesting there if they looked hard enough.

When the brothers had gone up to their bedroom last night, Noah had said that Daddy and Amber were being gross and it made him want to be sick all over the carpet and even on Amber's pink varnished toenails.

Before Amber had removed all the photos of Mummy, Daddy had sat them both down and explained that whilst they would always remember and love Mummy, now that Amber had moved in, perhaps it was a good time to take the pictures down. But Noah whispered to Josh that it was *never* going to be a good time, and when Daddy wasn't looking, he slipped one of the photographs under his jumper and took it upstairs to hide under his pillow.

And it was Amber who'd told Daddy to take their toys

upstairs. "They're not babies anymore, Ben, they're quite capable of playing upstairs in their bedroom when they come home from school."

She'd made them pack all the toys into a big white plastic box. Noah had kicked the Monopoly set and all the money and playing pieces fell out. When Amber told him off, he said the bad word, *bitch*, under his breath. If you said that word at school, you had to stay in at break time for a whole week.

Josh liked Amber. She smelled nice and sometimes she sat and helped him with his reading.

But Noah didn't like her at all. He made Amber annoyed, and she hissed things at him when Daddy went out of the room. Josh couldn't hear what she said and Noah wouldn't tell him.

They never went with Daddy to the park now to catch taddies in the washed-out jam jars that Nanny gave them. Daddy hadn't even played football in the garden with them for ages; he was too busy whispering with Amber.

Josh stared out of the window. The garden at Nanny and Grandad's house was much bigger than this one, and the grass was level and mowed smooth by Mr. Buxton, a neighbor who was also a retired landscape gardener but still did some *bits on the side*.

Last summer Nanny said they could invite some school friends over for a kickabout. Everyone had loved it, even Archie Jepson, who was a brilliant goalie in the year above Noah at school and whose dad had once trialed for Spurs. Archie had told all the other boys that their pitch set-up was brilliant.

Josh sighed and banged on the floor with the heel of his hand. "You've had your turn now, Noah," he said when his brother began on a new section of seating.

But Noah ignored him.

Josh might just tell Amber that Noah was being selfish. She'd sort him out, and if Noah gave her any lip he'd have to go up to bed, leaving Josh in sole charge of the stadium.

Even though by that time he knew it would be far too late. All the tiered seating would be completed.

CHAPTER TWENTY-SEVEN

Judi

On Monday morning, I dress for work in a pair of fitted chocolate-brown wool slacks and a pale coffee merino wool sweater that I bought years ago when we holidayed in Italy.

I open my jewelry box and my fingers hover above the pieces, waiting to pluck out the beautiful gold and citrine pendant that I know will match my outfit beautifully. Ben and Louise bought it for my fiftieth birthday, just before Noah was born.

I immediately spot that it isn't there.

My heart begins to thump. It's one of my most treasured pieces. I remember Louise explaining how she and Ben had spent a full day trawling the jewelry shops while on holiday in Cornwall before finding the piece they thought would be perfect for me.

"We both thought of you as soon as we saw it," she said, laying her hand on my shoulder. "So warm and beautiful, just like you, Judi."

I shake the jewelry box as if it might make my necklace suddenly appear, but of course, it doesn't. It isn't there.

"Oh," I say faintly, pressing the heel of my hand to my forehead.

"What's wrong?" Henry looks up from injecting insulin into his swollen belly. Increasingly, he spends lazy late mornings in bed, eating his breakfast and reading one of his military history books. Sometimes he doesn't get up until after I've left for work.

"My citrine necklace," I say. "It's gone."

"You'll have mislaid it, no doubt," Henry murmurs, wincing slightly as he pulls out the needle and dabs at his skin with a tissue. "You're very forgetful lately."

Was that it? Had I worn the necklace and taken it off elsewhere, forgetting to bring it back upstairs?

No. I remember taking out my diamond studs to wear yesterday morning before Ben and the boys arrived, and it was definitely in here then. I distinctly remember seeing it.

Amber came upstairs on her own during lunch.

The words offer themselves and I let out a small inadvertent cry.

"What is it now?" Henry says irritably. I notice the tissue he is holding is now stained with small spots of blood.

"Amber," I say faintly. "She came upstairs yesterday."

"And?"

"I think she might have taken it, Henry."

"What?" He removes his glasses and stares at me. "Are you serious?"

"It's the only explanation," I say, taking a step toward him and holding out my hands. "It was here yesterday morning and now it's not. And she's the only person who's been upstairs."

"She *had* to come upstairs." He speaks slowly, as if I might have a problem understanding him. "To use the bathroom."

"Yes, but don't you see, that could have simply been an excuse? She was annoyed at me about the food thing. She could've crept in here and taken the necklace out of pure spite."

"Judi, I really think you're—"

"I think she went into David's bedroom, too." I'm on a roll. I can't stop. "The first time she visited, his door was open and I know for a fact it was closed before she came up here."

He looks at me, but he doesn't say anything.

"Look, I know it sounds crazy, but I honestly think there's something strange, something underhand about Amber. She's a different person to who you think she is. She's managing to fool both you and Ben, but I can see there's something not right. I can't put my finger on exactly what, but—"

Henry shakes his head. "You can't say exactly what because it's all in your mind, woman. You're losing your marbles."

"No!" I take a stride toward him. I can feel my face flaming. "I'm sick of you always implying that stuff is all in my imagination."

He puts his glasses on again and picks up his newspaper. Completely blanking me.

I pick up the jewelry box and hold it out in front of me.

"I'm telling you, Henry, that necklace was in here. I'm a hundred percent certain of it."

"There's no reasoning with you lately, Judi," he says, looking up from his reading. "Think what you like, but the fact of the matter is that Ben has met a lovely girl and you just can't handle it."

"She told the boys off for being noisy in the hallway." I'm shouting now, rattling the jewelry box as I speak. "But you and Ben didn't even notice."

"The pair of them are young scamps. They need reprimanding now and again because *you* let them away with murder. Amber is a positive influence." He looks at me then and his voice softens a little. "They're all young enough to make a fresh start. The boys need a mother."

"Not her!" I yell at him, choking back tears. "*She'll* never be their mother." I punch my arm out as I shout, and the wooden jewelry box flies out of my hand and smashes into the headboard, narrowly missing Henry's head.

CHAPTER
TWENTY-EIGHT

Judi

That evening when Ben calls to pick up the boys, I'm both delighted and relieved when he accepts my offer to make him an omelet and salad for tea. It seems so long since he sat down and spent some time with us.

I carry the meal in on a tray, just in time to catch Henry chortling.

"Well, she seems a very nice young lady, son. And easy on the eye, too, if you don't mind me saying so." He gives Ben an exaggerated wink and then coughs and returns to his newspaper when he spots me at the door.

Earlier, I apologized to him for my outburst and for nearly decapitating him with my jewelry box. He thinks I'm losing it, but I'm very much in control of what I'm thinking and doing and I know for a fact that necklace was there yesterday morning. I just don't know how I can prove it.

I'm not proud of my behavior with Henry, but I confess that the nervy expression that settled on his face after my outburst gave me a certain satisfaction. It was preferable to being invisible to him, anyhow.

I give Ben his tray of food.

"Thanks, Mum, this looks lovely. Dad was just saying how much you both really like Amber."

"Oh, I forgot your tea," I exclaim. "I'll just get it."

Glad to find an excuse to wriggle out of discussing how wonderful Amber is, I return to the kitchen to pick up the mug of tea and check that the boys are OK watching television in the front room. Back in the sitting room, I hand Ben his drink.

"It's so nice you're not rushing off." I sit down next to him. "It seems we hardly see you these days."

"Actually, that's why I wanted to have a chat to you and Dad tonight." Ben chews and swallows a mouthful of food and then carefully puts down his knife and fork. I hold my breath. Something's coming. A moment later, he launches into what sounds very much like a rehearsed speech. "The thing is, it's daft you having to traipse all the way to school every day to pick up the boys when Amber works right next door."

"Nonsense, I like picking them up. It's no trouble." I hear the panic rising in my voice, and judging by their faces, so do Ben and Henry.

"But it's so *silly* you having to do it when Amber can easily pick them up and take them home each afternoon. It also saves me having to come over here to fetch them after work."

"It's a damn good idea in my opinion," Henry says cheerfully. "Your mother does too much, I'm always telling her so."

"That's exactly what Amber says too, Dad." Ben nods, relieved.

"Well, looks like everyone has agreed it, then." I stand up and look at them both in turn. My fists are balled and I can feel my fingernails cutting into my palms. "Suddenly everyone else is an expert on what's best for me."

"We're just worried about you, Mum." Ben looks wildly at his father. "You seem to take offense at everything just lately."

"Take offense?" I yell, stunned for just a moment by my own ferocity. "It would take a saint *not* to be offended by some of the things you both say to me."

"No need to get hysterical, Judi," Henry sighs.

"Don't you dare use your nasty little misogynistic terms with me," I snap at him. "Voicing my opinion is not being hysterical; it's doing what *you* do every single day of your life—without being challenged by anyone."

I glare at him, willing him to say something else so I can let rip. But he coughs and looks out of the window.

I turn and walk stiffly toward the door.

"Mum, please. Don't go." Ben springs up and comes after me, folding me into his arms from behind. "It's not like that at all, it's just—"

"It's just what?" My voice jumps an octave and I spin round, pushing back from him. "You've known Amber for five bloody minutes and suddenly she knows what's best for the boys? How can that be?" I feel furious with myself when tears spring into my eyes.

"Why is Nanny upset?" a small, worried voice pipes up behind me.

"Oh, darling, I'm not upset, not really." I crouch down and put my arms round Josh, pulling him to me. "Nanny's just being a silly billy."

"Nanny's a silly billy." Josh laughs loudly and wriggles out of my arms, hopping back into the other room. "Nanny's a silly billy," he sings as he goes.

It eases the tension a little.

"I'm sorry, Mum. The last thing I wanted was to upset you."

I look at my son's wretched face and I can see that whatever decision he's taken, it's not been made lightly.

"It's fine, honestly it is," I sigh. "But I worry, Ben. I worry there's a lot of change happening in the boys' lives. I worry—"

"And that's precisely the problem, dear," Henry interjects. "You worry far too much."

"I wasn't speaking to you, but if for some reason I want your esteemed opinion, I'll ask for it," I snap, and Henry shuts up. I fall quiet, surprising myself with my outburst but not regretting it one iota.

"The boys are fine, Mum, there's really no need to worry," Ben says softly. "Amber's brilliant with them. She's getting them into a proper routine. It's good for them."

"What kind of routine?"

"A regular bedtime, staying in bed later on a weekend, getting them to tidy up after themselves. Stuff I've never given a thought to."

I think about their new, sterile bedroom, the black-out blinds designed to keep them sleeping for longer. The absence of toys and family photos in the living room.

"She snapped at the boys yesterday," I tell him.

"What?"

"They were excited when they arrived, a bit noisy, and Amber snapped at them, told them to be quiet. That's not her job, Ben."

"She'd have been joking, Mum." Ben rolls his eyes at his father and suddenly they're a team again.

"I would think she's very good with the boys, considering her profession," Henry adds.

"How long have you known her?" I press Ben.

He shrugs. "A good few months now."

"That's no time at all. You can't *know* someone in what amounts to a few weeks. She shouldn't be telling the boys off and assuming parental responsibilities; it's really not her place to do that."

"Mum. It's like Dad says: Amber works with kids. She knows how to—"

"She doesn't know Noah and Josh. She's only just met them."

"Well, that will change." Ben's jaw tightens and in a flash his conciliatory demeanor vanishes. "Look, I was waiting for a good time to tell you this, because I know you won't approve. But Amber is moving in this weekend; she's coming to live with us."

CHAPTER TWENTY-NINE

Judi

Ben doesn't finish his omelet after our disagreement. He gets the boys ready and they all leave. I don't try to stop him; I know it's for the best.

I kiss them all goodbye, but I don't say much, and neither does Ben. We both silently acknowledge that a line has been crossed, a barren space forged indelibly between us.

"I'm going upstairs for a lie-down," I tell Henry calmly from the doorway. "I need to be quiet for a while."

"You're not being fair, you know," Henry says, staring at the television. "It should be a happy time for Ben after all he's been through, and you've just burst his bubble good and proper."

"I stand by everything I've said," I say tightly. "Things are moving far too fast for the boys. I'm only thinking of them."

"Are you?" He mutes the TV and glares at me. "Is that *really* your concern, Judi? Because it seems to me you're eaten up with jealousy of that girl. She's young and lovely and she cares about our son and the boys. What's your bloody problem?"

"She's not a *girl*. She's a thirty-year-old woman who knows exactly what she's doing to this family."

I turn and walk toward the stairs.

"She knows, you know," Henry bellows. "I bumped into her just by chance in town the other morning and she got quite upset, asked me why you don't like her. On Sunday, after you shunned her offer of cookery advice, didn't you see her face? She was hurt. Mortified, even, as was Ben tonight. There's only one person who's harming this family. Think about that."

I take the steps one at a time, the heat rising in my body. I look at the photos of David as I climb.

"You're losing your mind." Henry's voice floats up behind me through the open door. "Even Ben's worried about you."

Even Ben. When has he spoken to his father about me? What have they discussed?

I'm a little anxious, and I get rather hot sometimes. My body is changing, yes, but it's completely normal. There's nothing *wrong* with me, it's the bloody menopause. The elephant in the room that nobody wants to talk about. Why should I put up with Henry's snide remarks?

I wonder what did Henry and Amber talked about when they met *by chance* in town. I've noticed an awful lot of things keep happening by chance since Amber has been on the scene.

At some point, while my back was turned, a glass wall has sprung up between me and my family. And Amber has somehow managed to install herself on the other side of it, together with my husband, son and grandchildren.

I pad softly along the landing until I reach David's bedroom. Once the door is closed, I let the tears fall freely. I see Amber's face floating in front of me, her smug smile, the way she smiles so coquettishly at both Ben and Henry. I hear again the harsh tone of her voice as she reprimanded the boys.

She wants to break this family apart and she thinks nobody can stop her.

But she is wrong. They're all wrong.

Far from losing my mind, today I feel like I've actually found it again.

A quote springs to mind and it plays on a loop, echoing in my head.

Beware the wolf in sheep's clothing.

Beware the wolf in sheep's clothing.

I lie down on David's bed and close my eyes.

CHAPTER THIRTY

Amber

Amber hadn't expected that her chance to move out of the flat would come so quickly, but she felt very grateful that it had.

Although she hadn't told Ben, she'd started packing a couple of weeks ago so that she'd be prepared at short notice. Just the stuff she didn't use much: books she'd read but wanted to keep, and the box full of her sister's things that she'd taken everywhere with her since the family house had been sold, including Kathryn's precious diary. She had found it when her mother moved to the care home, buried in a storage crate.

For the past few weeks, Amber had hardly spent a single night at the flat. She felt as if she virtually lived with Ben already; it was just that all her stuff was still here and, of course, she was still paying rent on a crappy space she barely inhabited anymore.

But now the packing was finished. She and Ben had taken several carloads over to his in the last couple of days, and there were just two or three boxes remaining before she read the meters and locked up for the last time.

There were no feelings of regret or sadness that she was leaving. The music upstairs was as loud and intrusive as ever. Right now, the thudding, tuneless track seemed to be repeating endlessly on a loop, bouncing at full volume through the thin cracked ceiling. The shade on the single lightbulb situated above her head bobbed around in perfect time to the monotonous beat.

But just as Amber taped the final box closed, the noise upstairs abruptly cut off and several pairs of feet thundered down the stairs. Jeering, laughing blokes spilled out into the street, and she looked down from the window, watching as five men staggered off down the road toward the pub on the corner.

A rare peace descended on the building.

A worm of an idea began to burrow its way into her head, and instead of pushing it away and just leaving, finally, for Ben's house, Amber smiled to herself.

It involved a simple and very appropriate deed that could set right all the sleepless hours she and other tenants had suffered at the hands of the complete twats who lived upstairs.

It would be such a waste to pass up this chance.

CHAPTER THIRTY-ONE

Judi

Maura calls me late on Monday evening to say she's got a very bad cold and won't be in work for the next couple of days.

"It might even be flu; it's hit me like a freight train," she croaks. "If it is flu, I might need the week off."

"That's fine. Don't worry," I tell her.

"Judi, are you OK? You sound kind of…I don't know, funny."

I'm not OK, not really. I feel hollow after the argument with Ben. I keep pushing his hurt expression away, but I don't feel strong enough to revisit all the spiked words that flew back and forth between us.

"I'm fine. Keep yourself dosed up and wrapped up," I tell her. "And for goodness' sake, don't worry about work. I'll ring Esther."

When the occasion calls for it, rather than getting an inexperienced and expensive temp in from an agency, we call on Esther Cairns. If one of us falls ill or we need an extra pair of hands during busy times, Esther can usually be relied upon to help out at a moment's notice. She used to work at the surgery—for over thirty years, in fact—and she was the person responsible for taking Maura on many moons ago.

So although she has been retired for five years and has just celebrated her seventieth birthday, there really isn't anything that Esther hasn't seen or can't handle.

"Of course, dear, that's no problem," she says brightly, as soon as I explain that Maura is ill. "I'll see you in the morning, eight o'clock prompt."

I smile as I put down the phone. Esther is a stickler for timekeeping, and she'll no doubt let me know in no uncertain terms if she thinks our admin processes have slipped since her last visit. Those infamous killer observations of hers always start, "It's up to you, dear, but..." or, "Far be it from me to interfere, however..."

Still, listening to Esther's never-ending suggestions beats opening up the office on my own and running myself ragged placating difficult patients all morning.

When Henry has finished packing up a few bits of warm clothing for his overnight fishing trip, I take myself off to bed. I know he'll be long gone by the time I wake up tomorrow. I haven't a clue where he's going if I need to contact him in an emergency, but then I never do know any details, and if I'm honest, I don't particularly care.

We're not speaking since our heated exchange over Amber, and it feels better that way. Easier, anyhow.

Despite making a conscious effort not to, I keep thinking about Ben and the boys, and about the frustration that I sense is simmering just beneath Amber's surface. It showed itself when I dared to challenge her views on diet. And I'm irritated by the way Ben looks at her, as if he's almost in awe. Like she's some perfect angel that's appeared in his life and he just can't believe his luck.

I've always thought of my son as logical, sensible; as Henry is fond of saying, Ben has his head firmly screwed on.

I only hope these qualities will prevail when it comes to dealing with Amber. Especially now she's moving in. Now they are to become a family.

The following morning, it's a relief to get up and be alone in the house.

I heard Henry shuffling around in the bedroom next door at about five a.m., and then he crept into our bedroom, most likely to get something he'd forgotten. I pretended to be fast asleep, so there was no requirement to speak to him.

I take the car instead of walking and I get to the office a little earlier than usual, in the interest of looking super-efficient. Only to find Esther has already beaten me to it and is waiting outside at the back of the building.

"When I was in charge, I always liked to get here no later than seven thirty," she says pleasantly as I fumble in my cavernous handbag for the outer office door keys. "Personally, I think eight o'clock is cutting it a little fine, but far be it from me to interfere, dear. I'm sure you girls have everything running like clockwork here."

I smile to myself, making a mental note to tell Maura that Esther started early, before we even got into the building. We always enjoy a giggle—in a kindly way—when Esther has been in, gently reprimanding us.

Once inside, I begin the daily routine of turning on the lights, the heaters, opening the blinds, and booting up the computer. All the time, Esther follows me round, chattering on in the background.

I nod and smile in what seem to be the right places, try-ing to keep my mind on making sure everything is ready for surgery hours. I confess I'm not really paying attention to Esther's current rant about how the vet recently ripped her off when her Yorkie, Toto, stood on some glass whilst they were out walking.

Then, in the middle of it all, something she says snaps me to attention and I stiffen slightly, my fingertips hovering above the keyboard.

I turn round to face her. "Sorry, Esther, I didn't quite catch what you said there."

"I said, Ben's new girlfriend has certainly got her feet firmly under the table."

I push away the keyboard and straighten the already neat pile of prescriptions that Dr. Fielder signed yesterday.

"Would you mind telling me from the start again, about Amber and the boys, I mean?"

"I'm afraid this is how the job gets you, dear," Esther says. "Never a minute to yourself. That's why I recommend getting to the office a little earlier in the morning, so that—"

"Yes, I understand that. But you were saying, about Amber...Ben's girlfriend?" I say, trying to keep my voice level. "Something about her and the boys?"

But my efforts to appear unruffled fail miserably: Esther's eagle eye notices my fingers tapping nervously on the top of the stack of prescription slips. "Oh, it was nothing to worry about, dear. I was just a little surprised, that's all." Her voice softens. "I saw Ben and the boys at the park as Toto and I walked by. I think it was Sunday, but there again, it might well have been Monday evening, although I can't be sure because my—"

"And Amber was there too, at the park?" I cut across the senseless drivel again.

"That's right, yes, she was. And I remember thinking, how nice that Judi's lovely son has got himself such an attractive young lady, because you see, Maura had already mentioned he'd met someone, when I popped by the surgery one afternoon." Esther pauses, laying her hand over her heart and assuming a pained expression. "It was such a terrible thing to happen. Louise passing, I mean. Poor Ben . . . and your grandsons, poor mites. So young to lose their dear mother."

"Yes, they were," I say quietly. "But we're a strong bunch, you know; we've pulled together and got through it."

"Of course you have, and I could see that they're close. All of them, there at the park together like a proper little family. So much so that the young lady in question has quite got into her stride managing the boys. Your elder grandson, what's his name again now?"

"Noah," I reply, my mouth dry.

"That's the one, Noah. Well, from what I could see, he was being a bit of a monkey, in that way that young boys can be." She chuckles. "Sitting at the top of the slide, he was, and wouldn't let his little brother anywhere near to have *his* go."

I glance at the clock. Eight twenty. I'll have to open the doors for the patients just before half past. If only she'd get on with it. But I don't interrupt her. Instead I bite down on my irritation and wait.

"When I say being a bit of a monkey, it was just mischievousness, dear. That's all it was. He wasn't being naughty as such." She stares across the room to the big window that overlooks a small concrete courtyard, seemingly in her own world for a moment or two.

"So what happened, Esther, at the park?"

"Well, Ben called Noah down from the slide, but of course he did a splendid job of ignoring his daddy. So the girlfriend—Amber—off she trots, marching across the play area. 'Noah,' she calls to him. 'Get down here this minute.' And Noah, well, he must be quite a tough little cookie, because he starts singing at the top of his voice and looking the other way, the young rascal."

As she describes it, I run through the scene in my head. I can visualize it exactly and I manage to stop myself smiling. Noah is an astute child and he takes no prisoners. If Amber thinks she can make *him* her little puppet, the way she seems to be doing with his father, she's going to get rather a big shock.

The boys are very different. This is partly due to the three-year age gap, of course, but essentially they are totally different personalities. Noah has a defiant streak in him that reminds me of his daddy. When Ben was a boy, he had a stubborn streak that would show itself if anyone tried to rail-road him into doing something he didn't want to do. Ben, in turn, got it from Henry.

My David was always the more laid-back, affable person-ality. He'd always try to do the right thing and sometimes got taken for granted by his brother or friends.

I think about David and the traits that made him a bit of a doormat, and it occurs to me that I have to fight against the exact same thing virtually every single day.

I'm strong inside, though, where nobody can see. I don't think any of them quite realize that.

CHAPTER THIRTY-TWO

Judi

As fast as the thoughts of David come, I push them away. I'm so used to doing it now, it's become second nature. I haven't really had much choice: Henry has never cared for unbridled emotions at home.

Esther, meanwhile, is carrying on with her story.

"Well, while young Noah is singing and ignoring her, Amber starts to climb the steps of the slide herself." She laughs, a harsh, dry cackle. "When he sees her coming, he shoots off, straight down the slide, but quick as a flash, she's at the end of it to catch him as he lands."

"And then what?" The back of my neck prickles a little.

"I was only passing by and the hedge got in the way, but from what I could see, she grabbed his hand and gave him a proper dressing-down." Esther frowns. "A bit harsh really. I might be speaking out of turn, dear, but she's not their mother, is she?"

"A dressing-down, you say?" I swallow.

Esther nods gravely. "Enough of a reprimand to bring young Master Noah to tears."

The blood blazes in my veins. I think back to Sunday and

the way Amber snapped at the boys to quieten them down when they arrived. "And where was Ben while all this was happening?"

"I think he might have taken little Josh down to the stream at the bottom end, because when I looked around to give him a wave, he was nowhere to be seen." Esther tips her head and studies me. "Oh, I can see you're upset now, dear. I'm so sorry. I shouldn't have mentioned it."

"I'm fine." I shake my head, blinking rapidly. "I'm glad you told me, Esther. It's been quite difficult getting used to Ben having someone new around. And I worry, you know, about the boys. I need to know what's happening."

"But of course you do, dear," she says kindly, laying a hand on mine.

I'm surprised to hear myself openly admitting something so personal to Esther, who is, after all, just an acquaintance, and I quickly swallow down the unwanted emotion. Esther is a sweetheart and she means well, but she also loves to gossip with anyone in the community who'll give her the time of day.

By Thursday, Maura still isn't back at work. I haven't spoken to her, but she's texted me from her deathbed each day, giving me all the gory, phlegmy details of her now officially diagnosed chest infection.

I'm sitting at Maura's desk, shuffling papers and organizing the repeat prescriptions for the doctors to sign, but my heart isn't in it. I've virtually left Esther to her own devices, and essentially she's running the office, though she spends too much time chatting and catching up with the patients she's known for years.

Although I'd usually keep taking her off the reception desk periodically, today I let her talk to her heart's content.

Nobody has complained; in fact they seem to love telling her and the rest of the waiting room about every detail of their various ailments.

It's the perfect solution. Esther doesn't notice how quiet I am and I don't have to make senseless small talk while I'm fretting about her story about Noah and Amber locking horns at the park.

My stomach rumbles, but I can't face food. I haven't eaten breakfast for the last three mornings, although I've spent what seems like my entire life drilling the importance of the first meal of the day into both my sons and my grandsons.

Somehow I manage to make it to the end of the morning without snapping at Esther or breaking down in tears. I gather my bag quietly, and when Carole arrives to relieve me of my duties, I leave the office, calling my goodbyes and praying nobody finds anything last-minute for me to do.

Outside, I walk down the few steps from reception and stride quickly down the street. When I'm sure nobody can see me, I stop for a moment to gather myself. The air is cool and fresh on my face, and I feel glad that I decided to walk to work this morning.

For a few minutes I manage to clear my mind and concentrate on my own footfalls, counting my steps, breathing deeply and listening out for birdsong. It's soothing and meditative, but the effect doesn't last long. Within a very short time my mind is whirring again and my surroundings blur as I stare at the pavement in front of me, grit slipping and scattering as my sensible flat shoes scuff over the asphalt.

I've not heard from Ben or the boys since Monday evening. Each afternoon when I finish work, I slide into the same vacuous black space. A virtual no-man's-land where there is no cleaning or laundry to do for Ben, no boys to collect from school. No tea to cook and, as Henry is away on his fishing trip, nobody to talk to. Not that we talk much these days.

I don't want to bother Maura when she's ill, and I realize, with some shock, that there is absolutely no one else I can offload to.

I just can't seem to think straight. I can't decide whether, as Henry claims, I am being unreasonable and oversensitive... Is it *me* who's driving Ben away? Or is it perfectly reasonable to feel concern about my grandsons and the fact that everything in their lives is changing with breakneck speed?

I decide the second option is the one that feels right. Ben has had his head turned to the extent that he's letting Amber discipline the boys and destroy their stable environment at home. There's no telling the damage that might be done unless someone challenges her.

I haven't seen Noah and Josh for four days now. It's the longest we've been apart for over two years.

I feel a blast of heat inside as I consider the possibility that Ben is intentionally keeping them away from me, knowing it will cause maximum distress to all three of us. If someone had asked me even a week ago if he'd ever use the boys to punish me for a disagreement, I'd have laughed in their face.

But I'm not laughing now.

His reaction when I told him about Amber snapping at the boys last Sunday lunchtime clearly showed me where his loyalties lie. I am under no illusions about that anymore. The fact that he hasn't texted or called just adds further proof that he has no intention of holding out an olive branch to repair the situation.

As I walk on, the thoughts playing over and over in my head, I realize that I do in fact have a choice. I can wait until Ben deems it appropriate to bring the boys to see me, or for once I can push for something I believe in very strongly.

That is, my own right to see my grandsons. I won't gain anything by remaining quiet.

I glance at my watch. The boys' primary school is just a few streets away from the surgery, and I happen to know that their lunch break finishes at one twenty-five. If I pick up pace, I should be able to get to the wrought-iron fence that surrounds the playground in under ten minutes.

I turn around and begin to walk back briskly the way I came. I pass the surgery hoping and praying that nobody spots me, and thank goodness, nobody does.

I'm aware as I walk that I'm standing a little taller; my shoulders are pressed back now and I'm moving with purpose. I've been reactive to others for so long, it feels liberating to take even this small action that I, and I alone, have chosen. The mere thought of getting even a brief glimpse of my grandsons is enough to lift my spirits.

I hear the school playground before I see it. Children squealing, shouting, a messy merge of voices and sounds, released whilst running and jumping. River View Primary is one of the smallest primary schools in Nottingham and it has a good reputation. Both boys are doing well there, even though I feel they'd fare better in Lady Bay.

As I turn the corner, I see a small knot of school staff leave the building and fan out over the yard, and I know that lunchtime is about to come to an end. Soon the children will be escorted inside.

I run the last few yards, pressing my face up against the cool black railings. I see Josh almost immediately, over on the far side. He is with a group of boys all around his age and they are playing tag, or something similar. His face is ruddy and alive with mischief. He laughs and shouts, lost in a pretend world where adults and school no longer exist.

I am glowing within when I see him so happy and

relaxed; it's the balm I need to soothe my constant worry about him. My eyes scan the yard for Noah, picking out the slightly older children, but he is nowhere to be seen.

The electronic bell sounds and a whistle blows, and the children automatically begin to funnel rapidly into the building. I walk a little further along the perimeter fence so I can see behind the building, and that's when I spot Noah, leaning back against a wall. He is alone and staring down at his feet.

"Noah!" I call, waving my hands madly. "Noah!" But it's far too noisy for my voice to carry over to him.

One of the lunchtime supervisors walks past Noah and says something to him. He nods and takes his hands out of his pockets. I gasp out loud when I see that his left hand is bandaged.

"Noah!" He still doesn't hear, but his teacher, Miss Simpson, has just appeared in the yard. She glances at me and walks quickly over to the fence.

"Sorry, is there something I can help...? Oh, Mrs. Jukes, it's you."

Miss Simpson knows me far better than Ben, since I'm the one who's picked up the boys for the past two years.

"Yes, I was just walking by and saw Noah, so I gave him a wave," I say, a little breathlessly. "Is he OK?"

"As far as I'm aware." She frowns. "Is there a problem?"

"Well, he looks a bit downcast over there on his own," I say hesitantly, "and I see that his hand is injured."

"Ah yes, there was a note in the register." She holds her forefinger in the air as she searches her memory. "Apparently his stepmum called in at the school office a couple of days ago and said he'd hurt it playing football. It's badly swollen and that's why he's not playing with his friends, in case it gets accidentally knocked again."

"I see," I say tightly. "Well, I'd better get off now the bell has gone, but just to let you know, she isn't his stepmum. She's just Ben's girlfriend; he hasn't known her very long at all."

"Oh, I'm so sorry." Miss Simpson blushes furiously. "It's just that Noah brought a new contact form in this morning, and Miss Carr's name has been added as his stepmother."

My forearms prickle with goose bumps and an unwelcome thought pops into my head, which I voice without thinking.

"Can I ask...? Is my name and telephone number still on the sheet as an emergency contact?"

"Strictly speaking, I shouldn't really say." She looks at me and her face softens. "But off the record, no, Mrs. Jukes. I'm afraid it isn't."

CHAPTER THIRTY-THREE

Judi

I think I bid Miss Simpson goodbye, but I can't be sure, because I find myself halfway down the road, rushing away from the school at breakneck speed toward the sprawling academy just two streets away. Ben's workplace.

I'm forced to pause on the corner for a few moments to get my breath. Nostrils flaring, I lean a hand against the wall of Bilton's butcher's shop, where I often call for our Sunday joint, and stare into the window display with horror. The side of a pig hangs, still swinging slightly, on the hook, its glassy eye staring unseeingly. White gauze is draped on the surface below the head to catch the puddled blood.

I avert my eyes and look at the pavement. The white bandage on Noah's hand and Esther's story about what happened at the park fill my mind. My eyes sting and I bite down on my back teeth as I imagine Amber grabbing him hard enough to make him cry. I'm caught somewhere between wanting to sob with the hopelessness of the situation and scream with fury at both her and my stupid, naïve son.

"You all right there, Mrs. Jukes?"

I look up to see Simon, the butcher's lad, staring at me

with concern. His ginger hair and freckles are startling against the backdrop of his pale skin. I turn away. "Should I get Mr. Bilton?"

"No. No, thank you, Simon," I say, pushing myself away from the wall of the shop and standing upright. "I'm fine. I just rush around like I'm still a young woman at times. Catches up with me now and then."

"Ah, I see." He sighs, relieved. "I'll leave you to it then."

I walk away from the shop, brisk but steady, looking the other way so I don't have to see the curious stares from the customers standing inside.

Five minutes later, I'm striding up the driveway of Colwick Park Academy. I wonder how I'm going to manage to speak to Ben when I know for a fact he'll be teaching. I'm halfway up the drive when I see a signpost for the children's center, a narrow road leading off to the right. This is the place where Amber works.

I think about storming in there right now and challenging her about Noah's hand, but I know that's not the best way to deal with the situation. The fact that I had chosen to discuss my grandson's well-being with her at all would be tantamount to acknowledging her new self-appointed status as stepmother to the boys.

I can hardly bear to think of that word in relation to Amber Carr, never mind say it.

The reception area of the academy feels cool and spacious after my flustered walk. The receptionist is currently dealing with two people, so I sit down on one of the comfy chairs and slip off my jacket.

Underneath my white cotton blouse my skin is already damp and sticky, and a rivulet of moisture snakes its way down my spine, only stopped in its tracks by the waistband of my smart black work trousers.

The two people at the desk, who I assume are parents, walk past me, and I see that the receptionist is now free. I leave my jacket and handbag on the seat and walk over to the glass hatch. There are wide double doors to my right; entry to the main school is strictly controlled by a keypad lock.

The young woman on reception is counting money, her lips miming the numbers as her fingers leaf deftly through the tens and twenties. After a couple of seconds she looks up and smiles expectantly at me.

I introduce myself and tell her I need to see my son. I need to see Ben.

"I'm afraid he's back in class now, Mrs. Jukes. But if you'd like to leave a message, I can take it to his classroom right away."

I shake my head. "You don't understand." I'm struggling to keep calm. "This is an emergency. I need to see my son."

She glances at the clock. "Give me a moment, please." She closes the glass partition and I watch as she walks down the narrow office. She stops at a desk and speaks to the woman there for a moment or two. The woman looks at her, looks at me and pushes her glasses up on to her head before getting to her feet. She doesn't come to the hatch; she opens the office door and walks out into the reception area.

"I'm Christine Hopkins, the school's business manager." She extends her hand and I shake it, aware that my palm must feel horribly tacky. "I understand you're Ben Jukes's mother?"

"I am," I say curtly, fearful of a knock-back. "I explained to your colleague that I need to speak with Ben as a matter of urgency."

"Ben is teaching right now and we're under strict instructions not to disturb teachers unless—"

"It *is* an emergency," I say, my voice shaking slightly. "Please. I really need to speak with him."

"We could get him to ring you at afternoon break if—"

"I need to speak to my son!" Three uniformed students walking by slow down and stare curiously at the sound of my raised voice, but I can't stop now. "I just need to see Ben. For a few minutes, that's all."

And then I feel it, the powerful knot of rising heat that starts in my belly.

Not now, please.

Christine asks me to take a seat. "Please, Mrs. Jukes, try and relax. I'll see if I can arrange some cover for Ben, just for five minutes. Can I get you a glass of water?"

"No," I say shortly, heading for the chairs. "Thank you. Five minutes is all I need with him."

She scurries off, punching in a code at the double doors and then disappearing through them.

I press back into the cheap, squashy seat cushions. There's a school prospectus on the low beech table in front of me. I snatch it up and fan my face in a bid to offset the steadily building heat that burns on the inside like a bed of sauna coals.

I realize I'm no longer clenching my teeth. There's another feeling suppressing my initial anger. My scalp, face and neck feel as though they are covered in swarming insects; the skin on my forearms is crawling.

It's a feeling I'm beginning to get used to. Fear.

CHAPTER THIRTY-FOUR

Judi

"Mum! What's wrong?" Ben rushes out of the double doors and flies toward me, arms outstretched and face pale. "Is it Dad?"

The office staff hover at the glass with concerned faces. I stand up and take a few steps forward and open my mouth to speak, just as the rising flush breaks through into my face.

"Goodness, you're sweating buckets." Ben guides me back over to the seating area. "Are you ill? Speak to me, Mum, what's happened?"

"I'm fine and your dad's OK." I fish in my bag for a tissue and mop the moisture from my hairline and face. "I've come about Noah."

"What?" He looks wildly out of the big glass window behind me. "Where is he? What's wrong?"

"He's at school, but it's his hand, Ben," I say, gathering myself a little. "Amber has hurt his hand; she grabbed him at the park."

He stares at me and shakes his head faintly, as if I'm speaking in a foreign language.

"She made him cry," I continue. "You have to do something

Please, just think about what you're doing, asking her to move in with you."

"Are you talking about the bandage?" Ben sighs, visibly relaxing. "On his hand?"

"Yes. Amber grabbed him hard at the park a few days ago. I spoke to Esther Cairns at the surgery. She saw her do it, so don't let her deny it."

Ben rolls his eyes up toward the ceiling, saying nothing for a moment or two. When he speaks, he makes it crystal clear that I am testing his tolerance. It reminds me of how I used to speak to him as a boy when he'd misbehaved.

"Mum. Noah hurt his hand when we were playing footie in the garden two days ago. He tripped and broke the fall with his hand, spraining his wrist." He shakes his head and softens his tone. "It was nothing to do with Amber."

"But…how…? Did you actually see him fall in the garden?"

"Yes! I picked him up off the floor and Amber bandaged his hand, but it was just to make him feel better because she said it was only sprained. She's first-aid-trained so she knew right away."

I dab frantically at my brow, but the heat shows no sign of being assuaged.

"She's trying to damage us, Ben. All of us."

"What? Mum, get a grip. You're becoming paranoid," Ben hisses, his eyes darting over to the reception desk. "Look what you're doing to yourself…the state you're in." He gestures toward my streaming face as if that proves his point. "Amber is not trying to hurt us. On the contrary, she's trying very hard to build a relationship *with you*. But you're not making it at all easy."

"Then why has she taken me off the school's emergency contact list for Noah?" My tight, sharp words ricochet around the echoing space. "She's trying to get me out of the way because she wants you and the boys for herself. She's a conniving, lying—"

"Mum. Enough!" he snaps. "This is neither the time nor the place to discuss family business, as well you know."

"So when *am* I supposed to discuss it? I haven't seen you or the boys all week."

"I know, and I'm sorry about that." He pinches at the bridge of his nose. "I just thought we both needed a bit of space. After our conversation on Monday evening, I mean. Dad says—"

"You've spoken to your dad?" I say faintly.

"I...Only briefly, yesterday. Just to check you were both OK and see how the land lies." Ben is backtracking.

"And your dad says what, exactly?"

There's a beat of silence.

"He just said you seem a little stressed at the moment, a bit out of sorts."

"I'm not stressed or *out of sorts*; I'm out of my mind with worry!" I snap back at him before I can check myself.

I look at my hands, thinking about the implications of what Ben has just said. I haven't spoken to Henry once since he left for his fishing trip. I've just had a short text to say he's arrived and that the weather is holding up.

He never mentioned speaking to Ben.

I clamp my mouth closed and let the tracks of moisture run unchecked down my face. I feel like an outsider amongst my own family and I can't really make sense of how it's happened so quickly.

"Don't do this, Mum, please. Can't you just be happy for us?" Ben runs his fingers through his hair and I hear a door open and click closed behind me. "I've got to get back to my class. Listen, I'll call round after school today and we'll talk, OK?"

I don't answer him. I stare at the floor, wondering how on earth we ever got to this stage.

Ben stands up, briefly lays a hand on my shoulder and walks away. I watch him vanish through the secure double doors.

"Mrs. Jukes?" I look up to see that Christine, the business manager, is standing there, knotting her fingers in front of her. "Can I get you a cup of tea or something?"

I stand up. "No thank you. I'll leave now."

She nods, reassured.

Picking up my handbag and draping my coat over my arm, I walk slowly out of the automatic doors and head toward the school drive. Just before I get there, I spot a wooden bench set on a small, neat piece of lawn.

I stop walking and sit down, staring at the surrounding borders, neatly planted with rows of green leafy bunches that are yet to flower.

In one sense it seems a long way back, in the timeline of my life, that Ben was just a small boy. He and his brother were so reliant on me. Yet right at this moment it feels like that was only yesterday and I've woken up in a time-warp nightmare to find that my son is firmly under the spell of a woman who shows the world one face while carefully hiding another. A woman who wants to destroy all that we have.

And nobody else can see it.

It's not until a car stops and the driver lowers her window and asks if I'm OK that I realize I am quietly sobbing.

CHAPTER THIRTY-FIVE

Amber

It never failed to amaze Amber that the people who thought they were so clever in deceiving others never once stopped to think that two could play a dirty game.

Like the tenants upstairs at her old flat, whom she'd watched tumble out and down the street to the bar. She'd loaded the last three boxes into the boot of the car, taken the final meter readings ready to email them to the management company and then pulled on rubber gloves and taken a plastic bag into the overgrown back garden.

Several of the tenants had dogs, and the garden was basically the mutts' toilet. She'd retched and heaved while she collected as much stinking shit as she'd physically been able to carry, and then she'd taken it upstairs and systematically shoved the whole fucking lot through the letter box of the inconsiderate tenants' flat.

And when *that* little deed had been done, she'd turned the bag inside out and smeared what was left in it over the door, taking special care to fully coat the handle. She half wished she was sticking around a bit longer so she could witness the cries of outrage and revulsion when they returned.

She'd ditched the shitty rubber gloves at the door, popped back into her own flat to thoroughly wash her hands and she was off. She'd escaped at last.

She smiled at the satisfying memory.

This morning, she'd parked well down the road, away from the house. Judi was at the surgery and that daft old fart Henry was on one of his fishing trips. At least she laughingly gathered that that was what he liked to call his little jaunts away.

She'd had Henry and Judi's door key duplicated some weeks ago when Ben had been on a school trip with his class and had left the car and his keys at home. His parents' door key was on there, so Amber had simply whizzed down to the local Tesco store and had one quietly cut at the key kiosk there.

Now she walked up the drive and knocked at the door to make sure nobody was home before sliding the key into the lock and letting herself in. The nice thing about the house being detached and screened from next door with conifers was that it made life a whole lot easier for intruders like herself.

Inside, the smell of wax polish and then an after-scent of potpourri that whiffed of cloves and oranges assailed her nostrils, and she sneezed. The sound echoed around the hall-way and she froze for a few seconds, imagining what excuse she'd make if Henry or Judi appeared at the top of the stairs.

But of course she needn't have worried. She was alone . . . to do completely as she wished.

She climbed the stairs and walked straight to David's room. She opened the door and closed it behind her.

And then she began.

CHAPTER THIRTY-SIX

Judi

I don't remember much about the walk home from seeing Ben at the school. Just the feel of the cool air buffeting my face and the rolling heat inside of me.

Once I'm home, I don't bother with lunch or even a drink. I just sit staring into space for most of the afternoon. I must half doze off at some point because I start, jumping up from my seat, when I hear the gravel skid and fly at the top of the driveway.

I snatch up the remote control and flick on the television. Then I curl my legs up onto the couch and grab a magazine, opening it on my lap. I don't want Ben to see that I've been moping about.

I hear a key turn in the lock, the front door opening and then closing. I hear shuffling around in the hall and Ben appears at the living room door.

"Hello, Mum," he says, his arms swinging slightly like a shy little boy. It seems so odd to see him here in the house without Noah and Josh shooting up and down the hallway like bullets.

"Hello, darling, come and sit down."

On his way past, he stops and kisses the top of my head. I turn off the TV, close the magazine and look up at him. "Cup of tea?"

"No, I'm fine, honestly," he says, sinking down into Henry's chair. "I've got to get off soon."

Get off back to Amber, he means.

"Look, I've not dealt with all this very well, and I'm sorry, Mum." His fingers tap out an irregular rhythm on his thigh. "I shouldn't have just stopped coming over like that; it's natural you'd miss the boys. I really left you no choice but to turn up at school, but I so wish you hadn't."

"You should've talked to me, not just cut me off."

Ben sighs. "I'm finding it difficult to include you in things at the moment because you get so defensive about Amber's involvement in anything to do with Noah and Josh."

I try to think logically for a moment before answering.

"I've missed seeing you and the boys," I say softly. "But I came to see you at school today because I'm genuinely worried about them, Ben, not to tackle you about your lack of visits. In my opinion, Amber shouldn't have any involvement in disciplining the boys, and yet that's clearly what she was doing at the park."

He sighs and stills his fingers. "Mum, please don't start this nonsense about Amber again. This is the reason why I've stayed away. I told you, Noah hurt his wrist playing footie in the garden."

"So you say. But Esther Cairns is no liar, and she said—"

"You told me what the interfering old bat said and it's not true. Amber didn't hurt Noah, she'd never do that. She cares deeply for the boys."

"Esther said he cried but that you had taken Josh down to the stream. So you can't have seen what happened, Ben."

"Noah *always* cries in temper if he can't get his own way,

especially lately." Ben rolls his eyes. "He's turning into a bit of a behavioral nightmare, if I'm honest."

I look at my son and wonder how he can be such a wonderful teacher but not understand the first thing about his own children. "And have you stopped to think for one second why that might be?" I say quietly.

"Oh, I see. I suppose that's Amber's fault, too," he says smartly, staring out of the window.

"I don't think it's Amber's fault at all." That makes him sit up and listen. "*You* are the one allowing her to discipline the boys as if she's their parent. *You* are the one who's let her loose on the house so it can be transformed into a hippie's den."

Ben laughs, but he isn't amused.

"I didn't realize we had to ask for your permission to redecorate," he snipes.

"You don't need my permission to do anything, as well you know," I say, making a huge effort to stay calm. "But when you suddenly rid the house of Louise's memory and then cleanse the entire downstairs space of Noah and Josh's toys, don't be surprised when you see a negative reaction in their behavior."

Ben snorts. "That's one hell of an exaggeration, Mum. We've had a tidy round, that's all. Amber says it's good practice for kids to have separate playing and living spaces."

"Oh, there's nothing Amber doesn't know, is there?" I snort. "Despite having no children of her own."

He ignores my barbed comment.

"Look. Before we changed anything, I sat the boys down and explained that we were taking down the photographs and redecorating ready for Amber moving in," he says. "And they were absolutely fine about it."

The photograph under Noah's pillow flashes into my mind

"Perhaps they seemed fine, but beneath the surface they may have been upset, Ben. Maybe they felt as if they couldn't voice their true feelings."

"I don't think so. They seem more worried about when they're going to get the next Transformer robot for their collection."

"I couldn't help noticing that their room has been tidied, too. The walls have been stripped of their favorite posters."

"Like I said, we're redecorating, Mum." Ben tips his head to one side and narrows his eyes at me. I'm fairly certain he's remembering the other day, when I told him that I left the cleaning supplies in the hallway and didn't stay.

"Look, I'm just concerned that the boys' needs don't get forgotten in this whirlwind romance of yours," I say firmly, hoping to gain the upper hand. "Just lately, it seems to be you might be losing your mind as well as your heart."

"*I'm* not the one making wild accusations," he says grimly. "I'd never forget about my sons. Never. And it's very unfair of you to even suggest that. The boys' best interests are always uppermost in both mine and Amber's minds. I wish I could talk to you about our plans, but that's just not possible with you in this mood."

I don't want to hear what their plans are. Any luck and this relationship will burn out as quickly as it appeared. It's time to change tack.

"Can I ask why Amber has removed me as an emergency contact for Noah? I take it you've left your father on there as the additional contact?"

Ben shrugs. "Dad is still on there, yes. We talked about it; Amber didn't just do it of her own accord. Like she says, there are two of us there for the boys now; we don't need you to have to fly down to school if one of them is ill or something."

"But I don't mind."

"I know you don't, but like Amber says, it seems silly that you—"

"It seems I'm being cut out of anything to do with my grandchildren."

"Mum, that's not true." Ben sighs and runs his fingers through his hair. "That's not the case at all."

"I'm just saying what it looks like." I shrug. "You're their father and you should be the one making any decisions that affect them. Not some virtual stranger."

"Amber knows an awful lot about kids, and to be honest, it's nice having someone else to help me manage the boys. I know you think they're little angels, but they can be quite a handful."

"Don't you think I know that? The point is, it's not Amber's place to discipline them."

"You make it sound like she's a wicked stepmother or something." He scowls.

"Well, if the cap fits . . ." I bite down on my tongue, but it's too late.

"Come on." Ben holds out his hands to me in appeal. "I just want you to like her, Mum. That's all I want. You always said you hoped I would find someone else, after Louise. I want you to be happy for us."

"I *do* like her," I lie. "But the boys will always remain my priority. I can't help that and I'm not going to apologize for it. As long as I'm breathing, I will always look out for you and the boys."

"I know that and I love you for it. Honestly I do." Ben smiles. "Look. What about if we all come over on Sunday for one of your legendary lunches? Let's treat it as a bit of a fresh start and try to get things on track. I just think you and Amber have got off on the wrong foot. I really think that's all it is."

"That would be lovely," I say, keeping my real feelings off my face. "I've so missed you and the boys."

"Me too. And they've missed you," Ben says. He stands up and walks over to the couch, sits down beside me and slides his arm around me. "Do you know, they've asked for you every day."

He says it to make me feel better, but it almost tears the heart out of me to hear it. I lay my head on his shoulder and close my eyes, but I don't reply.

When Ben has left, I walk upstairs. I need to have a lie-down in my cool, quiet bedroom.

I pad down the landing in bare feet and stop outside David's room. His door is slightly ajar. I push it open with my foot and step inside. I swear it feels different in here, like the tranquil privacy of the space has been disturbed. But of course, that's impossible.

I scan the bedroom. That drawer...it seems not quite closed, and under the bed I see that David's box of stones is visible, just the corner. It's as if someone has been in here, touching. Meddling.

It crosses my mind that I might be starting to imagine things. I have no one to blame or accuse this time. Henry is away and only Ben has been in the house, but he didn't leave the living room.

Maybe Henry is right and I *am* going crazy after all.

CHAPTER THIRTY-SEVEN

Noah

She'd sent him up to his bedroom again for being cheeky. All he'd said was that he was too busy watching cartoons to help Josh with his homework.

It was just baby work his brother was doing anyway. It wasn't even going to be marked by the teacher. The real reason was that Amber really liked Josh but she didn't like him.

Amber was a really stupid name. Noah had looked it up online and amber was actually fossilized tree gunk, which was quite funny because it matched her gunky face perfectly.

She had turned the television off in the middle of his program and sent him upstairs. But Noah didn't care really because he hated being downstairs now, when Daddy wasn't home.

It used to be fun when Nanny had them after school, but now it sucked, just like everything else did since Amber had been around.

Noah got down on his hands and knees and reached right under the bed to the shoebox that he'd pushed behind the big plastic box of toys, nearly to the far wall. He'd had to be careful to hide his treasure trove well, because Amber was a neat freak, even worse than Nanny.

After listening for a few moments and satisfying himself that Josh, the creep, and Amber were still talking downstairs in the kitchen, Noah sat on the floor with his back against the bunk beds and opened the box.

He'd only recently started collecting the treasures—since just before Amber moved in—so he hadn't got that many yet. But that didn't really matter. Looking and holding the items in his box made him feel calm inside. He liked inspecting them in a certain order, as if that was his special job that nobody else was trained to do.

When his fingers dipped inside and brought out a treasure, his heart stopped blipping and he forgot about what might happen if Amber convinced Daddy to send him away and just keep Josh, who she liked. Noah had noticed that Amber could convince Daddy to do lots of things.

At the bottom of the shoebox lay the photograph of Mummy that Noah had rescued from the clean-up downstairs. On top of that, there was a folded piece of pale yellow tissue paper that had come with the new shoes that used to be in this box.

Noah had laid the other three items in a neat row on top of it like the display of Egyptian treasures they'd seen on the British Museum school trip last year.

There was a hairgrip of Amber's with little multicolored stones that glittered when you twirled it in your fingers. Noah wouldn't normally want anything that belonged to her, but this was simply too much treasure to pass up when he found it on the edge of the bath.

There was a small painted soldier that he had slipped in his pocket after Mr. Norton had shown his class the World War II display in the school hall last week. Noah supposed you couldn't really describe a figurine as *treasure*, but there was something about this soldier's face that made him wish they were friends in real life.

Noah thought the soldier might understand why he kept waking up in the middle of the night. It was always the same. Noah would be crying in his dream and then he'd let out a sob and that would wake him up with a jolt, and when he sat up in bed, his face was wet with real tears, not just dream ones. Yet he could never remember what it was that had upset him.

But the fourth treasure was his very favorite and one Noah knew he couldn't keep. He reached for it now, held it up toward the window and let the beautiful stone spin at the end of its pale gold chain.

Nanny had explained to them that this stone was called a citrine and that Mummy had chosen it especially for her birthday before Noah and Josh were even born. The citrine was see-through in some bits but then shone like a rainbow in others. It was beautiful, as his mummy had been.

Noah hadn't stolen the necklace; he would never steal anything from Nanny. He wanted to ask if it would be all right to borrow it, like they had done the Lilliput cottages, but Nanny had seemed to stop listening to him. She'd taken to wandering around the house as if she was looking for something, and snapped at Grandad if he asked her what she was fretting about. Sometimes she disappeared upstairs and Noah heard her crying behind Uncle David's door.

But that was before, of course. Nanny didn't collect them from school anymore. Stinking Amber picked them up now and gave them tiresome jobs to do around the house.

Noah couldn't wait until Daddy got a new girlfriend. One who liked children.

CHAPTER THIRTY-EIGHT

Judi

"I'm so glad you're back," I say, watching as Maura opens the office blinds on Friday morning. "How are you feeling now? You don't sound stuffy at all."

"No, it just sort of petered out and then disappeared completely," she says. "I'm so grateful, although I've still got three days of antibiotics to take. I wouldn't wish that on anybody."

I put down a steaming mug of coffee in front of her.

"I don't do things by halves, you know." She picks up her coffee. "Anyway, how've you been? Sorry to drop you in it like that."

"Oh, it's been fine. I just let Esther get on with it. As she told me several times, she could run this surgery on her own with her eyes shut." We both chuckle. "Things haven't been so good at home, though."

Maura raises an eyebrow when I tell her about Ben's house being transformed, how Amber has appointed herself stepmother to the boys and the way I've been sidelined when it comes to domestic duties and the daily school pickup. I also explain how I panicked when I saw Noah's bandaged hand.

"The worst thing is, I stormed into Ben's school yesterday

and accused Amber of hurting Noah when apparently, it turns out, he sprained it when he fell over playing football in the garden."

Maura looks aghast. "I don't understand how things could have moved this fast. It only seems five minutes ago that you met Amber for the first time."

"Tell me about it." I frown. "After seeing the boys virtually every day for the best part of three years, we've now got a situation where I haven't set eyes on them since Monday evening."

"And what does Henry have to say about all this?"

"He doesn't know most of it yet." I pull a face. "I haven't told him that I snooped at Ben's house, and he's away on one of his fishing trips, so he hasn't seen the state I've got myself into. I'm hoping Ben won't tell him about the scene I caused at school."

"I'm so sorry to hear all this, Judi." Maura touches my arm. "Have you spoken properly to Ben yet?"

I nodded. "He came over last night and we had a chat, but it's like she's brainwashed him, Maura. He won't have it that she is in any way to blame for anything. But they're all coming over on Sunday, so at least I'll get to see the boys then. There's nothing she can do about that, thank goodness."

This morning when I left for work it was pleasant and dry, so I decided to walk in. I brought my umbrella just in case, but when I finish at one o'clock, I'm pleased to see that the weather is still fine.

As I walk, I begin to plan Sunday lunch in my head. I'm going to make sure I cook Ben and the boys' very favorite dishes, so they know just what they'll be missing out on if they stop coming over.

This time yesterday I was in quite a state, stalking off to school to see Noah and then to give Ben what for. Today, I push thoughts of seeing the boys out of my mind. Now I know they're coming on Sunday, I can relax a little, safe in the knowledge that we'll have a wonderful afternoon together. Despite Amber's best efforts to spoil everything.

Walking past the park, I'm surprised to see Fiona Bonser there again, sitting on that same bench. The pushchair stands next to her thin mottled legs. I can't help noticing that her feet are encased in the same scuffed stilettos she always wears. She is clutching a woefully thin cardigan close to herself with both hands, her back turned slightly away from the prevailing breeze.

At least this time she doesn't appear to be sobbing, but after she gave me short shrift last time, I've no intention of stopping for a chat. I keep my eyes on the pavement ahead and continue walking.

"Hello, Mrs. Jukes," I hear her call.

I stop and look over the short hedge. "Oh, hello, Fiona," I say in mock surprise.

"Bloody freezing, i'nt it?" She wraps her arms tighter around herself.

"It's not so bad when you're walking," I reply. "But you're sitting there at the mercy of the wind, so I have to say you could do with a more substantial coat."

"Yeah, it's on my wish list." She gives a dry laugh and I think about the five or six coats I never use, currently gathering dust in my wardrobe.

"Well, I'd better get off, things to do. Take care of yourself, Fiona." I begin walking again. I've enough of my own problems to sort out without getting involved with hers.

"Do you like birds?"

"Sorry?" I look back.

"There's a blackbird just over there; she keeps taking worms to her baby." She points toward the bushes and her face lights up with a childlike wonder. Then her smile fades. "Do you know, she's doing a better job looking after her kid than I am."

Fiona sounds like she's carrying the weight of the entire world on her skinny shoulders. I feel bound to pass the time of day with her for a few minutes at least. So instead of walking on, I turn into the park entrance.

"Hank's asleep." She nods to the pushchair when I get close.

"Hank? That's an unusual name for a little one."

"His dad was American." She stares into the middle distance. "Reckoned we were going to get married and set up home together, didn't he? He was going to take my other kids on and everything."

"But that didn't happen, I take it?"

"Nah. He ran off back to the States soon as he found out I was pregnant."

"I see," I say quietly.

"Bastards, all of 'em." She looks at me, her eyes flashing. "Blokes. They treat you like shit, don't they, Mrs. Jukes?"

I give her a thin smile.

"I suppose Mr. Jukes is a nice man, though, eh?" she says as an afterthought.

"He has his moments," I say, peering into the pushchair. "Hank's cheeks look rather red."

"He's teething, little bugger. Keeps me up all night and then sleeps it off ready for his next go later on."

"There's some very effective teething gel you can buy. It numbs their gums nicely. I think it's called—"

"Can you get it free on prescription?"

"No. At least I don't think so, but you could always ask the doctor. I don't actually think it's that expensive."

She looks at me as if I've lost my mind.

"I bet it'll still make a big hole in the fiver I've got to last me until I get my Family Allowance on Monday, though."

I nod, understanding and feeling chastised. "How are you, Fiona? In yourself, I mean."

"Oh, you know," she replies flatly.

"I don't know, not really. To be truthful, you look very cold and a bit down in the dumps."

She sits thinking for a moment and then shakes her head as if she's decided against saying something. "I'm fine."

"Are you eating properly?" I glance at her bony blue-tinged knees.

"My kids don't go hungry, if that's what you're trying to say," she snaps. "I'd starve to feed them kids, I would."

"Fiona, I wasn't implying anything of the sort," I say hastily. "I know that you look after your children very well. The best you can." I say this despite little Hank lying there in his pushchair unprotected and quite underdressed for the cooler weather.

"Yeah, well, most people don't think that about me. I can see it in their faces. Disapproval."

"I'm not most people. It's obvious to me that you love your children very much."

"Thanks, Mrs. Jukes," she says with a smile. "I'd do anything for my kiddies. I would, you know. It's just that sometimes... well, it gets so bloody hard."

She looks at me and I can see she's starting to well up.

"Now come on. Cheer up, Fiona. You're doing an amazing job under very difficult circumstances, and for that, you're to be admired."

"It's just... it's just..." She can't get past those two words.

"It's just what, dear?"

"It's just so fucking *hard* at times." She wipes her eyes

with the back of her fingers. "I'm sorry, I didn't mean to swear."

"I've heard worse, don't worry about that." I pat her leg and it's freezing to the touch. "When was the last time you had a decent meal, Fiona?"

She shrugs. "I finished the kids' beans on toast that they left last night."

I glance at my watch. It's a quarter past one and Henry isn't due back until at least six this evening. I stand up. "Come on, let's go."

"Eh? Go where?"

"You're coming home with me. I'm going to cook you a nice meal, you can have a hot bath to warm you up and we'll collect some teething gel for young Master Hank on the way."

"But where...? I can't..."

"I won't take no for an answer, Fiona. I'd really like to do this; please let me."

She stands up, her high heels sinking into the soft ground beneath our feet. She turns to me as if she's going to object again, and I press my finger to my lips.

"Let's just go," I say.

CHAPTER THIRTY-NINE

Judi

The first regrets begin to surface in my mind after we've been walking for about ten minutes.

I start to think about what Maura might say if she finds out. Getting involved in a patient's personal life is never advisable, and I'm pretty certain that the doctors, my employers, would frown on it.

But I shrug off the grumbles. I can't just leave Fiona there to suffer alone. She seems so wretched. So lost and alone and in need of someone to offload to.

As we walk up the street toward home, Fiona looks open-mouthed at the large houses on either side. "Do you live in one of these, Mrs. Jukes?"

"Call me Judi." I smile at her. "I suppose our house is quite similar to these properties, yes. We're nearly there now, so you'll see it for yourself."

She doesn't reply, just keeps tottering along in her high heels, gawping at the properties as we pass. In the stark daylight, I notice that the old acne scars are clearly visible on her skin, the thick brown makeup sinking into the tiny craters, casting shadows that make the pitted hollows look much worse.

"Here we are," I say, turning into our driveway and reaching for the buggy. "Let me help you with that."

"Blimey, look at this. It's just like *Downton Abbey*."

I smile and take the pushchair handles, negotiating the buggy along the narrow pathway that runs over the graveled surface of the drive. I turn around to make sure Fiona is following, and see that her painted face is turned upward, taking in the scale of a house that is merely ordinary to me but extraordinary to her.

I step up on to the tiled porch step and unlock the door, pushing it wide open.

"In you go, Fiona, I'll bring the pushchair in behind."

Once we're both inside, I push the buggy down the hall to the open space under the stairs, and Fiona lifts Hank out. His eyes flutter and open and immediately scan his surroundings.

Fiona helps me make up his bottle in the kitchen. It feels so nice having a baby in the house again.

"It's a long time since I've done this." I spoon in the powdered formula milk. "Too long, in fact."

"Your kitchen, it's like something out of one of them posh house magazines." Fiona takes a long drink of the fresh orange juice she says she prefers over tea. "If I lived in this place, I reckon I might never go out again."

I grin and look at her but see immediately, by the way she is taking in the room, seemingly in awe, that she is deadly serious. To her, the spacious duck-egg-blue Shaker kitchen I barely notice anymore is the epitome of real luxury living.

For a moment I'm transported back to the day Henry and I looked around the house as prospective buyers. When the estate agent discreetly disappeared in order to give us a few minutes to chat things over, I clapped my hands together, stretched up onto my tiptoes and kissed my new husband on the cheek. It happened here, in the very spot I'm standing right now.

"It's my dream house," I breathed in his ear. "I love it. But I love you more."

"Glad to hear it. And I love you too, Judi Jukes." Henry never tired of calling me by my full married name for our first few years together; said he loved the alliteration, just the sound of it rolling over his tongue. "We're going to be very, very happy here. We'll raise our family and grow old together, pottering around in that beautiful garden until the sun goes down."

I remember smiling that day, looking out of the French doors on to the pretty planted space beyond, imagining us taking tea out there together of an afternoon, or maybe sipping a glass of chilled wine as the sun disappeared behind the sleek conifers. I remember stroking my rapidly rounding belly—our first baby, David—and thanking God for everything He'd given me.

Now Henry pays a nearby retired landscape gardener, Mr. Buxton, to mow the grass, and I can't remember the last time we spent any time together outside.

"Judi, are you OK?"

Fiona's concerned voice brings me back to the moment, and I smile and screw the top firmly on Hank's feeding bottle.

"Sorry, I was just thinking about when we first moved in here. I can hardly believe it's so long ago now. And do you know, Fiona, the strangest thing is that sometimes it seems a whole lifetime away, and then at other times the memories are as vivid as if it all literally happened yesterday."

Fiona shoots me a sideways glance but doesn't answer.

I pop upstairs, throwing my coat and handbag on my bed. From the wardrobe I select a mid-length feather-filled coat that

I haven't worn at all this year, and then it's on to the bathroom to run Fiona a scented bath. I lift two of our best high-thread-count Egyptian cotton towels out of the airing cupboard and lay them on the side of the vanity unit. Finally I hang a freshly laundered white cotton robe on the hook inside the door.

A trickle of pleasure runs through me when I think of Fiona enjoying the experience.

"Your bath is running now," I say when I get back downstairs. She's standing at the kitchen doors looking out at the garden. "Bathroom is up the stairs, first on the right." Her face lights up when I hold out the coat. "And this is for you. It should keep you a great deal warmer than that little scrap of knitwear. I'll pop it on the pushchair for when you leave."

I'm astonished how willingly she hands Hank over to me. "Thanks, Mrs. Jukes... Judi. All this... well, it's ever so good of you."

"Really, it's nothing. Enjoy your bath, and when you come down, I'll have a nice lunch waiting."

When I hear the bathroom door close behind her upstairs, I take Hank and the bottle full of warm milk into the living room. I pile a few cushions behind me and sit cradling him in my arms while he takes the milk, staring up at me with enormous trusting dark blue eyes.

When David was around five or six months old, he had trouble keeping his milk down. We got to the stage where we wore towels over our clothes after he'd fed because invariably, within minutes, up it would all come again. When the symptoms showed no signs of abating and David began losing weight, we were referred to the hospital. It was found David had gastro-oesophageal reflux and needed a minor operation to fix it. After that he was fine for a short time and then it started happening again. The doctors simply couldn't find what the problem was.

I remember it was a very worrying time, especially when we couldn't get any answers. Eventually the regurgitation of his food stopped and he began gaining weight again. But in the meantime, during those awful weeks of not knowing what was wrong, family and friends rallied round. Everyone looked after both me and David. Henry, who by this time had already seemed to have lost interest in me as a wife, transformed overnight into a knight in shining armor. He wrapped us both in cotton wool, took some time off work and basically wouldn't let me lift a finger.

It partly drove me mad, but although I never admitted it to anyone, it made me feel safe and precious, and for a short time it was just like the first few months of our courtship all over again.

I still get a warm feeling thinking about that time, even now.

CHAPTER FORTY

Judi

When Hank has taken half the bottle, I adjust him into a seated position and rub his back gently.

There is a line of dried dirt on his neck and underneath his ear, and his tiny hands are splayed like grubby starfish on my lower arm. I spot small patches of a biscuity crust bunched around the edge of his pale sandy-colored hairline.

His cheeks are ruddy and sore near his mouth and I feel annoyed that we called at the chemist for teething gel on the way over here and I could just as easily have picked up some shampoo and oil to treat his cradle cap too.

I know Fiona does her best with her children, but I'm afraid it isn't nearly good enough. I shiver when I consider that this precious, healthy boy, with his whole life in front of him, has already lost the lottery when it comes to his mother.

Hank releases a small burp of wind pretty much without any help, and I tilt him back down again. He takes the rest of the feed willingly and hungrily. When we get to the end, I feel certain he could easily have taken more, and it makes me wonder whether he is getting his three necessary feeds a day.

I use a spot of antibacterial foam on my finger, and when

it's dry, I squirt a blob of teething gel onto the tip and wait until Hank opens his rosebud mouth.

I begin to sing, jigging him very gently on my knee. "Half a pound of tuppenny rice, half a pound of treacle. That's the way the money goes, POP goes the weasel!" Hank lets out an amused little cackle and I slip my finger into his mouth, rubbing the numbing gel on to one side of his gums.

The wet skin is swollen and hot under my fingertip, and every so often I feel a rugged little bump as a tooth pushes up, ready to break through the inflammation. When I've done the other side, I wipe my finger on a tissue and lift him up in front of me.

Both Noah and Josh suffered terribly when they were teething. I can remember having each one of them for several nights when they were tiny to give Ben and Louise a rest. Louise was never threatened by my closeness to Ben and the boys. On the contrary, she was the first to admit how much she appreciated my advice and experience.

I hold Hank under his arms and bounce his feet lightly on my knee. His pale blue socks look bobbly and worn and are clearly in desperate need of a thorough wash, if not the bin.

"Is it time to change Hank's stinky nappy? *Is it?*" I chant in a silly voice. "I think Nanny Judi better had, *yes I do*!"

I'm just about to sit him down again when he lets out a sort of garbled sigh, and a sticky little hand shoots out and gently touches my cheek, lingering there. He looks at me with wide, trusting eyes and then gives me a big toothless grin, as if he can't believe his luck that he's here.

It's so wonderful to feel wanted again.

I quickly change Hank's nappy, trying to ignore how badly stocked Fiona's changing bag is. Its meager contents include one of the thinnest, cheapest nappies I've ever seen, a nearly empty tube of soothing cream and a dummy. And that's about it.

I peel off the existing sodden nappy to find that the poor child is rife with nappy rash, and after I've liberally applied the cream, the tube is completely empty.

I look up to the ceiling, hearing the telltale creaking of the floorboards that signals Fiona is out of the bath.

I carry Hank through to the kitchen and stir the lamb curry in the slow cooker. I made it last night, set it simmering on a very low setting, and now the meat is literally falling apart.

I stick a packet of rice in the microwave, amused to watch little Hank taking everything in, gurgling and pointing. It crosses my mind that Fiona might be guilty of keeping him strapped into his buggy in front of the TV or something similar. I don't want to judge or to think badly of her, but the child seems so entranced by new things around him, and I know from seeing her in the park that she has a lot on her mind.

With Hank happily perched on one hip, I drag out the old high chair. It was used for both Noah and Josh, and when they grew out of it, I relegated it to the corner of the pantry, never taking it up to the attic. I think a part of me likes to still see it there.

A few minutes later, Fiona appears with damp hair and a clean, makeup-free face, which makes her look younger. She is fully dressed again—although there is still more flesh on show than covered up—and we sit at the table that I've set simply with plates of rice and curry and tall glasses of iced water.

As she reaches for the salt cellar, her sleeve rides up on her arm and I give an involuntary gasp as a neat row of fingertip-sized bruises are revealed.

She glances at me, following my eyes, and immediately tugs down the sleeve.

"I'm always banging into things," she says, staring down at her plate and mixing the rice and curry together. "I can't remember where I get the bruises from half the time."

My mind flicks back to Maura telling me about her bruised inner thighs.

I choose my words carefully. "It looks rather as if someone has grabbed you by the arm, Fiona."

"No!" The words escape her mouth like a rush of hot steam. "I know it might look like that, but it isn't. I'd say if it was."

"I hope you would," I say, picking up my glass of water. "You can talk to me about anything, you know. I won't judge you."

She presses her lips together in a tight line.

"I felt like Kim Kardashian in that bathroom, Judi," she says, tipping the food off her fork and loading it up again. "All that hot water and bubbles. All I needed was a glass of Moët."

"I'm glad you enjoyed it," I say. "You deserve a little pampering."

She gives me a funny look, as if she thinks I'm being facetious.

"Listen, I really don't want to offend you, Fiona, but—"

She drops her knife and fork with a clatter and pushes her chair back. Hank visibly jumps in the high chair and yells in protest, banging the plastic tray with the heel of his hand.

"You want me to go? You don't have to say it, I know I've overstayed my welcome. I'm sorry, I never meant—"

"Fiona, sit down." I touch her arm. "That's not what I was about to say at all."

She sits back down and stares at her short, bitten nails.

"I wanted to say that I'd very much like to help you," I say gently. "Buy you a few things for Hank, even look after him now and then to give you an hour's peace, if you're happy for me to do that. What do you think?"

She stares at me. Something about the look on her face makes me wonder if everyone who has ever offered to do her a favor has a hidden agenda.

"Please don't be offended, and feel free to say no," I say. "It's just an offer, something I'd like to do. You don't have to accept if you don't want to, but know that I'm here to help you."

"Thank you, I—" She clamps her mouth shut and twists round in her chair.

We both sit up, alarmed, at the sound of the front door opening. There's a bit of scuffling and banging around and then I hear it slam shut. I stand up and walk quickly over to the kitchen door, looking down the hallway.

"Henry," I say faintly.

CHAPTER FORTY-ONE

Judi

"Now there's a welcome." Henry frowns and starts to walk upstairs with his small suitcase and overnight bag. The only man I know who goes fishing and takes a suitcase. "Nice to see you too, Judi."

"Sorry," I say quickly. "I didn't mean—"

Behind me Hank lets out an unbridled shriek of delight.

"Sshh," I hear Fiona whisper.

"What the hell was *that*?" Henry scowls and comes back down the three or four steps, putting both bags down. His eyes widen when he sees the pushchair jutting out from under the stairs.

"It's just Fiona who I know from work," I say over-brightly. "She popped in to see me with her little one and I asked her to stay for a spot of lunch."

I look back into the kitchen to see Fiona lifting Hank hastily out of the high chair and simultaneously grabbing her tatty handbag from the side.

"No need to go, Fiona," I say, aware that my voice sounds strained. "It's only my husband, Henry."

Henry walks into the kitchen and stands stock-still in the

doorway. His mouth falls open as he looks at me and then at little Hank in Fiona's arms. I stand there, silent and mortified. I can't quite believe he is being so openly rude.

"H-Henry, this is Fiona, and the little man's name is Hank," I stammer, looking from one to the other, a smile stretching falsely on my face. Fiona looks like a scared rabbit about to bolt.

Then she moves. "Sorry, I have to go." She rushes past Henry and into the hallway, stuffing her feet into her heels and shrugging on the coat I gave her.

"Fiona, no! You haven't finished your lunch." I rush after her, but Henry catches my arm.

"Let her go," he says in a low voice.

Two minutes later, the house is quiet again. Fiona and Hank have left and I'm still standing in the kitchen with my husband, wondering what just happened.

"Why did you do that?" My fingers curl inward and the nails sink slowly into the soft pad of flesh beneath my thumb.

"Do what?"

"Frighten the poor girl off. You were so rude, staring at her and not even saying hello. She looked scared to death."

"Do you know that girl well?"

"Well enough," I say, looking away.

"Judi, you need to be careful who you're befriending. You can't just bring any waif and stray into our home. It's not safe letting people see where we live, what we have."

My body stiffens with the injustice of his words.

"That's so unfair. You don't know anything about her," I retort, feeling my breathing growing more rapid.

"I don't have to *know* her. It's glaringly obvious that you simply felt sorry for her, tried to help her, but..." He hesitates. "Just don't let it get out of control, is what I'm saying. You can't help everyone."

"You're being totally ridiculous," I hiss. "I shouldn't need your permission to bring someone in for a chat and a bite to eat. And I know her from the surgery; she isn't a waif and stray, as you put it."

"I'm not going to argue about this." He walks past me, his face thunderous. He stops in the hall and, as if he's had an afterthought, turns to face me. "Don't let it happen again, Judi. It's not healthy."

"How dare you! I won't be dictated to in—"

"Judi." His severe tone stops me in my tracks. "We've all noticed you've become rather confused and hostile around the people who love you the most, and yet here you are offering hospitality and acceptance to a girl you only know fleetingly from the surgery. I'm not sure what's got into you, but it needs to stop, right now."

All noticed? I remember he's spoken to Ben while he's been away on the fishing trip.

"That's utter rubbish," I blurt out. "I don't know what Ben has told you, but it's not *me* who's at fault here."

"It might be best if I make you an appointment to see Phil Fern. Talk things through with a professional."

Henry knows Dr. Fern well. They went to Newcastle University together and are the same age. Even though Dr. Fern studied medicine and Henry was a business and finance student, they bonded on the rugby team and became good friends.

They still go out for the odd beer or to see a game, and Henry foolishly thinks that qualifies him to be party to my medical history, as his wife. I went to see Dr. Fern recently, and quite rightly, Henry hasn't got a clue.

"If I need to see the doctor, I'm perfectly capable of

making my own appointment, thank you," I say between clenched teeth. "All I need is for people like you to stop trying to tell me what to fucking do with my life."

And with that I storm past, ignoring his obvious shock and outrage, and stomp upstairs, slamming David's door behind me.

CHAPTER FORTY-TWO

Amber

It had certainly been a crazy few days.

Amber had felt her life had moved at breakneck speed, and for the first time she began to wish it was actually all real. She'd even begun to consider changing her perspective. If she did that, could this whole thing wipe out the horror of the past?

Even as she thought the words, she knew that could never happen.

Ben had never done anything to harm her; he'd simply been a vehicle to get nearer to the person she really wanted to hurt. Incredibly, he'd told her he loved her. Loved her! But he didn't know her; he only knew the face she allowed herself to show him.

Despite her best efforts, she found herself increasingly fond of little Josh. His childish charm and willingness to please were hard to resist at times. Several times she'd even wished he could loosen the steel casing that she felt was forever fused to her heart, but there was a dull acceptance that it was there to stay until she took her last breath.

Noah, however, was an altogether different animal to his younger brother.

She saw Judi in him. He was stubborn for his age, set in his ways. Sometimes, when she and Ben were sitting on the couch together at night, watching TV or talking, she'd glance up to see Noah watching her with eyes older than his years.

She wondered if Judi had instructed him to spy, to listen in to their conversations. He would make a useful little mole for his cunning nanny. Amber had noticed he was becoming morose and difficult to control, but she wouldn't let him win. When Ben wasn't around he was a different boy altogether: meek and quiet. Far preferable.

Ben didn't seem to mind at all that she had introduced a bit of discipline into the house. She told him it was for the boys' own sake, that they'd been allowed to run riot by his mother. Although of course she'd had to be careful not to go too far.

Still, yesterday's developments were going to change all that. Surprise was not a strong enough word for the way she'd felt when Ben had sat her down, the things he'd said. She'd felt herself getting ridiculously emotional and he'd seen it too, was happy at her reaction.

But she'd wanted to cry only because she wished she could enjoy it like a normal person without all the deceit and ill intent that bubbled away under the surface.

Yet it was nice to feel invincible at last. To know that everything was going perfectly to plan and that nobody could stop her now.

Least of all Ben's mother.

CHAPTER FORTY-THREE

Judi

On Saturday morning my phone buzzes with a message. It's heart-warming when I see it is a text from Ben.

I click on the notification and a photograph of Noah and Josh loads, waving from the front of the monkey enclosure at Twycross Zoo. I smile, loving the smiles on the boys' faces, seeing they're having a good time.

Something catches my eye at the corner of the shot and I pinch at the picture, expanding it on my phone screen. A hand with long pink nails is clutching Josh's hand tightly. Possessively.

Suddenly I'm seized by a compulsion to do something. Anything except sit here in this big, silent house, watching my family being taken away from me.

I grab my coat and handbag and head out to the car. Henry won't be back until much later from his photography group; he won't even know I've been out.

It's late morning when I get to the house. I feel a little nervous when I see Amber's Fiat parked out the front, even though I know for a fact they're all at the zoo and will have gone in Ben's Ford Focus.

On the way here, I've thought of a suitable excuse, just in case they return unexpectedly. I've lost my reading glasses and I remembered that the last time I had them was at their house. It's a plausible tale because I don't use them that often. I do most of my reading on my Kindle, where I can easily increase the text size.

The street is relatively quiet and there is no sign of any nearby neighbors, so I get out of the car, walk briskly to the front door and let myself in.

Inside, I feel like I'm in a different house to the one I used to clean. I already know Amber has made big changes to the decoration of the rooms, but now there's a new hall table and a mirror above it. No coats hanging over the banister, no shoes piled in the corner near the door.

And the house smells different; there must be incense burning downstairs every night, because the odor is quite strong, even now.

I double-lock the door behind me and slip off my shoes. I don't know what I'm looking for or why I've come here. I just know it's a starting point.

Something about Amber Carr is not adding up and I'm going to do my best to find out why.

I head straight up to the main bedroom. The room seems smaller, more closed in, and I realize that a new double wardrobe has been purchased and pushed up against the other wall. This one is white, without mirrored doors, and when I look inside, I find it is full of Ben's clothes, packed too close together.

I get down on my hands and knees and look under the bed. There are a few neat piles of magazines under Ben's side and nothing but a pair of fluffy slippers under Amber's

I'm looking for something Amber wouldn't necessarily want anyone else seeing. It feels like the definition of madness—that I don't even know what it is I'm looking for—but I'm utterly certain there is something to find.

I ignore the chest of drawers and the bedside table. I've no wish to see the contents of *those* again. I throw open the doors of the mirrored triple wardrobe and unsurprisingly find that Amber has commandeered this bigger space for her things.

I disregard the clothes hanging from the rail and crouch down, sweeping longer items aside to see the floor of the wardrobe. There are a lot of shoes here, all neatly paired and stacked in double rows. I can see right to the back, because the light from the window is good, but there is nothing else here but footwear.

I stand up on my tiptoes and peer at the shelf that runs across the top of the double bit of the wardrobe. As I've now come to expect of Amber, it's neat. I lift a folded blanket and a spare pillow, peer inside a large velveteen wallet that contains dress jewelry.

I'm very careful to replace everything exactly as I find it. I glance nervously out of the window, imagining what I'd do if Ben's car suddenly pulled up outside. But his car isn't there. I'm still OK for time.

The single wardrobe making up the triple door space has been used to store Amber's coats and heavier jackets. I can see that Ben's winter coat is in here too. There are three pairs of long boots on the floor, including the over-the-knee suede pair she's fond of wearing with her ripped skinny jeans.

There is nowhere else to look.

With a heavy heart, I close the third wardrobe door, and then, just before the magnet clicks to, I have a bit of a light-bulb moment and pull it open again. Coats and jackets have pockets, places people can forget they've put things, especially when they've no reason to believe anyone is looking.

As far as Amber is aware, I'm no longer coming to the house; she's managed to convince Ben he doesn't need my help anymore. I haven't been here since before she moved in, so I'm sure she feels no threat that I'll be snooping around.

I ignore the prod of conscience that spears my gut and think instead of Noah's injured hand. I begin a systematic check of outer and inner pockets. A denim jacket, a faux-fur coat. A long black coat with a glossy fur collar. There are no inside pockets in the silky lining. There's just a waxed walking jacket to go. I plunge my hand into the deep pocket and my fingers close around an envelope.

I take it over to the window and peer inside. I pull out the photos and take a look. Two young girls: in the sea, eating ice creams, petting a dog.

I replace them and push them back into the coat, disappointed.

I check the other pocket and pull out a screwed-up business card. I straighten it out enough to read the print. It's for a care home in Sheffield: Sunbeam Lodge. Scrawled on the back in pen are the words "Mum: Room 15A."

The first time we met her, Ben told me Amber's parents had both died in a car accident.

Bingo.

CHAPTER FORTY-FOUR

Judi

Sunday morning I rise at six a.m. I slept in the spare room last night and I had the best rest I've had for a while. No snoring from Henry for starters, and no need to be civil to him after the way he behaved in front of poor Fiona.

I make the bed and take Henry's pills and diabetes medicines into the bathroom. I've repeatedly asked him not to leave his medication lying around. The boys are both very sensible, but still, you never know what might happen if they're feeling mischievous.

I can't stay annoyed for long. The precious find of the care-home business card has really boosted my spirits. It's too early to get excited, but it's a possible lead into Amber's murky past. If indeed her mother is alive and well and stuck away from prying eyes in a care home, then it's a way I might be able to trap Amber and reveal her terrible lie to Ben. He'd surely wash his hands of her if she was proven to be so deceitful.

I searched online for Sunbeam Lodge and it looked anything but bright and sunny in the photographs. I also found an online newspaper report dated two years earlier, describing how the place had been under investigation for neglect and narrowly avoided being closed down. If Amber's poor mother is there, it looks as though she has a sad and miserable existence.

Yesterday, after calling at Ben's, I drove down to the park in the hope that I might see Fiona. The weather was dull and drizzly and I kind of knew she wouldn't be sitting there in her usual place on the bench, but I had to at least try, to apologize again.

I'd insisted that Fiona come back to the house with me and I felt responsible for the awful experience she had to endure, courtesy of my husband. During his feed, Hank felt so vulnerable and comfortable in my arms and Henry somehow managed to violate that warm maternal feeling I'd enjoyed so much.

I force myself to push thoughts of Fiona's broken life away, at least for now.

Downstairs in the kitchen, after a first, essential cup of tea, I begin the early preparations for lunch.

I make Ben's favorite, cauliflower cheese, so it's ready just to pop in the oven. I've decided to include Henry's first choice: mustard mash. Josh's preferred roast parsnips will make an appearance and then it will be Noah's choice for dessert.

"Plenty of nice duck-fat-roasted potatoes, too," I murmur to myself, smiling in anticipation of the sour look that will no doubt settle on Amber's perfectly made-up face. Saturated fat will be the least of madam's worries if my Sunbeam Lodge investigation comes up trumps.

Henry puts in an appearance about nine, mutters a cursory "good morning" and makes himself a bowl of cereal. Half an hour later he disappears into the garden in his overalls without saying anything further.

I let his grouchiness go over my head. Nothing is going to spoil my precious time spent with my grandsons today.

I pace myself throughout the morning, not doing so much that I get flustered, and I manage to keep any worrying thoughts at bay by thinking of Noah and Josh. They'll no doubt be bubbling over with everything they've got to tell me about their week, there'll be another intricate robot toy to inspect, and I simply cannot wait.

When they arrive, I'm ready. I'm dressed, my hair is neat and I've even put a bit of lipstick on. The house is sparkly clean, and aside from the last bits of veg to chop, all the food is prepared and most of it is already in the oven.

"Hi, Mum, Dad," Ben calls brightly as he steps into the hall, followed by a subdued Noah and Josh, who slip off their shoes without a word.

Amber stands on the tiled step outside, watching them.

"Heavens, I've never known you two boys to be so quiet," I say, trying to brighten my voice. "Are you feeling OK?"

"Yes," Josh says, and Noah nods silently.

Something doesn't feel right. I hold my arms out, and as Amber steps inside, both boys lean into me, one on either side. I pull my arms in and hold them close.

"Hello, Amber," I say.

For a few moments it feels like Ben and Henry are both holding their breath to see how things lie between the two of us.

"Hello, Judi," she says, taking off her shoes and avoiding my eyes. "How are you?"

I open my mouth to answer her, but Henry beats me to it.

"Oh, we're very well, Amber dear," he booms, far too enthusiastically. "It's so lovely to see you again. To see you *all* again, isn't it, Judi?"

"Yes," I say. "It seems like forever since we last saw the boys."

"Noah, Josh. Straighten your shoes, please," Amber says shortly. "You've already kicked them halfway across the hall."

"Oh, that doesn't matter." I hug the boys to me. "We've more important things to do than tidy shoes, haven't we, scamps?"

Josh grins and nods up at me. But Noah stiffens slightly and looks at Amber.

"Fine then," Amber sighs. "If your nanny is happy with that, then it's fine." She turns to Ben. "Just popping up to the bathroom."

She disappears upstairs. I glance at Ben, who opens his mouth and closes it again. I feel like waiting at the top of the stairs to make sure she doesn't sneak into any of the bedrooms.

"Come on, chaps, let's have a catch-up in here," Henry whispers conspiratorially to the boys, and winks at Ben.

Noah and Josh follow Ben and Henry into the living room and I return to the kitchen to finish everything off for lunch.

My heart feels full, my step is light and I want to sing from the rooftops that my grandsons are here. I don't give a toss about upsetting Amber bloody Carr.

Just a couple of minutes later, Ben sidles into the kitchen. I look up from chopping and smile at him. "You know, it really doesn't matter if there's a bit of mess in the hallway when the boys are here, love."

"It doesn't hurt to make them think about being a little tidier, though, Mum." He tucks his chin to his chest and widens his eyes at me.

"I know, I know. I'm too soft on them." I grin. "I'm hopelessly guilty of loving them to bits."

"Mum, could you just leave the food for just a moment and come into the living room, please?"

"What?" I stop draining the potatoes and look at him, suddenly ridiculously afraid of what he's about to say. "I can't...I mean, can it wait until—"

"Please, Mum. I just need a few minutes of your time. We've got something important to tell you."

CHAPTER FORTY-FIVE

Judi

I set the saucepan down with a clatter. My heart is already pounding and I suddenly feel very hot.

I'm vaguely aware of Ben gently taking my arm and leading me into the hallway, where Amber flashes me a wide, smug smile and disappears into the living room ahead of us.

When I step into the room, Henry and the boys are in there waiting with beaming smiles, and Amber herself hands me a glass of champagne.

"Mum, Dad, Amber and I, we want to tell you the most amazing news." Ben nods, and Amber steps forward and raises her left hand, wiggling her third finger at me. It sports a solitaire diamond ring. "We're engaged! I proposed to Amber yesterday . . . and, well, she said yes!"

"And then we went to the zoo!" Amber squeals, spinning around in glee, and little Josh jiggles and grins widely, looking up at me.

"Well, now, that really is splendid news," Henry declares, raising his glass. "To Amber and Ben. Congratulations, you two!"

I watch as they all clink glasses, sipping champagne and

smiling at each other. Their voices sound muffled, as if I'm underwater and watching events around me unfold in super-slow motion.

"Engaged to be married?" I hear myself whisper in the midst of the din.

"Isn't it wonderful?" Henry slaps Ben on the back and kisses Amber on both cheeks. "Welcome to the family, my dear."

"Thank you, Henry." She flutters her long lashes, and then the room falls silent and I become aware that everyone, even the two boys, is waiting for my reaction.

"You're officially engaged?" I say slowly, putting down my glass. "So... soon?"

"We're not in our teens, Mum." Ben winks at Amber. "We're old enough to know that what we have is real."

"We both feel very lucky, Judi," Amber simpers, leaning into Ben. "And there's not just us to consider; there's the boys, too. It's so important to their stability that we become a proper family unit. That's why I had no hesitation in saying a big fat yes when Ben proposed."

Ben beams at his new wife-to-be.

"How long have you been planning all this?" I manage to ask.

"I'd been thinking about proposing for about a week," Ben says, looking at his father. Henry opens his mouth to speak and then falters. He won't look at me and it suddenly clicks why that is.

"You knew." I narrow my eyes at him. "You *knew* they were going to do this."

"Not until a few days ago," Henry says quickly. "I mean, Ben rang to say he was thinking of proposing and to ask if I thought you'd be OK with it."

"I didn't feel I could tell you beforehand, Mum," Ben

mutters, looking at the floor. "I would've loved you and Dad to have known, but I realized that probably wasn't the best thing, considering."

"Considering what?" I snap. "Considering I would've told you to slow down and not be so utterly reckless as to rush into something so important?"

"It's a shame you feel like that about our happy news, Judi," Amber says quietly. "It was all very low-key; we had a little celebratory lunch with the boys and then we went to the zoo. It seemed the most natural thing in the world to do."

"I bet it did," I mutter, looking at Ben.

"Come on, love." Henry picks up my glass of champagne and pushes it at me again. "Be glad for these two young love-birds, eh?"

I look at the boys. Josh is smiling, but Noah is po-faced. He doesn't look over the moon at their news either. I meet Ben's eyes and see his immense happiness and his silent pleading for my acceptance.

"Congratulations," I sigh, grudgingly taking a sip of champagne. "I can't deny it's a shock, but I do hope you'll both be very happy."

"Thank you for your blessing, Judi." Amber smiles and leans forward to give me a peck on the cheek. "We'll definitely all be very happy. I'll make absolutely certain of it."

CHAPTER FORTY-SIX

Judi

After another five minutes of feigning good wishes and clinking glasses, I can't bear it any longer. I make my excuses and get back to the kitchen before the food is all but ruined.

As I begin to chop the final vegetables, I get the strangest sensation. I feel as if I'm standing back watching myself go through the motions, detached from the awful reality of the mistake Ben is making.

The Ben I know, the sensible boy I raised, has been replaced by a rash, gullible fool who can't see any further than the end of his nose. Amber Carr must have counted her blessings the day she met him.

Nothing I say, nothing I tell him makes the slightest bit of difference, and time is running out because soon they'll be married. But I thank my lucky stars I found that Sunbeam Lodge card. Desperate times lead to desperate measures, and in that moment I resolve to use anything I can to get through to my son and bring him to his senses.

I turn at a shuffling noise behind me and see that Ben is watching me from the doorway. He smiles and his face is animated, joyous. I can see how happy he is with this person, this virtual stranger, who has changed the dynamics of our family in record time.

"Thanks, Mum." He kisses the top of my head.

"For what?"

"For . . . well, you know, not having a hissy fit when we told you our news."

"Well, you've gone and done it now, Ben," I say tersely. "It's a bit late for lectures, however much I'd like to give you one."

"Yeah, I know. It was a crazy thing to do, I admit it. But it felt like a *good* craziness, if you know what I mean. We're so happy together, you know, Mum. All four of us."

"Dare I ask, have you planned the wedding yet?"

"Not yet. We don't want to wait long, though," Ben replies, his voice upbeat. "And it's easier because Amber doesn't want any fuss, just something nice and simple."

And as quick as possible, no doubt.

"Pass me the other chopping board, will you?"

"Amber thinks Noah might have ADHD," Ben says casually, pinching a raw carrot baton from the small pile I'm building.

"What?" I take the chopping board and frown at him.

"Noah. Amber thinks he might suffer from attention deficit hyperactivity disorder."

"I know what it stands for, Ben." I see enough kids with the condition at the surgery. "I just wonder how on earth she's come to that highly unlikely conclusion. She's only known him for two minutes."

My face flushes as Amber appears. I didn't see her at first, skulking back there in the shadows of the wood-paneled hallway.

"I've noticed that Noah finds it very difficult to keep on

task with anything, Judi," she says, reaching for Ben's hand. "And he doesn't always listen when he's spoken to."

"He's eight years old!" I laugh, thinking this must be a joke. "All eight-year-olds are like that."

"Actually, no they're not." Amber looks at Ben.

They step aside to let Henry through. He puts his empty glass on the side and chirps up, unhelpfully, "I'm sure Amber knows what she's talking about, dear. Best leave it to the experts."

"With respect, I know what I'm talking about too. Everyone seems to have forgotten I managed to raise two sons without them ending up in therapy or gorging themselves silly on junk food."

"Oh, come on, Mum," Ben sighs. "Nobody's saying that. Please don't start, not today."

Amber lets go of his hand and steps forward.

"Times change, Judi." She's speaking slowly, as though I'm senile or stupid. Or both. "Through research, we know much more about child development than when Ben was young."

"Oi, how old do you think I am?" Ben nudges her in mock outrage and they share an intimate giggle.

I can't smile. My face feels twisted and frozen.

Henry and Ben are both looking at Amber like she's the damned Oracle or something. But she is far from the font of all knowledge, and I, for one, am not letting her get away with preaching such nonsense in this house.

"Noah is like every other eight-year-old I've ever met," I say tersely, turning to the sink when I feel my eyes unexpectedly prickle. "There is absolutely nothing wrong with him. Nothing at all."

"Well, as far as I'm concerned, there's no harm in getting him checked out," Ben replies lightly. "Do you need us to lay cutlery out or anything, Mum?"

I whip round.

"What're you talking about, *checked out*?"

"A behavioral therapist," Amber supplies in clipped tones. "I have a contact through work, she's very good. Early intervention is the key with these conditions. If Noah *is* found to be suffering from ADHD then the medication can be very effect—"

"Are you completely crazy, the two of you?" I pull a china cup out of the bubbles and smash it down onto the draining board. Thin dribbles of blood form between my fingers and quickly ooze down my hand and forearm.

"Oh!" Amber exclaims and turns to Ben with wide eyes.

The boys run into the kitchen and stop dead in the middle of the room.

"Nanny's cut herself," Noah calls out in alarm.

"For God's sake!" Henry grabs a hand towel from the side and thrusts it at me. "Wrap it up to stem the flow so we can see how bad it is. What on earth were you thinking of?"

CHAPTER FORTY-SEVEN

Judi

"I'll deal with this, Dad." Ben steps toward me and gently wraps the cloth around my bloody hand.

I can't speak at first. I'm shocked by the mighty pull of the twisted barb that runs through me like a relentless undertow.

Ben tears off some kitchen towel from the roll on the side and dabs gently at the two small cuts now visible in the thin skin between my fingers. He is surprisingly attentive. "They're not that deep," he says, looking back at Amber.

She walks over and peers down.

"You'll survive," she says blankly. "It'll stop bleeding soon, just keep pressure on it."

She steps back again.

"I'm sorry." I look up at Ben, my eyes shining. "I didn't mean to break the cup."

"It's all right, Mum," he says soothingly. "You're tight as a drum at the moment. You need to find a way to relax."

"I've been trying to get her to see Dr. Fern," Henry tells him pompously. "But she won't have it."

"I am here, you know," I snap. "And last time I checked, I

was still quite capable of making my own medical appointments, thank you very much."

Henry grumbles under his breath and rounds up the boys, following Amber out of the kitchen into the other room.

"There's nothing wrong with Noah, Ben," I whisper. "*Please*, just this once, listen to me. You could do him more harm than good getting these so-called experts involved. Don't believe everything Amber says, even if she is your fiancée now." Just saying the word makes me feel bilious. "I can't explain it, but don't listen to her."

"All right, Mum," Ben says in a soothing voice. "Try and calm down. Forget about it now and let's have a nice family lunch together. The boys have really missed you."

I remove the paper towel and see that the cuts have almost stopped bleeding. I stick two small plasters over the awkwardly placed slashes and Ben helps me get the vegetables boiling on the hob. A few minutes later and we're ready to go.

As I carve the meat, I push my concerns about Noah away, refusing to waste another second worrying about Amber's influence. She might soon be his wife, but she's not Ben's keeper, and surely he'll have the sense now not to get therapists involved.

I carefully set aside Noah's portion, making sure I include the slightly charred bits he loves the best. Amber will not win when it comes to the welfare of my grandson. I will not stand by while she has him studied and prodded by some self-appointed *therapist* who'll determine whether to attach an ADHD label that could affect him for life.

Love conquers all, and so long as my motives are pure, I have nothing to fear from Amber's judgment or anyone else's, and that includes Henry and Ben.

All that matters right now is spending time with my

family and doing anything I can to show Amber up for the devil that she is.

"Apple pie!" I announce as I carry in the homemade dessert.

Despite the drama, we've managed to enjoy a hearty Sunday lunch that everyone seemed to relish, apart from Amber, who merely pushed a few vegetables around on her plate.

"Noah's favorite dessert, this one, and I even added cinnamon, too. How's that? Now, Master Jukes, will it be cream or custard today?"

I wink at my grandson only to find he is looking warily at Amber. As soon as he arrived today, I noticed that the bandage on his hand had been removed. I decide not to mention it, but I notice he's still moving it a little gingerly as he rubs his eyes.

"Remember what we said this morning about choices, Noah," Amber says quietly, maintaining eye contact with him.

"Choices?" Puzzled, I place the pie on the table mat and perch on the edge of my chair.

"I chose to have Frosted Shreddies for breakfast," Noah says meekly, his eyes glistening.

"And?"

"The boys are eating too much sugar, Mum," Ben explains as Amber nods in agreement. "They're allowed one sweet treat a day now, and they chose to have it at breakfast time."

"But I want some of Nanny's pie," Noah whines, pulling at Ben's arm.

"I've made the pie now," I say reasonably. "And we always have dessert after lunch..." I wink at Noah again and then smile at my son. "Maybe just this once?"

Ben turns to Amber and she looks back at him meaningfully.

"No, Mum. Sorry." He turns back to me. "It's for their own good."

Noah bursts into tears and launches his robot toy into the air. When it clatters to the floor, he growls and kicks it away from him.

"Well, the odd dessert never did you any harm growing up," I say to Ben, getting to my feet. I'm trembling. I refuse to stay in here trying to make them see sense any longer. "If the boys can't have pudding then neither will anyone else."

Henry avoids my glare. I've noticed he's been quieter and is pleasingly wary around me since my recent outbursts.

I pick up the pie and take it through to the kitchen. I slam the white and blue tin dish down onto the worktop, and then a better idea occurs to me.

Flinging the back door open, I stalk out to the bin and throw in the pie, dish and all. I close the lid with a thump, feeling triumphant.

When I return to the kitchen, Henry is waiting, an incredulous look on his face. Ben and Amber appear, looming up behind him.

"What?" I throw my hands up at their open mouths. "If my grandson isn't allowed dessert then none of us will have it. How's that?"

I pull the back door closed behind me.

"Mum, that's just downright ridiculous," Ben says.

Noah squeezes through the cluster of adults and snuggles into my side.

"You're behaving like a child yourself, Judi," Henry huffs. "I was looking forward to a piece of that pie."

"Well, so was Noah," I say, ruffling his hair. "But as we've all learned today, you can't always have what you want."

I glare at Amber, my eyes glowing, and she looks coolly back at me.

A thought pops into my head, a kind of epiphany, if you like. This woman is like a cancer in our lives. She's taken hold, been allowed to flourish and now we have a real problem.

At the surgery, Dr. Fielder is fond of saying that there is only one attitude worth having when it comes to cancer, and that is to be prepared to battle tooth and nail. To have the best chance of surviving, you have to fight it with every fiber of your being.

CHAPTER FORTY-EIGHT

Amber

The weekend had been just brilliant. She couldn't have planned it better if she'd written a wish list of Judi's emotions and reactions.

It was little wonder Judi had been put out by their engagement news, and what she'd said had been quite true.

It *was* crazy that they were getting married.

It *was* too soon and Ben *didn't* know her.

He had never thought to question why she was suddenly here, in the middle of his life. Sometimes she wondered if he was frightened of losing her. Perhaps after Louise died, he'd convinced himself that he'd live the rest of his life alone. Just working, bringing up his two sons and calling at his mother's for tea every day. A grim thought for anyone.

But then there were times when life ruthlessly dealt you your worst nightmare; some people had no choice in the matter. As she herself knew only too well.

Ben had followed his heart and acted rashly by almost anyone's standards in proposing so early on, but Amber didn't care about that. It more than suited her purposes.

She'd watched Judi carefully in the midst of all the

engagement furor. She could see clearly that she was having a great deal of trouble processing what had happened, what had gone wrong.

This woman who'd got used to covertly controlling her family thus far.

It occurred to Amber that a less observant person than herself might easily assume it was that blustering old fart Henry who was the figurehead of the family, but that was just a smoke screen.

The selfless super-cook image that Judi had fostered over the years had certainly stood her in good stead, almost disguising the quietly domineering matriarch alter ego that operated from the shadows.

Denial was a better word to use to describe Judi's reaction to the happy news...denial that she had finally lost the struggle to keep her son and grandsons firmly in her iron grasp.

Once they were married, the process would be complete. Judi's hold would be gone, and she knew it.

And Amber had watched with great pleasure as the realization had dawned on her haggard face like the sun finally setting at the end of a very long, troubling day.

CHAPTER FORTY-NINE

Judi

Later, when they've all left, I run a bath and relax back into the bubbles, allowing the warm water to lap over my cramped shoulder muscles.

The day hasn't been the success I hoped it would be; in fact it has been quite the nightmare. I feel like my son and grandsons are on a runaway juggernaut that moves farther away from me every hour of the day.

Although I fully intended to enjoy our family afternoon without any concern as to what Amber made of proceedings, she has managed to poison our family time from here on in.

Of course, she couldn't have done this without Ben deferring to her every time she makes one of her ill-considered judgments about what is best for the boys. She has grown in power and danger because Ben has every intention of making her his wife and therefore the boys' legal stepmother.

I realize something worrying. Just lately, every time I think about my son, I feel a twinge of resentment that after everything we've been through together after losing Louise, he has turned out to be such a lightweight the second an attractive woman appears on the scene.

It's so rare these days that I get to speak to him on his own, but the couple of times it's happened, I can't get past his passionate defending of Amber, no matter how unreasonable she's being. Now I know why, after seeing the contents of her bedside drawers. She's casting a well-planned, seductive spell on him and he doesn't even realize it.

Ben is university-educated, a committed father who works with young people every day, and yet he's taking advice on his precious sons from a woman who is...some kind of childcare expert? We don't know. As with most things, we've simply had to take her word for what she tells us about her life before Ben.

Of course, I can understand there might be unresolved trauma in her past life according to the very scant details Ben told me, but she seems very well practiced in changing the subject or feeling unwell every time something doesn't suit. And my Sunbeam Lodge discovery goes some way to offering a possible explanation of why this might be.

I've given up hoping that Amber might furnish us with more information. I'm going to have to find out about her past for myself.

I don't stay in the bath long. I'm antsy and finding it increasingly difficult to relax. I used to enjoy reading a novel while I bathed, but my mind is too active for that now.

Thinking about a plan to find out more about Amber has excited me, given me a feeling of control again, which is a welcome change from the frustration and hopelessness that's been the norm up until now.

I have two things particularly on my mind: a visit to Sunbeam Lodge and inquiring a bit more into Amber's job.

I dry myself in the bathroom and slip on the unused cotton

dressing gown that's still hanging on the door from Fiona's ill-fated visit on Friday.

In the bedroom, I comb through my wet hair and smear a little moisturizer on to my dry face. I used to take great pleasure in keeping a good skincare routine, but the last few weeks it's gone to pot and now my skin feels tight and flaky.

I realize I've still got my earrings on, so I take them out and open my jewelry box to drop them in. And I freeze.

The gold and citrine necklace is back in there, sitting on top of everything else.

It's as if it was never missing in the first place.

When Henry gets in from his monthly local history group meeting just after nine, I meet him at the door. He doesn't see me at first; he's busy looking at his phone. All thoughts of continuing the silent treatment have now evaporated. I stand there, my hand drifting in mid-air.

"What is it?" He stuffs his phone back in his pocket and looks alarmed. "Whatever's the matter?"

"Sh-she put it back," I stammer. "It's in there again."

"What?" He frowns. "Who put *what* back?"

"The necklace," I whisper. "It's back in my jewelry box."

He shakes his head and moves past me. "I doubt it was ever missing in the first place, Judi. You probably just didn't look thoroughly enough."

"I did look, and I'm telling you, it wasn't there," I protest, following him into the living room. "Amber put it back again. It's the only rational explanation."

"Judi." He spins round and claps his hand to his forehead. "Enough of this. I can't take it anymore, this...this utter nonsense you're constantly peddling. You're about as far from being rational as you could be."

"I don't care if you believe me or not," I tell him. "I know I'm right and before long you'll realize that. I just hope Ben sees through her before it's too late, before something really bad happens."

"Save it, will you? They're to be married now." Henry sits down and flicks on the TV. "And frankly, I've heard enough. We've *all* heard enough."

Despite Henry's insults, and purely to keep myself busy, I make him a cocoa on autopilot, out of habit, and take it through. While he drinks it, I tidy round in the kitchen and set the dishwasher going before I head off to bed. I know I'll be tossing and turning, probably for hours, before a nightmare-twisted sleep descends, but I crave the peace of being alone, away from Henry's cutting words.

I'm finding it very difficult to make sense of the reappearance of the necklace. Even I am surprised that Amber would have the sheer audacity to firstly take it and subsequently replace it. Yet it's the only thing that makes any sense at all, and she *did* go upstairs again on her own earlier.

"Judi," I hear Henry call in a bored voice from the other room. "Your phone's going off."

I run through and manage to snatch it up, pressing the answer call button at the same time that I register it is Ben's name on the screen.

I decide in a split second that I'm going to tell him about the necklace right away. Put an end once and for all to the spiteful games Amber is playing.

CHAPTER FIFTY

Judi

"Mum?" Ben sounds breathless.

"Ben? Is everything all right?" Henry's head snaps up as I grab on to the back of his chair.

"It's Noah, Mum. He's really ill. We've brought him to A and E. The doctor's just seen him and says he's got food poisoning. Probably E. coli, they say. Poor little chap's severely dehydrated, so they've put him on a drip."

"Oh no!" I think about the lunch he ate here earlier and swallow hard. "Are they keeping him in?"

"For a while, but they say he's lucky we got him here when we did, because the next stage could've been kidney failure."

"My God." I widen my eyes.

"What?" Henry stands up, holding out his hands in frustration. "What's happened?"

I cover the mouthpiece. "It's Noah. He's got food poisoning," I say in a hoarse whisper, then return to the call. "What happened, Ben? How did you first know he was ill?"

"When we left your house, he was a bit quiet all afternoon. Amber took the boys up to bed at their usual time. An hour later, Noah's in the loo shouting for us. He had the most terrible diarrhea, Mum, passing blood."

"Oh, my poor Noah." My hand flies to my mouth and I can feel my eyes starting to prickle.

"They've taken a stool sample for tests, but the doctor is ninety-nine percent certain it's E. coli."

"And how is he now?"

"He's in a bit of a bad way. I..." I hear my son's voice crack. "They say he'll pick up quickly once he's rehydrated, but I can't stop thinking what might have happened, Mum."

"Oh, darling." I wipe my face. "Dad and I will come right now." I look at Henry, who is still standing, and he nods with some urgency.

There's a silent pause at the end of the line.

"There's no point you coming down, honestly, Mum. Amber's here looking after Josh. She's been brilliant, I honestly don't know how I'd have coped without her. Noah is completely out of it, sleeping, but they seem confident he's out of danger now."

"But—"

"He'll be off the drip soon and they say he'll probably be fit enough to be discharged. It'd be best if you come and see him tomorrow, at home."

I hesitate, but then I just say it. "No, Ben, I want to see him. We can be there in fifteen minutes flat. I won't sleep otherwise."

"We're OK, Mum. It's best you stay put. I just called because I thought you should know what's happening. That's all." He falls quiet for a moment. "Amber and I are coping just fine."

I beg him to keep us informed, and end the call. Then I sit down heavily in the chair.

"So what's happening?" Henry asks.

I can't speak for a few moments. I think about Ben's face when he was a young boy. Inquisitive and loving, always on the go and trying something new. I was the person he ran to back then when life didn't go the way he'd planned. Bruised from a playground spat, or the time he found his pet rabbit cold and still in the hutch when he went to feed him before school. These were things I could help with, simply by wrapping my arms around him and holding him close.

As our kids get older and become adults themselves, there's a stage we unknowingly pass, from which point forward our role as parents diminishes in their life.

Now Noah is very ill and Ben and Josh are with him at the hospital. Amber is there too. Only a matter of weeks ago, I would have been the one there, supporting them.

I don't know how or exactly when it began happening, but my son has moved on. They are a family now.

I hear Henry speak again, but his voice sounds far away. I close my eyes and allow myself to properly feel the cramping pain that fills my body. Today I've reached a new understanding. A cold, gray place I didn't even know I was headed for.

Today is the day when, finally, my son doesn't need me around anymore.

I don't sleep, of course. Tossing and turning all through the night, I come up with scenarios I've read about, stories I've heard at the surgery.

All those times the medics believed a child was out of danger and then *bam*. Inquiries, investigations, excuses follow. What comes after doesn't really matter anymore, because the child is gone, leaving behind a maelstrom of emotions that the family will never recover from.

Twice I get up and get dressed. I go downstairs and look at the car keys. I stare out of the front-room window, at the dull sodium-orange streetlamp that reflects up from the bottom of the driveway like a muted stagelight. Both times, Ben's voice, in that determined tone, echoes in my ears: *Amber and I are coping just fine.* It cuts deep, but I can't stop playing it on a loop in my head.

I lie on my back in bed and stare up through the darkness. The heat begins to churn in my solar plexus, writhing like a knot of vipers awaking from slumber. I can't see the ceiling or the walls, but I know they're there, containing me, restricting me. Henry snores softly beside me and I listen to the backdrop of my own breath; a faint rasp, shallow and irregular.

As sleep tries yet again to claim me, David's face floats in front of mine. Forever young and vibrant. To me, he is alive, preserved in that place and time. He can't grow older and cast that vulnerable boy aside.

Nobody can ever take him away from me now.

CHAPTER FIFTY-ONE

Judi

I snap awake before it's even light outside.

I reach across and press my phone screen, snatching it up when I see there's a text from Ben, sent at one thirty this morning.

Hi Mum, we're home. Noah is OK, will ring later. x

A quick check of the clock tells me it's five thirty now, and that's far too early to call Ben, but I can't just sit here for hours wondering how Noah is. I just can't.

I silently slip out of bed. The sheets are damp to the touch thanks to my tormented night. God knows how long this stage in my life is going to last. It didn't count as a really bad episode on my personal hot-flush scale, though it was certainly bad enough to warrant changing the sheets. But I can't do that now and risk waking Henry. The last thing I want is another lecture, telling me how everyone is saying there's something wrong with me and I need to go see Dr. Fern.

I grab yesterday's clothes—jeans, a long-sleeved top and my discarded underwear and creep downstairs. I allow myself a cup of tea—I can't function without it—and then I quickly get dressed, running a brush through my hair and slipping my bare feet into my work flatties. I shrug on the old walking jacket that's hanging in the hallway, grab my handbag and keys and leave the house.

It's dark and cold and my actions feel illogical and somewhat clandestine. But now I know that Noah has been discharged from hospital, my mind burns with a need to see my grandson with my own eyes, to satisfy myself he's OK. It feels like the right thing to do.

It's a short drive to Ben's house, but the journey seems never-ending. The roads are long and empty and, despite the street lighting, I feel enveloped in gloom.

I turn into Ben's road, but I don't park outside the house. I drive past, turn the car round and find a spot a little farther up where I still have a clear view of the front door and windows.

There are far more cars parked here than I've seen before, as it's too early for most people to have left for work. Amongst the properties, there are only one or two windows lit behind closed curtains. Ben's house is shrouded in darkness. The blinds are down on the lower floor and the curtains closed in the front bedroom.

I close my eyes and think about Ben and Amber, asleep in bed, their limbs entwined. The faint tick of Ben's traditional alarm clock—he prefers it to a digital display—and the wardrobes stuffed with Amber's clothes. I blink away the images when I recall the contents of the two drawers I had the misfortune to peer into.

It's six fifteen now. The sky isn't yet light, but it's changed from being pitch dark. The sun will be coming up in about twenty minutes. I need to sit here patiently, taking comfort from the fact that I'm physically as close to Noah as I can get at this moment in time.

It's the most terrible thing that he became so ill, but hopefully it will have shown Ben that he needs his family around him at times like this. On reflection, I wish I'd insisted on going to the hospital and ignored his instructions to stay at home.

Still, I'm here now and that's what matters. With both Ben and Amber working full-time, they're going to need my help while Noah is off school, recovering. I know Maura won't mind me taking a few days' annual leave, and if it needs more of my time than that, then Henry will just have to sacrifice his social calendar to stay home with Noah until I get back from work each afternoon.

Something catches my attention and I look up to see that Ben's bedroom window has just lit up. The shadow of a person passes by the curtains, looming large and out of proportion like a predatory figure in a nightmare.

I sit, transfixed, as outsized, jolting shadows move back and forth like a macabre puppet show. Then the lights snap on downstairs and I know someone is in the living room and, I'd guess, very probably in the kitchen at the back of the house.

I twist the keys from the ignition and open the car door, reaching over for my handbag. My heart sinks as I catch sight of the time on the dashboard clock. It's only six twenty-two. I can see the glow of the sunrise beginning, a glorious haze still trapped and contained under a bubble of thick, smoky-looking clouds.

By anyone's standards, it is too early. I consider waiting in the car until seven o'clock, but then another thought supersedes it. Ben has forced me to do this. If I had been able to see Noah for myself last night at the hospital, I would no doubt have slept better and felt reassured enough to visit later today.

Well, I refuse to be put off again. It's clear that Ben is receiving specific instructions, and they're not from me.

I grab my handbag and lock the car. It seems that with every second, the sky becomes a smidgen lighter, and I feel more confident, more comfortable in my right to be here.

But when I get to the pavement in front of the house, I hesitate again, thinking for a moment or two. I grudgingly decide that rather than use my key, it feels right to knock quietly at the front door. This would have been unheard of only a few weeks ago, but now I feel a bit like an intruder. The annoying thing is that my decision would be quite different if Ben and the boys were alone in there.

There again, if *she* wasn't around, I'd have been by Ben's side throughout Noah's trauma.

I pat my hair tidy, take a breath and knock.

CHAPTER FIFTY-TWO

Judi

After rapping on the door, I let my hand fall. I clench my fist and silently pray that it's Ben who answers the door and not Amber.

A few seconds elapse and I'm just about to knock again when I hear the chain being released and the door swings open.

"Oh," Amber says hesitantly. "It's you, Judi."

"Yes," I say levelly, glancing at her skimpy pajamas and the sparkling ring on her left hand that changes everything. "It's me. I know it's still early, but I couldn't sleep. I had to come and see how Noah is."

"Ben," she calls over her shoulder, before looking back at me. "Your mother's here."

She's standing in the doorway and I'm still outside.

I take a step forward. "I'll come in off the street if you don't mind."

Somewhat grudgingly, she stands aside.

"Mum!" Ben appears, clad in his Marks and Spencer stripy pajama bottoms, the ones I bought him last Christmas. "What the...? Why are you here so early?"

"I couldn't sleep, Ben. I've been awake half the night, worrying. How is he?"

"I don't know, he hasn't woken up yet."

"We didn't get back from the hospital until one a.m.," Amber adds. "I just came down to make us a cup of tea to take back upstairs to bed."

I receive her subtext loud and clear: *Leave us alone.* I ignore it.

"Well, I'll have a cup if you're making one," I say, slipping off my coat and shoes. The raw fury that passes across her features is well worth the trip over here. "Can we have a quick chat, Ben?"

He looks at Amber and back at me.

"I just want a few minutes of your time, if that's not too much to ask," I say quietly. "I'd like to know what the hospital said. I'm surprised they didn't want to keep Noah in overnight to monitor him."

He sighs. "He was out of danger, Mum, I'm sure the doctors know what they're doing. Let's go into the living room."

"I'll just get on with the tea then, shall I?"

"Thanks, love." Ben smiles at Amber and their eyes meet briefly, but she doesn't smile back.

"I'd like to see Noah," I say.

"'Course," Ben says. "Do you want to pop up now?"

"Do you really think that's a good idea, Ben?" Amber turns back at the door. "He was exhausted when we got back; surely he should be left to just sleep so his body can repair itself."

I squeeze hard on the handles of my handbag. "I won't wake him." I hate the note of pleading I hear in my own voice.

"He's been really restless, Judi. I looked in on him a couple of times in the night and he stirred." She shrugs and looks at Ben. "Up to you, sweetie, but I think we should let him rest."

"Let's leave it for now. I'll tell you about what happened at the hospital." Ben ushers me down the hallway with his arm. "He might wake up before you go and then you can pop up."

He opens the living room door and we enter the gaudy den that used to be a perfectly nice, tasteful living area. Ben leaves the curtains closed and snaps on a new, purple-shaded lamp that barely gives any illumination at all.

"My, how things change," I say, looking around.

"You know what they say." Ben nods cheerfully. "A change is as good as a rest."

I don't comment.

Ben relays a rather rushed account of what happened at the hospital.

"The main problem was the dehydration, but the drip sorted that out. They said he's out of danger now, just needs plenty of rest and fluids."

I sigh. "What a relief. You must've been terrified, darling." I reach across and place my hand over his. "I'm assuming he's going to be off school for quite a while?"

"They said only about a week. Kids bounce back incredibly well, don't they?"

"They do, but it goes without saying that we'll have him over at our house. I'll take a couple of days off work and then—"

Ben holds his hands up. "There's no need for you to do that, Mum."

"Nonsense, your dad and I don't mind a jot. In fact, we wouldn't have it any other way." There's a feeling of rising panic in my chest. "Anyway, you work full-time; how on earth will you cope otherwise?"

Ben takes a breath. "Amber is going to look after Noah. I can't believe how fantastic she's been, Mum. She's taking her role as stepmum to the boys really seriously. She's even putting her career second."

I look at my son, bewildered.

"Please don't look like that. Noah will be fine, Mum. And like Amber says, he's much better off here, in his own home, than somewhere else."

Somewhere else? No. He'd be staying with his grandparents, who've helped looked after him since the day he was born. I feel a sudden, curious emptiness inside.

I know I should keep quiet, but I can't. I just can't do it. "Noah probably doesn't even regard this as his own home anymore. Everything here has been changed beyond recognition."

"I'm sorry you feel like that about the house, Judi." Amber carries in a tea tray with three mugs on it. I take it she'll be joining us. "I just wanted to make it a bit more comfortable, more of a home, you know? Left to the three boys for the past two years, it felt a bit plain and sterile."

I flinch at the insult but say nothing, and Ben at least has the decency to look away. He knows full well that I helped Louise choose all the furnishings and decoration in this house, and I've continued to help him since she's been gone. For a crazy moment I almost feel like I want to lash out at Ben for letting everything we've worked for together slip away so easily.

Amber smiles sweetly at us both and sets down the tray on the bare coffee table, the one that used to be covered with framed family photographs. Precious memories for the boys, now removed.

Ben picks up a mug and holds it up in front of his mouth as he speaks.

"I just told Mum that you're going to be looking after Noah," he says pointedly to Amber.

"That's right." She smiles as she passes me a mug of tea. "We'll soon get him fighting fit again."

An uncomfortable silence falls over us like an invisible shroud.

I'm torn between remaining silent and avoiding causing offense to Amber and saying what I mean. But this is my only chance to speak to Ben before crucial decisions are made about Noah's recovery. I was hoping to do it alone, just the two of us, but now she's made that impossible.

If something happened to Noah in her care, I'd never forgive myself that I didn't put up a fight for him.

"My concern is this," I say, putting down my tea and looking purposefully at Ben. "Amber doesn't really know Noah very well yet. If he were to deteriorate again, she might find it difficult to spot the signs."

"I work with children all the time. I can assure you I know *all* the signs of them feeling unwell." She smiles and speaks easily, but I see the tense way she's holding her shoulders, how her fingers chafe against her pajama bottoms.

"Remember, Amber is also a trained first-aider, Mum," Ben adds.

"But not a trained doctor," I say quickly.

"There again, neither are you," Amber states calmly.

"I might not be a trained doctor, but I've cared for my grandson since he was born and I—"

"Please don't worry," she interrupts. "Noah will be in very safe hands here with me."

There's a finality to her words. A sense of drawing the conversation to a close.

I look at my son. "I think you're making a mistake, Ben," I say tersely. "No offense to Amber, but Noah doesn't know her well enough yet. He'd be far more relaxed at our house."

Ben's cheeks start to flush as both Amber and I focus our gazes on him, waiting for a decision.

He sighs and shrugs his shoulders.

"We really appreciate your offer, Mum, but you do far too much for us as it is. It's been decided now that Amber will look after Noah. He'll be fine and you can visit him every day. You know that."

He looks down at the floor and Amber stands up, walks over to him, and slips her arm around his shoulders.

"Please don't worry, Judi," she says. "I promise I'll look after *all* your boys."

I stand up and my handbag falls from my lap, knocking the untouched mug of tea over. A large dark-tan stain spreads over the carpet, saturating the soft beige fibers and ruining everything it touches.

CHAPTER FIFTY-THREE

Judi

I can't bear to be in Amber's company a moment longer. I mumble a hasty goodbye and rush out of the house, and cross the road to my car. As I pull away, Amber opens the living room curtains and waves.

I don't wave back.

It's only six forty-five, but it's now light outside. The roads are still fairly quiet, although there is more traffic than when I drove over. The journey home is a bit of a blur. I'm hot and my stomach feels bloated, even though I haven't eaten anything since last night.

I pull up onto the drive, rush into the house. Henry sits staring vacantly at his laptop screen in the kitchen. I hesitate, a little breathless, at the door and his head jerks up.

"Where have you been?"

I pull up a stool to the breakfast bar where he is sitting. "I couldn't sleep. I..." To my horror, I well up.

"What's wrong?" He squeezes his eyes shut and pinches at the bridge of his nose. "Judi, we can't keep going on like this. The way you're rushing around and snapping everyone's head off... it's very worrying."

A solitary tear drips down my cheek.

"Come on, it can't be that bad, can it now?" He reaches over to pat my damp cheek. "What's wrong, love?"

"They wouldn't let me see Noah," I whisper.

"Sorry?"

"I've been to Ben's," I explain. "I know it's early, I just had to go. But they wouldn't let me pop upstairs and see Noah."

"I should think not. You can't just turn up unannounced like that, Jude. It's not just Ben and the boys now, is it? There's Amber to consider."

"You don't understand. I need to see Noah. I need to make sure he's OK. It's my responsibility to do that."

"He's his *father's* responsibility and anyway, we'll see the lad soon enough. I'm guessing you'll be nursing him here while Ben's working?"

"That's just it. I won't, Henry. *She's* taking time off to look after him." I spit out the words and bang the heel of my hand on the kitchen counter. "She's cutting me out. Stopping me from seeing my own grandson."

Henry shakes his head and rolls his eyes. "Come on now, Judi. You've got to calm down. Your imagination is running riot. I'm sure Amber will do a perfectly fine job. Ben's very lucky to be marrying someone who—"

"Nothing will change when they marry, Henry. The boys don't even *know* her. They're not used to having her around yet."

"Rubbish. She's living with them, for goodness' sake; she's going to be their stepmother. Of course they know her. You should be glad they're giving you a break and coping by themselves at last. It's about bloody time."

"I don't want a break. I miss the boys terribly. I just want things to feel normal again."

He puts his hand on top of mine and his voice softens slightly.

"Judi, when are you going to realize that it's not about what *you* want anymore? Things have changed. Ben, Amber and the boys—they're making a new life together. You've got to let them get on with it. Let them go a little, do you understand? It's time, love."

I pull my hand away and slip down from the tall stool.

"Never," I say, my jaw setting in a hard line. "Nobody else might be able to see through her, but to me it's clear what she's up to. Ben and the boys, they're my family. They're part of me, Henry. And I will *never* let them go."

I leave the car on the drive and walk to work. I barely feel the lash of the cool wind and fine rain on my tear-streaked face.

Henry tried to carry on the conversation, but I knew I'd said enough. In the end, I decided to save my breath, because he just can't seem to see the danger that Amber poses to all of us.

I couldn't just stay in the house, pacing around and thinking of all the awful things that might happen if Noah takes a turn for the worse, if they don't get him the help he needs.

As I walk, keeping up a steady pace, the stream of traffic chugs by. The rough burr of white noise fills my ears and takes the edge off my troubling thoughts.

"Good Lord!" Maura exclaims when I step inside the office a good fifteen minutes later than my usual arrival time. "You're wet through." She rushes up and takes my mac as I shrug it off, hanging it on the coat rack. "Jude, are you all right?"

"I look like a drowned rat, I know." I give her an apologetic little smile. "I had to come in to work, though. I couldn't stand to stay at home and..." I dissolve into tears.

"Oh come here, hun." Maura puts a comforting arm around my shoulders and at the same time expertly plucks a tissue from the box on reception. "That's it, just let it all out."

"Thanks." I snuffle, taking the tissue and holding it to my face. "It's truly been the weekend from hell."

"Well, we've got a good ten minutes until surgery begins." She glances at the wall clock. "Sit down and tell me all about it."

I leave out the fact that I took Fiona back to the house, because I know Maura will give me grief over that; she'll probably even agree with Henry in his waifs-and-strays assessment. I begin my story at the point when Ben, Amber and the boys arrived for lunch.

Maura's mouth literally drops open at the news of their impulsive engagement. She shakes her head and rolls her eyes as I tell her about Amber's unofficial ADHD assessment for Noah, how I accidentally cut my hand, and the ban on the boys eating sugar, imposed by their new stepmum, as Ben now allows her to refer to herself.

She widens her eyes in horror when I tell her about Noah's E. coli infection and the fact that Ben is refusing to let me care for him while he is off school recuperating.

"Try not to worry, though, Jude. I'm sure Noah will be fine now if the doctors say he's out of danger," she comments. "But I know it must feel like a slap in the face for you, after everything else Ben and Amber have stopped you doing."

"Thanks, Maura." I snivel gratefully into my tissue. It feels so nice to have someone understand and be on my side for once. "I texted Ben asking him to let me know how Noah is throughout the day, but he hasn't replied yet."

Then I remember the missing necklace that mysteriously reappeared in my jewelry box. I quickly relay the story to Maura.

"Don't take this the wrong way. I'm not suggesting you're losing it"—she nudges me playfully—"but is there any chance at all the necklace could have been tucked behind your other pieces and you just didn't spot it?"

"Zero chance," I say firmly, shaking my head. "When I opened my jewelry box, there it was. Right on top. I couldn't have failed to see it before if it had been in that position. There's just no explanation other than that Amber put it back again."

Maura looks at me but doesn't say anything for a long moment. Then she shakes herself.

"Tell you what." She speaks in the same bright tone one might use to encourage a child to cheer up and forget their troubles. "Pop in the back and freshen yourself up. You can use my hairbrush. It's on the shelf under the mirror. I'll make us a cuppa and then we'll let the stampede in."

I nod and smile at Maura's diplomatic way of telling me I look a mess. Walking in this morning without an umbrella, I never gave a thought to how my hair might look when I got into work.

Later, when Dr. Latif calls Maura in to brief her on the patients' hospital referral letters and, mercifully, there's a short lull on reception, I access the patient database.

I type in "Fiona Bonser" and her file immediately pops up. I double-click on the link, scan the file and select the last two pages of notes to print, together with her personal contact details.

For the few seconds it takes the printer to crank up, I glance around guiltily, my heart knocking on my chest wall. When it's finally finished, I stand up and grab the sheets from the printer, folding them tightly and stuffing them down the side of my handbag.

"Judi?"

I jump in my chair and look up to see Maura standing

behind me. My face heats up as I wonder if she saw me pushing the wodge of paper into my bag.

"Don't look so worried." She grins. "You jumped a mile there. Good news, you can get off an hour early. I need to do some file updating on the server, so I might as well sit on reception and do it. Carole will be in soon; she's usually early."

"Oh! Are you sure?" I immediately think of what I'll do if I get off early.

"Don't talk me out of it." She laughs. "You get off."

"Thanks," I say, grabbing my bag and logging off the system.

I don't need telling twice.

CHAPTER FIFTY-FOUR

Amber

Judi had acted like one of Ben's sons: a spoiled brat who didn't know how to handle the fact that she couldn't do as she wanted anymore.

But Amber had been proud of the way Ben stood up to her. They'd already had a lengthy conversation about how she might react, at the hospital during the hours they'd waited around for Noah.

Amber could clearly see that refusing to let her look after Noah had caused Judi immense pain and frustration.

Still, she wasn't hurting enough for Amber's liking. There was a long way to go before she reached her goal.

Judi liked to stand around the edges of her family, playing the "poor me" role, but a thread of steel ran through the woman and Amber knew she'd do well never to underestimate her.

Instead, she would keep chipping away at the core of her, taking away the things that mattered most to Judi little by little until one day she would wake up and realize she had nothing left in life. Until there was only one sweet relief left for her and finally, they'd all be free of her and Amber would sleep again at night.

Yes, she'd focus on the smaller actions that would bring her down and ultimately destroy her.

Like a boxing match, where the consistent body blows did the real damage—not as flamboyant as the knockout punch, but just as deadly if sustained over time.

CHAPTER FIFTY-FIVE

Judi

As I walked in this morning, I call a cab to take me home. It feels like an extravagance, but I don't spend that much really, certainly not on myself. And a bit of extra time this afternoon will be useful.

It's not through circumstance that I tend to be quite frugal—we can certainly afford for me to splash out if I want to. I suppose I just naturally lean toward spending less. Perhaps being raised in a working-class family, where it seemed that we consistently had nothing growing up, has something to do with it. Henry and I are financially comfortable now, compared to most people I know, at least.

Fortunately, the cab driver is the silent type. I'm not in the mood for endless pleasantries, so this one deserves a tip. I take my purse out of my handbag and fish around for coins. I never carry much cash.

Henry has always sorted out the money matters in our relationship. I know some women would frown on that, but I've honestly never wanted anything to do with it. Having a banking background, he's fastidious about keeping financial paperwork organized in various color-coded folders, locked in a filing cabinet in the study.

"Never know who might be snooping around," he always says briskly when he takes his mail straight upstairs from the letter box. Although I often wonder who he might be referring to, as we don't have many visitors, only Ben and the boys. And now *her*.

I was surprised a couple of weeks ago, therefore, when I found a letter with a new debit card attached by his side of the bed. It must've dropped out of his folder at some point.

I saw that the communication referred to our Platinum Reserve account. There was a short statement showing regular large cash withdrawals and the balance of the account which was far less than I remembered as I know Henry paid his redundancy lump sum in here when he retired.

I was also surprised, considering his usual paranoid security measures, to see that Henry had scrawled four digits—I assumed the pin number—in the top right corner of the A4 sheet. I expect he must have intended to file it directly in his locked cabinet, not noticing it had slipped underneath the bed.

I pushed away a feeling of unease and folded the letter around the debit card, tucking it all in my trouser pocket to return to him later. I felt sure there would be a perfectly logical reason. I really ought to ask him if he's depositing the cash he's withdrawing into another account; it wouldn't hurt to start taking a bit more of an interest in such matters.

During the short journey home, I leaf through my copy of Fiona's patient file.

Thoughts of the confidentiality breach bring the twinge of guilt again. It nips at my chest like a spiteful adder, but I dismiss it.

Ben might not need me now, but young Fiona has no one.

No one to look out for her, to offer her guidance and support raising little Hank.

I scan the printed report. It appears that Fiona first came to see Dr. Latif back in January with pains in her lower abdomen. The doctor made a note at the beginning of her appointment: *Patient insists she is not pregnant. Patient refusal—pregnancy test.*

She examined Fiona and found nothing of concern. She diagnosed possible inflammation and bloating and prescribed a course of anti-inflammatories.

At the beginning of February, Fiona was back. The pain had got much worse and she had problems passing water. Dr. Latif took a urine sample and speculated that it might be a urinary tract infection. She didn't prescribe anything but told the patient to return for her test results in five days. Judi could see immediately from the notes that Fiona had, in fact, not returned for those findings.

The next entry in the file was for Fiona's appointment just last week, the one that Maura had taken it upon herself to investigate. Dr. Latif had carried out another examination and had documented bruising to Fiona's inner thighs. She wrote:

Patient appears to be in moderate to severe pain. Tests negative for UTI. Attempts made to engage patient in discussion over her injuries. Patient rejects suggestion that injuries are sexually related. Unable to diagnose or prescribe as patient left the surgery, terminating the consultation.

I frown, mulling over the details in my head. Fiona is obviously ill. She's reaching out for help but then seeming to pull back and withdraw at the last moment. Almost as if she's afraid of something. Or someone.

I don't know anything about Fiona's background, her childhood. But it has occurred to me before now that she has a problem trusting people. The look on her face whenever she visits the surgery, the first time I came across her in the park—the look that says she is immediately on her guard and expecting the worst treatment from people, like a whipped dog.

My hand drifts up to my throat and I swallow hard as I think of Noah's pale, drawn face. I haven't seen him since he fell ill, but I've seen him enough times in the past when he's suffered with minor childhood illnesses. I remember his colorless lips and dull eyes.

I squeeze my own eyes shut and consciously replace my grandson's troubling image with Hank's sweet, plump features. I summon up the feeling of warmth I enjoyed whilst holding him close, his small, neglected body, cradled safely in my arms. Trusting and innocent.

Fiona and Hank are both so desperate for someone to care.

I pick up the contact details sheet and study it.

> *Patient name*: Fiona Heather Bonser
> *DOB*:   None given
> *Address*:   Flat 6, 8th Floor, Calvin Chase,
>   St. Ann's, Nottingham
> *Tel no*:   None given

I know exactly where this block of flats is. I've walked by it many times over the years, staring up in a kind of fascinated dread at the rows of clean laundry that some tenants peg across the rusting balconies like bunting.

I pay the taxi driver and walk up the driveway, but I don't go into the house. I get straight into my car.

I have something very important I need to do.

CHAPTER FIFTY-SIX

Judi

When I googled for information about Sunbeam Lodge, I made a note of the visiting times, gratified to find they slotted in nicely with my working hours.

Now I belt up and program the postcode of the care home into the sat nav, and five minutes later, I'm on the road.

I haven't got a clue what to say to Amber's mother, if indeed she is still at the home—I've no idea how long that business card has been in her pocket. I don't know exactly what I'm hoping to find, just that Amber has given me no choice but to grasp at straws. If her mother is alive, then she has lied about both parents being killed in a road accident, and there has to be a reason for that. Perhaps something she is keen to keep concealed about her past?

That's it. That's exactly what I'm hoping to find out.

An hour later, I park the car on an expanse of cracked concrete in front of a poorly maintained two-story building.

A bent and broken sign out front identifies the place as

SUNBEAM LODGE CARE HOME, the rays of the smiling sun logo faded and discolored.

I reach into my handbag to check my phone. Despite the fact that I texted Ben twice that morning to inquire after Noah, there is still no response from him.

I lock the car and walk toward the glass entrance porch with its peeling, splintered wooden frame. My shoes scuff on hardy weeds that have somehow forced their way up through the crumbling concrete path and bled into the narrow borders, choking any signs of floral life that might have once inhabited the space.

I step inside the damp, grubby porch, where a visitors' book lies open on a crooked shelf underneath a button marked RING FOR ADMITTANCE.

I ignore both the book and the bell and wait. In only a couple of minutes, I see a shape approaching the patterned opaque glass and a woman around my age opens the door from the other side.

Obviously a visitor herself who's now leaving, she kindly holds the door open to allow me to enter the building.

My stride falters a little once I'm inside. I've never been in one of these places before, and now I'm getting older myself, I feel uncomfortable and infused with a sense of dread.

The fusty, moldering smell, the grim fluorescent lighting, and the noises…a troubling backdrop of groaning accompanied by the sounds of tasks being carried out and brisk footfalls.

I pass through a small communal area with mismatched plastic furniture. A small television is blaring out a daytime talk show, but nobody is in here. Part of me wants to turn and run back outside, but instead I grit my teeth and move toward a corridor marked RESIDENTS.

As I walk, the numbers rise, evens one side, odds the other. I arrive at room 15A. The door is slightly ajar. Just as I raise my hand to knock, a care worker in navy trousers and a white tunic walks briskly toward me.

I get ready to try to wriggle my way out of why I'm here when I'm not a relative and haven't even signed the visitors' book, but her pace continues. She gives me a nod and an uninterested smile and carries on walking.

Heart pounding, I tap on the pale-green-painted door and push it gently open.

An old lady sits by the window dressed in a drab dress with three-quarter sleeves, her hands frail and shaking as she stares out over the car park area. There is no net up at the window and the light floods in through her hair so pink scalp is clearly visible.

"Kathryn, you came!" She turns, smiling, sees me and frowns. "You're not Kathryn. Who are you?"

"Just a friend." I smile. "I came to see how you are. Who is Kathryn?"

She looks indignant. "My daughter!"

"Of course, I'm sorry."

There is a letter on her bedside table. She watches without comment as I reach for it and see it is addressed to Martha Carr, c/o Sunbeam Lodge.

"It's Martha, isn't it?"

"That's me," she says firmly. "Do you know where Kathryn's got to? She should have been here hours ago."

"I think she's on her way," I say kindly. "And Amber is coming too. Your other daughter Amber?"

"Pffft. She can stay away. Nothing but trouble, that one."

"Does she come to see you often, Amber?"

"Who are you?" She leans forward and peers at me. "I don't think I know you."

"Yes, of course you do. I'm Mary," I say, my middle name jumping into my head. "I used to live near you, remember?"

The old lady frowns and stares into space, probably trying to grasp a wisp of memory.

I certainly don't want to distress her or cause her any grief. I'm pretty sure, even though I've only been here a matter of minutes, that Martha has symptoms of dementia. A firm grasp and memory of happenings from years ago but a mind like a sieve when it comes to things that occurred just five minutes ago.

The doctors regularly assess similar patients at the surgery.

"So, Martha, does Amber visit you here?" I repeat my question in an attempt to bring her back on track.

"Never." Martha folds her age-spotted arms in a huff. "Never see her. But my Kathryn, she comes nearly every day. We're going to London together soon, you know."

"How lovely." I smile. "Why do you think Amber doesn't visit?"

"There's no telling with her. I suppose she was never the same after the accident."

A static prickle raises a strip of hairs on the back of my neck. "Accident?"

"When Kathryn died." Her eyes swim, diluting the already pale blue irises. "Her sister."

"I thought you said Kathryn visited you here?"

Martha scowls, shaking her head as if she's trying to get her thoughts to fall in line. "My Kathryn died. Who are you again?"

"I'm Mary," I say softly. "It's very sad that Kathryn died. Perhaps it's your daughter, Amber, who visits you here?"

"Never see her," she snaps. "Don't want to see her. I tried my best to help her, you know. But she wouldn't be helped. Kept running through the barrier trying to get to them, and when I tried to hold her back, she hit me. Really hard." Martha touches her cheek gently and winces.

"Who was Amber trying to get to?" I swallow, wishing I had a glass of water. I haven't a clue what Martha is talking about, but it feels like there's a nugget of truth tangled up in amongst the confused words. I can sense something profound hanging in the air around us. "Where was this?"

"At the roadside," Martha says impatiently. "Don't you listen? She kept trying to save them, but they were already dead, you see. All of them."

"Amber's parents?" I hazard a guess. I'm hopelessly confused. Maybe there was a car accident after all and Martha isn't Amber's real mother. Perhaps her biological parents were killed and—

"Not her *parents*, silly." Martha rolls her eyes and looks away from me, out of the window. "Her family. Her husband and children. Dead. All of them."

CHAPTER FIFTY-SEVEN

Judi

Back in the car, I sit for a moment going over the things Martha told me, trying to allow the possibilities to fully sink in.

It's like putting together a jigsaw when half the pieces are missing.

I look back at the building, the windows reflecting back dark and empty. Martha sits behind one of them, but I can't work out which one it might be. She has probably already forgotten me. I hope so. The last thing I want is to make her life any more miserable.

There's a sour taste in my mouth. I'm not proud of my interaction with an old woman who has nothing left to look forward to. Spending the late winter of her life sitting at a window waiting for, it sounds like, her dead daughter to visit.

I am lucky. My son and grandsons are still very much alive. I have something left to fight for and I'd like to think that if Martha were of sound mind, she'd understand that, she'd understand I had no choice.

Underneath her garbled words she seems to acknowledge Amber's failings and see her as someone to be avoided, to keep out of one's life.

I start the car and reset the sat nav for home. As I drive out of the car park and down the street, Martha's words echo through my head.

Her family. Her husband and children. Dead. All of them.

What can it mean? Who is she exactly, Amber Carr?

And what happened to the family that she has never mentioned?

CHAPTER FIFTY-EIGHT

Judi

Back at the house, I fire up my little-used laptop and begin searching for an article about a road traffic accident where a whole family were killed.

It soon becomes apparent that it's a thankless task, akin to searching for the proverbial needle in a haystack. There's too much I don't know. When was the alleged accident? Where did it take place? What was Amber's married name?

The online search for *Amber Carr* is disappointing. It simply brings up anyone with the same or a similar name on a whole roster of social media platforms.

I click on a few links and accounts, but none of them appear to be her, so far as I am able to tell from the available photographs.

I sigh and close the laptop. Every way I turn, I'm faced with a dead end.

Frustratingly, it feels too soon to confront Amber with the information I've gleaned from her mother. After all, what does it actually prove?

Ben told me there had been a fatal car accident but that it had claimed her parents and her sister. He's never mentioned that Amber was married with children, though that doesn't necessarily mean that she hasn't confided in him.

It's all a nasty mess made up of half-truths and omissions.

I have to tread carefully here. I can just imagine Ben attacking *me*, accusing me of snooping and believing a senile old woman like Martha.

The more I think about it, the more it seems likely that Ben could be fully aware of her past but that Amber has begged him not to tell me the full story . . . why, I don't know.

There's only one thing I feel certain of, and that is that the more I find out about Amber Carr, the more afraid I am of what she could do to my family.

I only have one real chance of finding out the truth: by asking Amber myself.

But first there's something else I must do. Another piece of the jigsaw may be at hand.

CHAPTER FIFTY-NINE

Judi

I turn into the driveway of Ben's school and take the right-hand turning into the children's center car park.

During the drive over here, I have concocted two of what I hope are believable stories. If there is someone I know working at the nursery, it's no use me pretending I don't know Amber. I will simply act surprised that she isn't working today.

If I'm lucky, I won't know any of the staff and I can pretend I am sourcing a place at the center for my grandchild.

I lock the car and walk toward the long, flat building, my feet crunching into the gravel. I ring the bell and wait until the intercom buzzes into life. When I explain I'm here to look around the nursery, the door releases.

Inside, the center is a whirlwind of color and noise. Small children scatter in all directions and cluster around the mostly female staff. My eyes scan the large open-plan space and I'm gratified to find I don't spot any familiar faces.

"Can I help you?" A young woman with mousy hair and stark black-framed glasses approaches me, smiling. Stacks of finger-painted masterpieces drape over her arms. "Sorry it's a bit hectic, it's nearly going-home time."

"Yes, I can see that. I hope you don't mind me just dropping in," I say a little nervously. "I just wanted to see the place in view of my granddaughter coming here."

"Of course, that's fine. I can make you an appointment to come back when there's a bit more time, if that's OK." She smiles. "Just wait one sec while I set this artwork down."

While she's over the other side of the room, I walk across to a long wall displaying information about the place. It appears they cater for children aged 0 to 5 years—preschool, in other words. As I walk along the wall, my heartbeat increases when I spot a "Who We Are" staff photo display at the end.

My eyes flit quickly over the faces, searching out Amber's cropped blond hair and pert nose. Frustratingly, I don't spot her right away, but there are around fifteen faces in all, so I start again at the beginning, looking at each of the portraits, from Anna Ross, Center Manager, to Wendy Ratner, Childcare Worker—the young woman I've just met—and then Mary Bower, the center's cleaner.

Amber's photograph isn't up there.

I can't remember how long she said she'd worked here, but it's more than possible that they simply haven't updated the display. I do recall, however, that she said her title was "Lead Parent Support Worker."

There are two parent support workers on the staff display: Maisie Poulter and Dean Grant. Definitely no Amber Carr.

"I'm Wendy." The young woman appears again, holding out her hand. "I'm a childcare worker here—I see you've already found me on the display."

She smiles as I shake her hand.

"You have quite a lot of staff," I say, nodding to the photographs. "Though I'm surprised there's not a photo here of my friend's daughter. She's the center's lead parent support worker."

"Oh." Wendy frowns. "We don't actually have a lead worker as such, just Maisie and Dean."

My heartbeat moves up into my throat.

"Her name is Amber Carr," I say.

"Oh yes, I know who you mean now," she says, and I slump a little inside. "She worked here for a bit, but she's just a temp from an agency. We had a busy period due to the new intake and she was helping out as a care assistant."

"She doesn't work here now?"

"No, it's been a while."

"Oh, I must've got it wrong," I say. "I felt sure she said she worked here as a lead parent support worker."

Wendy laughs. "Sounds like Amber; she likes to exaggerate. She actually looked after the children fully supervised; cleaned them up and helped them with their words and numbers. That sort of thing."

I knew it. I knew she was lying. It's all lies, even about who has or hasn't died in her life. A sick feeling rises in my chest.

Wendy looks at me a little curiously. "Did you say you were here because you were interested in your granddaughter starting?"

"Yes, but I'm sorry." I glance wildly around me, not sure what to do for the best. "I've just remembered I'm supposed to be somewhere else, so I have to go. Sorry."

I reach up for the door release button, rush out of the double doors again and run to the car.

Amber is a liar. She is a psychotic liar and she is looking after my grandson, unsupervised.

I call Ben's phone, which, unsurprisingly, as he'll be teaching, is turned off. But it won't be long now until the end of school.

"Ben, ring me back the second you get this message," I splutter. "It's urgent. It's about Amber. Please, ring me as soon as you can."

I can see the roof of the comprehensive school building jutting out over the hedges that frame the small gardens at the center. Ben is in that building and yet I know I won't get to speak to him if I just turn up like last time. He's probably told the reception staff not to fetch him again. It's so frustrating.

I'll just have to wait until he contacts me and do what I can in the meantime.

I open the car door, toss my handbag on to the passenger seat and start the engine. I sit for a few moments, forcing myself to take a few calming breaths before I set off.

I look over to the main window of the center and see that Wendy is standing there, looking out at me with a concerned look on her face and speaking on the telephone.

I raise my hand by way of telling her that everything is OK, and then I steer the car out of the center car park and down the school driveway.

I'm headed for Ben's house. I want to see my grandson, and this time nobody is going to stop me.

CHAPTER SIXTY

Judi

When I get to Ben's house, I knock at the front door but then let myself in with my key. After what I found out today, I refuse to stand on ceremony waiting for Amber to allow me admittance to my own son's house.

"Hello," I call out in the hallway. "Only me."

The house is silent and still. I slip off my shoes and dart into the kitchen, put my head into the living room. There's nobody down here.

I climb the stairs.

"Hello? Amber?" I call a little more quietly, in case Noah is asleep. "Are you up here?"

There's no answer.

I walk into the boys' bedroom and gasp as Noah peers over his bedcovers with wide, fearful eyes.

"Oh, darling, there you are!" I kneel at the side of the bottom bunk where Amber must have put him for convenience during his illness and I lay my hand across his clammy forehead. "Are you feeling a little better, sweetheart?"

He nods. "Could I have a drink, please, Nanny?" he asks in a raspy voice.

"Of course you can." I look around me, aghast that Amber hasn't even left a glass of water at the side of his bed. I turn to fetch him one and then stop in my tracks. "Noah, where is Amber?"

"I don't know," he says faintly. "I just woke up and called her, but she didn't come. Then I heard the door downstairs and it was you."

Dread crawls over my skin in one swift movement. I rush out of the room and into Ben's bedroom. The bed is made, the curtains are drawn. I look down on to the road and realize her car isn't there. I check the rest of upstairs and then fly downstairs and do a thorough search of every room.

My fears are confirmed. That bitch... that absolute *bitch* has left my sick eight-year-old grandson alone. Alone in the house.

I pick up my handbag and take it into the kitchen. Once I've finally pushed the anger back, I get together what I need and prepare Noah's drink.

I have to stop her. I have to make everyone see what she is and that she can't be trusted. Especially Ben.

Upstairs, Noah gulps down his water and I rub his shoulders.

"Are you achy around your neck and shoulders, darling?"

"Yes. Everything aches, even my toes," he says, yawning. "And I keep going hot and cold and then hot again, Nanny."

"And are you hot right now?"

He nods. "And my tummy hurts."

I take the small medicine case from my handbag, then peel back the covers and dab a little of the cool, numbing cream on to his stomach.

"You just close your eyes, sweetheart, and Nanny will rub your poorly tummy."

His face is pale and he looks thinner than when I last saw him. I can feel my fury for Amber lodged hard as a nut in my throat.

"Oww." He flinches, his eyes flying wide open. "That hurts."

His hand flies down to his belly and I fend it off with my free forearm while I finish.

"I know you're in pain and very sore, but you'll feel better soon," I say quickly. "There we go, darling. Now just relax. Nanny's here and I'm not going anywhere. You can trust me to do what's best for you, Noah. Do you understand that?"

He nods faintly.

I sit with him a few minutes longer, holding his hand and speaking low, soothing words. When I stand up, his eyes open. They seem unfocused and his paleness has risen to a new, worrying level.

I try not to panic as I pluck my phone out of my bag and call 999.

"Ambulance," I say urgently. "Please send one quickly. My grandson has taken a turn for the worse."

I ring the school and leave a message for Ben, and one on his answerphone, too. Half an hour after I initially arrived at the house, paramedics are loading Noah on a stretcher into the ambulance when Ben's car pulls up and he jumps out.

"What's happening?" His eyes fly to the back of the ambulance. "Oh God, Mum, is he OK?"

"She left him alone, Ben," I say out of earshot of the paramedics and as calmly as I can manage. "I called on spec to see how he was and he was all alone."

Ben doesn't answer me, but runs to the open ambulance doors.

"Can I see him?" he implores.

The man nods and Ben climbs into the vehicle, stroking Noah's head. As I walk nearer, I spot a solitary tear rolling down my son's cheek. From my position at the doors I can see Noah shaking and shivering.

"We've stabilized him," the paramedic says. "He's OK for now. They'll tell you more at the hospital."

"The doctors told me he was going to be fine, that he was over the worst," Ben says accusingly.

"Your mother told me he's had an E. coli infection?"

"That's right," Ben replies. "They put him on a drip and sent him home. Said he'd be OK."

"Well, I'm not sure if this episode is connected." The paramedic frowns. "The symptoms could be because he's not eaten for a while, but we wouldn't usually see this severe a reaction."

He looks over at me.

"It's a good job your mother caught him in time."

Ben visibly pales. "My fiancée, she was supposed to be looking after him…" His voice falters.

"I'll be looking after Noah from now on," I say quickly, before Ben tells him Noah was left alone in the house and the paramedic feels duty-bound to get social services involved.

I feel a pang of guilt as Ben hangs his head, looking utterly wretched.

"He'll be OK, son," I say.

"Thanks, Mum. I mean, thanks for being here. I'm sorry…I'm so sorry for everything."

"Well, no harm done this time, thank goodness." I put my arm around him as he climbs from the ambulance. "I'm here now. But please don't ask me to leave him again. I want to take over caring for Noah until he recovers. But there's something you need to know about—"

We look round in alarm as a screech of brakes sounds. Amber jumps out of her car and runs toward us, staring wildly at the house and then the ambulance. Fear is apparent only when she realizes she's been found out.

"Ben! What's happened? I just… Where's Noah?"

Ben glances over at the paramedics, who are busy preparing to set off.

"How could you leave him?" he hisses, his cheeks flushing dark red. "Where the hell were you?"

"I...I..." She glares at me. "The center rang me. She...Your mother has been down there asking questions about me."

That's the least of her worries; little does she know. But I decide I'm not going to mention my visit to Sunbeam Lodge until I'm good and ready. I need Ben to focus, to absorb the true impact of what I have to tell him.

That sly young woman, Wendy, at the center. I saw her on the telephone when I was sitting in my car. She must've called Amber the second I left the building.

"What?" Ben shakes his head in confusion, frowning first at Amber and then at me.

"They said she was still in the car park, described your mum and her car and read me the registration number, so I dashed down to see what she was playing at. I was only gone ten minutes or so."

"I've been here at least half an hour," I say curtly, looking at the ground. "And you were nowhere to be seen when I arrived."

"Judi, why have you been to my workplace, asking questions?"

They both look at me then, but I won't be silenced.

"You don't work there anymore, though, do you? So it's hardly your workplace. We can talk about this later. There's something far more important to get straight, and that is how could you leave Noah alone in the house?"

I'm gratified when Ben ignores Amber's protest about work and instead follows up on my comment.

"Thank God Mum came by. What were you thinking?" he says through gritted teeth.

I take a sideways glance at Amber, feeling gratified at the pure panic and confusion that has settled on her usually devious and confident expression.

"Ben, I'm sorry. Truly I am. He'd been fast asleep for ages. I thought he'd be fine, just for ten minutes or so." She looks at me. "Just for a short while. It unnerved me when I heard Judi was down at the center; it was just a knee-jerk reaction."

"It's a very bad show, you know, leaving a poorly eight-year-old alone like that." I'd like to wring her scrawny neck, but I keep my voice nice and level. "It amounts to neglect in my book, and if social services knew what you'd done—"

"They don't know, though, do they?" she says briskly.

"No. Thanks to Mum keeping her mouth shut, they don't," Ben snaps at her, and then he turns and smiles gratefully at me.

"Thankfully Noah is going to be OK this time." I look at her. "But understand this. I *will* do whatever it takes to keep my grandsons safe. Anything that's necessary. My loyalty lies only with them."

She stares back at me and our eyes lock in a brief silent battle.

"Ready to leave now," the paramedic calls.

I move toward the ambulance without looking at her again.

"I'll travel with him," I tell Ben firmly.

"That's fine. I'll follow in the car," Ben says.

I watch as he turns away from Amber. And I can't help myself. I smile. At last, it feels like the tide is turning.

CHAPTER SIXTY-ONE

Amber

Amber slammed her palm against the steering wheel of the car when the lights turned red.

That bitch. That total and utter *bitch*. She had clearly enjoyed every second of Amber's downfall in the eyes of her precious son.

She wasn't sure whether to be more furious with Judi or with herself for taking her eye off the ball so completely. She had been stupid, there was no other word for it.

When she'd got the call from Wendy Ratner to say that a woman was down at the center asking searching questions about her, Amber had panicked. She'd looked in on Noah and he'd been dead to the world. He'd been like it all morning; he'd never stirred once.

In her haste, she hadn't stopped to think that if she managed to get there in time to confront Judi, the first thing she'd do would be to question who was looking after her precious grandson back at the house. But of course the meddling cow had already left, and Amber had only stayed to chat briefly with Wendy.

Without doubt, Amber had made a serious error that

could compromise everything she had worked for so far. It was the kind of error she'd promised herself at the beginning she wouldn't make. If Judi was curious about her work, what else might she be sticking her nose into?

Trust the stupid kid to wake up and have some kind of seizure... with Judi ready and waiting to witness it all and exaggerate the drama in any way she could.

It would almost serve them right if something *did* happen to Noah. Teach them a lesson. Not on Amber's watch, of course. It would be so much better if Judi were somehow to blame for Noah coming a cropper.

Both Ben and Judi treated Noah as if he were some kind of little prince, so delicate and needing to be wrapped in cotton wool. It was ridiculous.

When Amber and her sister were kids, they were basically left to raise themselves. Their mother never cared if they were out late at night or if they had enough to eat—which most times they didn't. She might be old and vulnerable now, but Amber often thought of her mother's negligence when she visited Sunbeam Lodge. Kathryn had been her favorite, so Amber always suffered worse.

She'd been all too aware that her mother wished it had been her that died that day and not Kathryn. The therapist had said that had served to compound all the negative feelings of guilt and sadness she had experienced after her sibling's death.

It sickened her to see how the Jukes family consistently indulged the two boys and expected everyone else to follow suit. Yes, they'd lost their mother, but plenty of people had to deal with life's setbacks. Some kids had to deal with them alone.

She refused to fall in line as far as *that* was concerned.

Quite the opposite: once she and Ben were married, she intended to kick the little runts into line.

After all, Noah and Joshua Jukes had had it far too soft for far too long.

Life would be very different for them soon.

CHAPTER SIXTY-TWO

Judi

When we get to the hospital and the ambulance doors open, I'm surprised to see that only Ben is there.

"Where's Amber?" I ask, readying myself for a battle over who is going to accompany Noah inside.

"She's picking Josh up from school and waiting with him at home until we get back," Ben says, looking sheepish. "If we'd had more time I'd have made other arrangements. I realize it's far from ideal that Amber is watching him after what just happened."

"Ben, you must keep Amber away from the boys, at least until we have time for a proper chat. There's something—"

"Mum, not here, please. Just let it go for now; we've got Noah to worry about."

"We've got Josh to worry about too," I snap. "Why don't you go back and get him now? When you hear what I've got to tell you—"

"Here's Noah," Ben says, distracted.

A hospital porter meets the paramedics at the door and we walk alongside Noah as he is wheeled through and into a private cubicle.

I look down at him and feel like sobbing when I see his poor pale face. His big brown eyes are open but look unfocused and diluted somehow. I squeeze my own eyes closed and look away. It's breaking my heart... Why did it have to come to this?

"I'm so sorry, Mum. I should've listened and let you look after Noah."

I nod. "I'm sorry too, Ben. I never wanted Noah to end up in this state. I'd have done anything to stop this happening."

"Amber's not a bad person, you know," he continues. "It was a terrible oversight and I feel so angry with her for what she did, but just between you and me, she does care about the boys. I know what you think, but you should see how she looks out for them."

"Don't make excuses for her, Ben." I glare at him. "She loves to tell us how she's an expert when it comes to children, and then she does something as dangerous and wrong as this. It beggars belief."

"Yeah, I know," he replies, chastised. "It was stupid. I can't believe she did it either. I don't know what to do about it."

"You need to hear the full story," I say. "Before you decide what action to take."

He shoots me a sideways glance.

"What Amber said about you going down to the children's center... Is that true?"

"I did call at her alleged workplace," I say, making sure there's no trace of regret in my voice.

"You did? But why?"

"Because I won't just swallow her lies like you do. She doesn't work there anymore, and she never had an important role there like she tried to have us believe. According to the member of staff I spoke to, she was only one up from being a cleaner."

"Don't be spiteful, Mum, it doesn't suit you." Ben frowns. "Amber had already told me she'd left the job. She wanted to look after Noah and she's looking for other opportunities; she's capable of more."

My nostrils flare.

"I'm telling you she has outright *lied*, Ben. She was just a temp, not a bloody lead worker or whatever fancy title it was she claimed she had. Did she tell you *that* too?" I glance at little Noah, conscious that he might be taking in our conversation. "We'll need to talk about this later; this is no place for us to be arguing. I'll go with you to the children's center and you can hear it for yourself."

I shake my head in frustration when Ben looks away. She gets to him before me every single time. But I won't let this drop. It's important and it's one of two lies I can prove; two lies she can't wriggle out of.

The curtain is pulled back and a short, slightly chubby man in a white coat appears. "I am Dr. Kareem," he says, smiling at a listless Noah. "Now, what has been happening to this young man?"

"Can you explain, please, Mum?" Ben says, a worried look on his face. He's leaving it up to me to reveal Amber's neglect—or not.

I briefly explain about the E. coli poisoning incident and how we expected Noah to recover without complications. "He was at home, asleep. When he woke up, he wanted a drink and I remember him saying his tummy hurt. Then he started shaking and his eyes went all unfocused, so I called the ambulance."

Dr. Kareem nods and consults his clipboard. "You did the right thing, well done."

I smile gratefully at the doctor, basking in the glow of having done something to help Noah. Ben reaches over and touches my arm in gratitude, and it feels wonderful to have my son back on my side again.

"We are going to need a urine sample," Dr. Kareem says. "Can you try and get young Noah to take some water?" He nods to a glass and a water jug on the side and a small glass sample bottle next to it.

I nod, and Dr. Kareem disappears again, stating that he'll be back later.

"Thanks, Mum," Ben says awkwardly. "For not telling the doctor about what happened."

"I did it for you and Noah," I say shortly. "Social services would whisk both boys away in an instant if they found out what she did."

Ben swallows and draws back the curtain. "I'll go and get us a couple of coffees from the café," he says meekly.

I look down at Noah and smooth back the hair from his forehead, resting a warm, protective hand there.

"Do you think you could drink some water for Nanny?" I pour from the jug.

Noah doesn't say anything, but when I support the back of his head, he gulps thirstily from the glass I hold to his lips. He drinks half the water and I top the glass up again from the jug.

Then I pick up the sample bottle and unscrew it. While Ben is busy getting our drinks, I make sure everything is ready.

By the time Ben returns, Noah has used the thick cardboard bedpan provided and his urine sample is complete.

It's seven o'clock before we see the doctor again.

"We have his results." He frowns. "It is confusing. We have found glucose in Noah's urine, which can signify diabetes, among other conditions."

"Oh no," Ben groans. "Poor lad, don't say he's going to be like Dad."

"However," Dr. Kareem continues, "to add to the confusion, his blood test has come back with normal levels; in other words, no high blood sugar. I am afraid we will need to do more tests."

"If Noah needs to remain in hospital, I can stay with him," I offer, glancing at Ben. He nods.

"There should be no need for that," the doctor says. "Noah has now stabilized and thankfully there is no imminent danger, but of course you should bring him back in immediately if there are any more instances like what happened earlier today. In the meantime, we'll make an appointment for the tests."

"So he can go home?" Ben says hopefully.

"Not just yet, I'm afraid." Dr. Kareem hesitates and gives Ben a strange look. "Maybe in an hour or two; there are just one or two loose ends we are required to tie up first."

"I really think Noah needs to come home with me, Ben," I say when the doctor leaves us. "Not back to your house."

"Mum, I don't know..."

"What don't you know?" I pick my handbag up and let it drop on to the bottom of the bed again. "Are *you* going to take time off work to look after him?"

"As much as I'd like to, I can't," he replies grudgingly.

"Exactly."

"But Amber isn't working at the moment and—"

"Are you seriously telling me you'd leave him in *her* care again?"

"No! Of course not, but... I worry about you coping, Mum. You seem really het up. I don't like doing it, but I could always ring in sick myself."

"Is it any wonder I'm het up, after what she did? Noah is coming home with me and I'll care for him until he's better." I pause. "I only kept my mouth shut about Amber's negligence because I assumed you'd let me have him."

"Mum, that's not fair!" Ben's face reddens. "Are you going to hold that over my head every time I make a decision that you don't like? I need to think about what to do. I don't want to decide this second."

"Of course I'm not going to use it as a threat. Stop exaggerating," I reply. "Look, let's just get Noah right again and let things settle down. You know he'll be perfectly fine with his nanny."

"Mum," Ben sighs. "I hate what Amber did. I'm shocked and disappointed, just like you are. I'm going to have to have a serious talk about it with her, make sure it never happens again. But we are engaged and soon to be married…we're a family now. We've got to work on our mistakes if we're to make a real go of it."

I look at him.

"Go home for a couple of hours, Mum. Just chill out a bit and rest."

"How can I chill out, not knowing how Noah is?"

"He's going to be fine. I'm not going anywhere. It makes no sense you sitting around for hours as well."

Our eyes meet and I know he wants some space, some time to think. I honestly feel like anything I tell him about Amber right now will just fall on deaf ears.

I turn and pull the curtain back, walk out of the ward.

I don't think I've ever felt so unwanted, so alone.

CHAPTER SIXTY-THREE

Judi

I get a cab back to Ben's house so I can pick up my car. Amber's Fiat isn't there so I assume she's on her way to pick up Josh. I force myself to go back to the car and drive away. I can't confront her at school or in front of Josh. I must pick my moment.

I find myself driving the long way home, toward the flats where I now know Fiona lives.

I haven't thought much about her and little Hank because of the chaos that's ensued in my own life. Funny that. Fiona probably needs me more than anyone at the moment and I may well be the only positive influence in Hank's life.

My son has as good as sent me packing from the hospital and I can't trust myself not to fly at Amber like a mad harridan if I set eyes on her right now, so there's nothing I can do but sit it out for the time being.

A numbing separation has crept in between myself and my son. An invisible wall of silence that has somehow sprung up that he seems not to want to acknowledge or talk about.

They'd all have me believe it's in my head, but I know better.

Whatever cunning spell Amber Carr has cast on the male members of this family, thankfully I remain immune to it.

There is something about this woman that makes me incredibly uneasy, a sort of ticking dread. I feel it in the prickle that hovers over my skin when she's close by, the way I find myself worrying about her seemingly positive influence on Ben and the boys. And now the evidence I'm gathering seems to back up my concerns.

As I drive toward the railway crossing and the flats come into view, it strikes me that I might as well do something useful with the day.

I park across the road from the block and count up to the eighth floor. I'm not sure whether Fiona's window faces the road side or overlooks the plethora of industrial units at the back. Neither view will be up to much.

Faded England flags flutter from several balconies, while others are being utilized as temporary storage areas, stuffed with bicycles, toys and piles of unidentifiable scrap items.

I grab my handbag and get out of the car, locking it before I cross the road and head for the entrance to the flats. Once inside, I immediately spot the OUT OF ORDER—ENGINEER NOTIFIED notices attached to both battered metal lift doors.

I didn't count them, but there looked to be at least another six floors above Fiona's level. I assume people of all ages live here; what would an elderly or less mobile person do when faced with these redundant lifts? The realities of struggling up all those stairs with shopping bags is a sobering thought that I doubt the lift repair company fully appreciates.

I steel myself and begin to climb. I'm fine until floor two, and then the labored breathing starts. I make it to floor three and stop to take a breather. I look out of the small, murky window at the busy road beyond.

I can see my car from here, and the queue of traffic waiting at the crossing for a train to pass.

I hear a door slam above and spin round at the sound of

quick footsteps behind me. A little girl of around Josh's age smiles at me as she skips easily down the stairs from the floor above.

"Hello," I say, looking up above her and realizing that she has no accompanying adult. "What's your name?"

"Lily." She beams and stops shyly on the bottom step.

"And where's your mummy, Lily?"

"Home." She jabs her finger toward the flight of stairs behind her. "She's busy feeding our Ryan and I've got to get some bread from the shop."

She uncurls a sticky fist to reveal the single pound coin that nestles there.

I know there is a Spar shop quite close, about a hundred meters from the entrance to the flats. Still, a hundred meters for an unaccompanied five-year-old is quite a distance, and certainly far enough for her to get lost... or worse.

I wonder if I should offer to accompany her when a door flies open above us and a young woman of about Fiona's age appears at the top of the stairs.

"Lily! I thought I heard your voice. What the bloody hell are you playing at?" She looks at me and frowns, self-consciously smoothing down her greasy topknot. "Who are you? Are you from social services?"

"No, no," I reply quickly, smiling. "I'm visiting someone here. I was just passing the time of day with little Lily here."

She scowls at the girl. "What've I told you about speaking to folks you don't know?"

"Sorry, Mummy." Lily's eyes widen as she looks up.

"Well, stop gassing and get going. I've got to stand up here at the window like a prat so I can watch you to the shop, remember?"

Lily nods and smiles and continues her skip downstairs without looking at me again.

"Sorry," I say to her mum as I start to climb the flight of stairs toward her. "I didn't think. She's a lovely little thing, isn't she?"

The woman glares at me and turns on her heel without answering. A few seconds later, the door to her flat slams shut.

Another two rests and endless panting and finally I reach the eighth floor. The stairway is located up through the middle of the building, so there's a choice of left or right, both leading to a corridor of identical doors with different numbers.

I correctly choose left and walk past the decreasing numbers until I'm standing outside flat 6. The door is patchily painted, blue over white, and is covered in scuff marks. I can clearly see the black outline of an entire sole of a shoe about a third of the way up.

I raise my hand to knock and then freeze mid-air as a screech comes from within, followed by a torrent of abuse and foul language. I step back in alarm as I realize it is Fiona's voice I can hear.

"I won't say anything." Then, calmer, "Please, just leave me alone. I want out."

It takes me a moment to register that there are gaps before the shouts and swears, but no other voice, and that's when I realize she's on a phone call.

CHAPTER SIXTY-FOUR

Judi

Outside Fiona's flat, I shift from one foot to the other, trying to decide what to do.

Should I leave right now, go back home and call again another day? Or wait out here until she quietens down and then try to speak to her?

I glance up and down the corridor, wondering how it will look if one of her neighbors sticks their head out to see me lurking around in the hallway, obviously listening at the door.

But the corridor is empty, and apart from some muffled music coming from inside one of the flats behind me, there's no other sign of life on this side of the corridor.

I step closer to the door and tilt my head a little. I can still hear Fiona's voice, but thankfully she seems to have calmed down somewhat and is actually just speaking loudly now, not screeching or swearing.

I wonder if all her children are home from school, witnessing her outburst. Will they be afraid, or are they used to it? I decide it's very probably the latter. Little Lily who I met on the stairs didn't look like she'd be fazed by such behavior one bit— maybe it's just a way of life to the kids who live round here.

I hold my breath and listen for a few moments. Fiona seems to have stopped speaking now and I can hear only the muted tones of a television.

I knock on the door and wait, unsure of what to say when she opens it. I haven't really thought about it; just that I need to apologize for Henry's behavior the other day and ask how Hank's teething problems are.

There is no response from inside the flat. I wonder if she's afraid to answer the door for some reason. There's no letter box to call through; I passed a vast lattice of tenants' mailboxes downstairs.

I knock again and step closer to the door.

"Fiona?" I call. "It's Judi from the surgery. I just called to see if—"

Suddenly the door flies open inwards and I nearly fall straight into the flat after it.

"What do you want?"

Fiona's face is bloated and tear-stained. She's dressed in just knickers and a vest top with a short silky robe draped over her shoulders, leaving her arms free underneath the fabric. I'm shocked how much skinnier she looks without the benefit of her flimsy clothes.

Behind her I see her daughter, Kylie, eyes wide and clutching little Harrison's hand, his face covered in chocolate.

"I . . . I just came to apologize for my husband's behavior the other day," I say hurriedly. "And to see if Hank's gums have improved any with the teething gel."

Fiona doesn't speak, but stares at me in such a way I find myself literally squirming on the spot. She looks me up and down, and her exhausted expression becomes twisted and sneering.

"Come to gloat, have you?" I open my mouth to respond, but she raises her voice. "I've nothing to say to you; I can't believe I ever trusted you. Now fuck off and don't come here again."

"Mummy?" Kylie sounds tearful, anxious.

Fiona whips round suddenly and the silky robe slips from her shoulders to the floor. I gasp out loud at what is revealed and my hand flies to my mouth.

But before I can utter a word, she steps back and slams the door in my face.

For a moment or two I can't move; I'm rooted to the spot in shock. Then I knock on the door again.

"Fiona! Please, let's talk. You need to speak to someone about what's happening to you."

Silence. I can't even hear the television now.

I knock again. "If not for yourself, then get help for the children's sake."

I wait but there's no response, so I walk down the corridor and stop at the top of the stairwell, holding my breath against the stench of urine that wafts into my face courtesy of an open window.

Reaching into my handbag for my phone, my mind is cloudy with the dilemma of the situation. After what I've just seen, surely I have no choice but to call the police...or perhaps social services. If something happens to Fiona or her children, I'll never be able to forgive myself.

I activate the screen with my fingertip and stare at the brightness, waiting for the right answer to come.

A flutter of panic starts inside me and I suddenly decide I ought to think about it before taking any rash action. I'll go back home and consider the right thing to do. My actions could change Fiona's life; the authorities could take her children away, which will probably finish her off.

There's no doubt that Fiona is a rather poor example to her kids. She isn't a textbook mother or a smiling middle-class poster parent like the ones we display on the surgery notice-board, but after spending a little time with her, there is one thing I can be certain of.

She loves her children, and I happen to know that currently they seem to be all she's got that is good in her life.

Back in the car, I sit for a while looking up at the flats. I know now that Fiona's apartment faces out over the other side, so even if she's looking out of the window, she won't be able to see me down here.

I take my phone out of my handbag and glance at the screen. There's no text from Ben to say how Noah is.

My head feels full of pressure. Just lately, it seems that every way I turn, I hit a brick wall in my life. It feels like I've truly become the invisible woman: nobody hears what I say or sees what I do; my actions appear to have no impact on anyone around me.

A thought crawls into my head and just sort of sits there, tingling at the back of my mind. I've felt the sensation before and just ignored it, but this time I close my eyes and try to get in touch with the feeling it has created inside me.

It's a sort of defiance, the beginnings of a drive to do something. As soon as I put the label on it, I feel the sensation swelling, becoming more powerful.

The old Judi, the one who knew how to make everything better, is still in there somewhere. I can feel her stirring.

I'm sick to death of sitting in the shadows. It feels like high time I did something about all the crap in my life.

CHAPTER SIXTY-FIVE

Judi

I go home to freshen up and somehow manage to kill another couple of hours pottering around, but then I just can't stand it any longer.

I text Ben to say I'm on my way back to the hospital and turn off my phone. I've heard nothing from him all afternoon and I'm going back whether he likes it or not.

When I get there, he looks tired and concerned.

"They still haven't told me when he'll be discharged," he says.

Noah keeps drifting in and out of sleep, and although he looks impossibly pale, he seems comfortable enough.

I bite my tongue when thoughts about discussing my visit to Martha Carr begin to stir in my head. Now is most definitely not the time.

We're both sitting by Noah's bedside in companionable silence when the curtain is pulled back.

"Amber!" Ben looks up and frowns. I can see he's fighting with himself.

Little Josh is with her and I pat my knee. He walks over and climbs up on to my lap. I'm struck by how big he's getting, how tall. He's far from being my baby now.

"I couldn't just sit at home worrying," she simpers to Ben. "I'm so sorry, darling. Please forgive me."

"We can't talk about it here," he says tightly. "To be honest, I can't even begin to get my head around what you did. I've done nothing but turn it over in my mind for the last few hours, and I'm no nearer understanding. I still can't believe you'd leave Noah like that."

"I know." She hangs her head, ever the actress. She hasn't even acknowledged that I'm here. "It was a moment of madness. I was so . . . I don't know . . . so scared that your mum was going to make trouble for me at the center."

"If there's been trouble, you've only made it yourself, Amber," I tell her. "Telling lies is never going to lead to a good outcome."

"I haven't told any lies."

"You told us you were a lead worker when actually you were just a—"

"Can you two just *stop*?" Ben glares at both of us and I seal my mouth. "You're like some of the kids in my class: constantly bickering and trying to get one up on each other. Why can't you just get along?"

I press my lips together, afraid of what might come out if I try to speak. Amber looks at me but obviously thinks better of trying to communicate.

She puts her handbag next to my chair and steps outside the cubicle with Ben. I hear them speaking in low voices. Then Amber comes back inside and smiles at Josh.

"Joshy, your daddy is going for coffees; can you go with him to help?"

Joshy? I frown to myself.

Always helpful, Josh jumps from my knee and runs after Ben. I stand up and fiddle with the bag of fluid on Noah's drip, which seems to have slipped slightly.

"I am really sorry, you know, Judi," Amber says softly when they've gone. "I accept I should never have left Noah alone like that. I just thought he'd be fine for a few minutes. I couldn't work out what you were doing at the center. I mean, why would you go down there, asking questions about me like that?"

"Save it," I reply, sitting down again. "You'll find I'm not such a pushover as my son."

"You're right, I was never a lead support worker at the center," she says, catching me off guard. "I exaggerated a bit about the job, but I'm not a liar. All I wanted to do was to impress you and Henry at our first meeting."

"You can dress it up all you like, but the fact is, you *did* lie, Amber. Your colleague told me you were just a temp from an agency, and as such you couldn't even work unsupervised with the children."

"And what about you?" Her eyes flash. "Haven't *you* ever lied?"

"What?" I'm distracted by the drip again. The tube looks like it might have a kink in it.

"Have you never told a lie before to cover something up or make yourself feel better?"

It's a good attempt to shift the blame, but I see through it immediately. I get up and trace my fingers down the slender tube to make sure it's straight enough for the solution to slip through.

"This isn't about me," I say without turning round. "It's about *you*, Amber and the fact that you left my sick eight-year-old grandson alone in the house."

"All of it is down to that? All the animosity and suspicion you have toward me is down to that one mistake I made today?" She smiles and shakes her head, keeping her eyes on me as I move back to my seat. "I sense you run very deep,

Judi. Like a calm stretch of water with a current beneath the surface strong enough to drag someone under."

I throw my head back and laugh. "Full marks for trying the psychoanalysis angle, Amber, but as usual, you're way off the mark." This unexpectedly honest exchange between us feels both refreshing and troubling, but I'm giving as good as I get.

"No, really," she goes on, narrowing her eyes as she watches me. "What are you so scared of, Judi? Is it because Ben and I will soon be married and there's nothing you can do about it? Isn't it much healthier to just accept that things are changing? That your boys don't need you any-more?"

I stand and pick up my handbag. "I haven't time for this, I need the bathroom. Rather than coming up with far-fetched stories, why don't you try straightening that?" I point to Noah's drip. "The bag keeps slipping and I've tried to do it but can't. All the nurses are so busy."

"I'll have a look." She stands up, suddenly seeming eager to please.

I stand for a moment watching from outside the curtain, and then I pull it closed and approach the ward manager. I speak quietly to her and she walks back to the cubicle with me.

"May I ask what you're doing?" she asks crisply, stepping forward. Amber jumps a mile and spins round.

"Oh! Sorry, I was just trying to adjust the bag. It's slipped, you see." She glances at me and back at the nurse. "Why are you looking at me like that?"

The ward manager doesn't speak but turns on her heel and walks briskly away, her flat shoes clipping the floor.

"What was all that about?" Amber pulls a face.

"I've no idea," I say. "When I went to ask how long before

Noah is discharged, she asked me if you were alone in here with him."

We look at each other in silence.

A few minutes later, Dr. Kareem appears with the ward manager and I hold my breath when I see that Ben and Josh are behind him.

"What's happening here?" Ben says, looking at Amber and then at Noah. "What's wrong? Is Noah OK?"

Josh moves closer to me and I hold him tight with one arm. Amber steps closer to Ben.

Dr. Kareem turns to Ben. "We have reason to believe someone may be purposely harming your son, Mr. Jukes."

"What?" Ben presses a hand to his forehead. "What on earth are you talking about?" He looks warily behind him, back into the ward. "Do you mean another patient has hurt Noah?"

Dr. Kareem coughs. "No, that is not what I mean. As you know, Mr. Jukes, our medical tests so far have proved inconclusive, and yet Noah's mystery condition appears to be getting worse." He looks at Ben and then addresses Amber. "I have to ask you if you have tampered with Noah's intravenous drip in any way."

"What? For God's sake, of course I haven't."

"Then can I ask what you were doing when I came in earlier?" the ward manager demands. "You appeared to be touching the fluid pouch."

"I was just trying to secure the bag!" Amber gasps.

"Why didn't you simply ask a nurse?"

"Because you were all busy—I was actually trying to do you lot a favor." She looks at me. "Tell them, Judi."

"This is madness." Ben's voice rises. "Amber would never do that. I mean, why would anyone do something so awful?"

"To make Noah appear to be ill when he isn't really," I

say faintly. "You also said she'd never leave Noah, but she did."

Ben's eyes open wide and he looks at Amber. "You wouldn't. Tell me you wouldn't do that."

She shakes her head, apparently dumbfounded. She reaches for him, but he pulls his hand away.

"I saw her," I whisper, turning to Ben. "She was messing about with his drip when I came in with the nurse."

"*You!* You asked me to..." Amber is breathless now. The hair around her face looks damp and she gulps in air like a dying fish. She grabs at Ben's shoulders with both hands. "Ben, this is madness. I wouldn't. You know I wouldn't do that!"

Ben looks at Dr. Kareem. "It doesn't make sense, Doctor, this—this accusation. What on earth would Amber gain from doing something so heinous? It's ridiculous."

Amber is silent, her face pale and drawn.

When I pick up her handbag and root inside, she doesn't try to stop me. There is a small bottle in there, filled with liquid. I take it out and hold it in the air so everyone can see it.

"What's that? That isn't mine!" she cries.

Dr. Kareem takes the bottle from me and inspects the label. "Glucose," he says gravely. "The very thing we've found in Noah's urine samples and yet not in his blood sample, which has been taken directly by the nursing staff."

"Someone must've put it in my bag." Amber begins to cry. "Ben, I swear to God it isn't mine."

My son's face is deathly pale and he seems to have shrunk in stature.

"You understand we'll need to inform the police," the ward manager says quietly. "We have a duty of care."

"No!" Amber looks wildly around the room. Her eyes

settle on poor, listless Noah in the bed. "I'd never hurt him like this. I wouldn't."

Ben walks over to stand next to me and I look up at him, unable to speak, my own eyes and heart full of the horror of it all.

CHAPTER SIXTY-SIX

Judi

The next day, Josh is at school, Noah is tucked up safely on my sofa and Maura has been informed that I won't be in work for at least the next few days. Social services have been in touch with Ben and I'm struggling to deal with the way everything has blown up in my face. I decide to immerse myself in housework for the rest of the day.

It might seem odd to some, but I can get lost in the routine of cleaning and household chores. Something about the mechanical actions that I can do on autopilot just takes me out of myself and gives me temporary respite from the constant chatter and worrying of the voice in my head.

I don't know what's happening with Amber and the police. I've left Ben to deal with it and I'm concentrating on caring for my grandsons. Before we left the hospital, the term "Munchausen by proxy" was mentioned several times and Amber descended into a real mess.

I start with the dirty laundry bin in the main bathroom. As I seem to have worn the same things day in, day out lately, the clothes in here are mainly Henry's.

I don't know where he is today. He never leaves a note

and I don't expect him to, but I know from his usual schedule that he probably won't be back until teatime.

I take great handfuls and throw them on the bathroom floor to sort into piles: whites, darks and coloreds. I gather the dark clothes together, and just as I'm straightening up, something catches my eye on the whites pile.

I drop the laundry in my arms and peer more closely at one of the white T-shirts that Henry is fond of wearing under his V-neck woolen pullovers. There's a mark approximately two centimeters long just under the shoulder seam.

I reach for the garment. I sniff the mark, touch it lightly with my fingertip and see that it is a smear of pale pink lipstick. It looks like he's up to his old tricks again.

I'm not stupid; of course I've known there has been no emotional bond between me and Henry for a long time now.

If I'm honest, we drifted apart years ago. It started slowly, almost too slowly to notice, but then I found we were speeding away from being a couple toward becoming separate people again. It's just something we've both got used to.

The difference, I suppose, lies in needs. I no longer feel the need for a sexual connection. Hugs and emotional closeness are what matter to me, and I can get those from my son and grandchildren. At least that's where I used to get them, before Amber appeared on the scene.

Henry is out of the house a lot at his various meetings and social gatherings, and it's never occurred to me to question that. I simply assumed these places were where he satisfied his own friendship needs, but it seems I've been looking the other way for far too long.

I have never stopped even for a moment to consider if Henry is telling me the truth about where he is going when he steps out of the front door.

Yet as I look at the lipstick mark, the long-standing

simmering resentment toward my husband that I've held inside for so long turns into a searing heat that burns like acid in my stomach.

It's a total surprise to me that my feelings for him run so deep.

I honestly thought I no longer cared at all.

I leave the piles of clothes, including the offending shirt, on the bathroom floor and go back downstairs.

I take Noah a tray through. I feel gratified to see he has regained a splash of color in his cheeks.

"I'm not hungry," he croaks when he is properly awake and sees the mashed banana and the slice of toast I've prepared. At the hospital, the doctors suggested some light foods to try him on when he felt up to eating again.

"Just a mouthful," I urge him, but he presses his lips together and looks away.

I'm not going to force him; he's only just feeling a tiny bit better after his worrying relapse yesterday.

"Is Amber kind when she looks after you?" I say tentatively, knowing that really, it's out of order to quiz Noah.

He shrugs but doesn't answer me.

"I bet she does fun things with you two boys, doesn't she?"

"She likes Josh more than me," he says in a small voice.

"Oh, I'm sure she doesn't." I smile at him. "What makes you think that, sweetheart?"

"She reads with him and he never gets into trouble like I do."

"Trouble?"

"She tells me off and sometimes she sends me upstairs to my room."

Something pulls tight inside me.

"Have you told Daddy about this?"

Noah shakes his head.

"Well, maybe you should have a chat with him. Just you and Daddy. What do you think?"

"But he's always with Amber," Noah whispers, his eyes dark. "He's never on his own anymore."

I squeeze his hand and pull the fleecy blanket up to his chin.

"You rest a little now," I say soothingly. "Perhaps you might have a bite to eat when you wake up again."

I can't think of anything else to say to comfort my grandson.

My scalp is crawling and I feel like screaming.

By late afternoon, Henry is skulking around the house and trying to cheer Noah up with his silly jokes.

I realize the lipstick mark on Henry's T-shirt has completely slipped my mind amid all the drama of Noah's illness. The whole hospital-recovery thing has swallowed me up, just like it did when David was small.

The fact that I'm right in the middle of it all, keeping it together for Ben's sake...for the boys' sake...that takes importance over everything else.

Everyone needs someone to trust, which gets me thinking about Fiona again, and my unresolved visit to her flat.

"Would you mind just holding the fort here while I pop out?" I say to Henry. "I could do with some milk and bread, just bits we're out of."

"Hmm?" He looks briefly at me before his eyes drift back to the TV. "Yes, that's fine."

I collect my handbag from the kitchen and grab my car keys. "Won't be long," I call from the doorway.

He doesn't answer and I'm reminded of how ignorantly he behaved when Fiona visited the house.

I was on the brink of ringing the police about the awful bruising I saw on Fiona's upper arms and back when her robe slipped from her shoulders.

Angry purple and blue contusions, bunched like exploding storm clouds all over her pale skin. Who is abusing her? Are the kids safe? I shake my head, saddened that in the midst of my own family drama, I've forgotten this young woman's plight so easily.

CHAPTER SIXTY-SEVEN

Judi

I park up outside the flats and discover the lifts are still out of order.

I puff and pant up to the eighth floor and listen at Fiona's door. I can hear the television and the voices of children but no screaming and shouting like before, thank goodness. I knock.

"Who is it?" a muffled voice calls from within.

"It's Judi, from the surgery," I call back.

I hear a bolt slide back and the key turns in the door.

"Why are you here again?"

She looks awful. Thinner than ever, with heavy dark circles under her eyes. Her blond hair looks darker, scraped back and greasy, but she's dressed in leggings and a long-sleeved T-shirt so thankfully I can't see the dreadful marks that I know mar her body.

"I just came to see how you are," I say.

She laughs and holds her arms out from her sides. "So look. This is how I am." She steps back to let me into the flat. "As you can see, I'm pretty shit."

"And I really did want to say sorry about how my husband treated you."

She looks at me for a long moment and then says simply, "I don't want to talk about it."

I step inside on to a square of floorboards far too tiny to refer to as a hallway. She leads me into a small, cool room where I can immediately smell damp. It is filled with noise from the television, and clutter; piles of stuff—mainly clothes as far as I can see—lean against the walls. An illuminated bare lightbulb hangs from the ceiling and the matted carpet sticks to the soles of my shoes.

"It's a mess." She sweeps her arm unapologetically around the room. "We basically live in here; it's warmer than the other rooms. Sometimes we all sleep in here too."

Hank sits on a ripped fleecy blanket on the floor. I'm seized by a compulsion to whisk him away, out of this hole.

When he spots me, he grins and bounces on his bottom.

"Someone's pleased to see you," Fiona says, looking forlornly at her son and turning down the volume on the TV. "He doesn't know what's happening."

"Hello, little man." I smile and move toward him. "Can I?" I ask before picking him up.

"Feel free. You usually do." Fiona sits down and picks up a magazine, seeming already to have lost interest in my visit, but I can tell she's not reading it, just flicking through the pages.

I talk to Hank, sing him a nursery rhyme, tweak his cold, ruddy cheeks. His nappy smells and feels full, but he blossoms like a flower with my attention; he smiles, laughs, squeals. It's wonderful to see.

"Fiona," I say, and she looks up from her magazine. "Who's hurting you?"

She shakes her head, lets out a bitter laugh and stares at the small bare window that's dripping with condensation.

"Is this person hurting the children, too?"

"No way!" She closes the magazine and glares at me. "I'd never let anyone hurt my kids."

"You need medical attention." There's nothing her GP can do about bruising, but I dread to think what might be hurting her inside where no one can see. Not that I can own up to knowing she's already sought advice for internal injuries.

"I'm going down the surgery in the morning."

I think about how Maura's jaw will drop when she reads Fiona's notes afterward, and I'm glad I won't be there to witness it.

"I nearly rang the police," I confess. "When I saw your injuries."

"Well, you've no right; it's got sod-all to do with you," she snaps, her face coloring. "Stop trying to interfere in my life, will you? You'll wish you hadn't, trust me."

Was that a threat? I ignore it.

"The police would help you. Protect you."

She looks at me, shaking her head slowly. "What planet are you on? You're so far removed from real life you can't see what's happening even when it's right under your nose, you silly cow. If I go to the police, they'll laugh in my face."

"I don't understand." I sigh, tired of her casual insults. "Nobody is going to laugh if you report what's happened to you, that you were attacked."

"Nobody attacked me, you daft bitch. I let someone do this to me. For money. Understand?"

I look at her, not understanding at all.

"There's a whole different world out there that you've never seen. You don't even know it exists."

"What world are you talking about?"

"The world where men pay you for sex. Get it now?" She stuffs her tongue under her lower lip to emphasize my stupidity.

There's only one way to get those kinds of injuries. The dirty cow. Maura's words bounce back at me.

"That's silenced you, hasn't it?" She gives a mirthless laugh. "Don't look so shocked. You'd be amazed what people will pay for. The kind of people who pay for it, too. That would definitely surprise you."

"Where do you...?" I struggle to find polite words. "I mean, do you bring them here?"

"What do you take me for?" Her face darkens. "I'd never let my kids see stuff like that. I'd never bring men back here." She gets up and stalks out of the room.

This is intense stuff and I'm way out of my comfort zone when it comes to giving advice on such matters.

My phone beeps in my bag. I reach around Hank and pick it up. It's a text from Ben.

I'm at yours. Noah woke up asking for apple juice. Could you pick him some up pls? x

I smile. This is a sign that Noah is feeling better; he loves his apple juice.

"I think you ought to go," Fiona says flatly from the doorway. "This isn't your world, Mrs. Jukes."

"Judi," I correct her, wriggling my little finger free of Hank's sticky fist. I stand up and place him back down on his blanket, then turn to face Fiona. "You're right. This is not a world I understand, but that's not to say I can't fix it, make things better for you."

"Eh?"

"How much do they pay you, these men?" I look at her and she shakes her head slowly, as if I've spoken in a foreign language.

I widen my eyes in anticipation of her reply, but she stays quiet.

"It's a simple enough question, Fiona. How much do they pay you to hurt you? For sex?"

"I'm not having this conversation," she says.

"Why not? It's a simple enough question. Is it twenty, fifty—"

"Twenty quid for full sex, ten for a blow job," she says. "Satisfied now?"

These were the sums that would buy the body of this young mother of three. The amount that someone, somewhere had deemed to be a fair price.

"I'll pay you," I say quietly. "I'll give you what you need so you don't have to do this anymore."

"Have you lost your mind?"

"No," I say, looking over at little Hank. "But you might have, if you're thinking of turning my offer down."

"Why?" She whispers the word and her eyes glitter. "Why would you do that for us?"

"Because I can make a difference," I say, taking out a wad of twenty-pound notes that I drew out using the debit card I'd found by Henry's side of the bed. I hold them out to her. "If you let me, I'll help you all I can."

"Judi, I think you're the one who needs to get some help," she says. "You need to look at what's happening closer to home."

"What?"

"Your husband. He's one of those men you're talking about. Not with me, thank God, but I saw him once, with my friend . . . That's why he looked so shocked and angry at your house. That's why he wanted me out of the way."

Henry's face . . . his fury . . . the awful things he said about Fiona. The lipstick mark on his T-shirt.

I walk over and pick up Hank again, hold him to me, feel his comforting warmth, his neediness.

"I still want to help you," I say. "I'll give you money, anything you need."

Fiona walks over and takes Hank from my arms.

"I know you mean well, Judi," she says with a sad smile. "But my baby, he isn't for sale."

CHAPTER SIXTY-EIGHT

Judi

I open my eyes and Maura is there. I try to raise my head from the softness behind it, but it feels like a lead ball sitting on my shoulders.

"It's OK, you're at home," she soothes. "You took some sedatives; you've been asleep for a few hours. Henry was worried."

I vaguely remember being back home, screaming at Henry that I knew what he'd been up to, throwing things at him that smashed against the wall. And then, upstairs, I reached to the back of the drawer for the tablets that Dr. Fern prescribed.

My mouth feels as if it's grown a layer of fur on the inside.

Then the terrible reality drifts into my mind from the midst of a numbing fog. Noah ill, Fiona rejecting my help . . . Henry sleeping with prostitutes.

A tear traces down my cheek and clings to my jaw before falling.

"Everything's going to be OK, Judi," Maura says gently. "Henry is staying away for a few days and you're going to Ben's house. To be with him and the boys."

"Thank you," I whisper. "And Amber?" Her face is imprinted on my mind like a hateful tattoo.

"No one's heard from her," Maura says grimly. "Looks like she's off the scene, for now."

It's like music to my ears.

CHAPTER SIXTY-NINE

Judi

The next day, Ben drops me back at the house to collect a few things before I go to stay with him for the weekend.

I'm in the kitchen, packing up a few bits of the boys' favorite food to take, when I hear a noise in the hallway. I move to the kitchen door and stagger back a step when I see Amber standing there.

"What are you doing here? How did you get in?"

She holds a key up and wiggles it. "I've had it for ages."

I walk backward into the kitchen and she strides toward me, stopping in the doorway.

"They let me off, you know. Did you hear?"

I say nothing.

"Not enough evidence, you see. Despite your best efforts: your lies and the glucose you planted in my handbag."

I turn away from her and begin loading Tupperware boxes into a carrier bag.

"You won," she says.

"What?"

"You won, Judi. We hate each other. I wanted to do you in and you wanted to do me in. And I suppose, in a way, we've both lost the game, but you win really because I'm leaving Nottingham today."

My heart leaps inside, but I stay poker-faced.

"You can have Ben and you can have your precious boys—on one condition."

I look at her.

"Tell me why. Just this one time, let's leave the crap behind and speak honestly."

I shrug. It's like a dare; I feel strangely amused by it. But I remain cautious.

"Look!" She turns out the pockets of her coat. "I'm not recording it or anything, if that's what you're worried about. And I admit, I didn't really want Ben, Noah and Josh. I did it because I wanted to hurt you. But we'll come to that later."

She shows me her phone and lays it on the side so I can see the screen isn't activated.

"You were the one who skewed Noah's test results, right?"

I look at her and swallow.

"I know it was you. What I don't know is why. Why did you do it when it could have harmed him?"

I tune her voice out and I'm back there for a moment. All those years, melting away like ice.

It started by accident, the first time, when David was just a baby. I was used to being ignored by my husband and feeling so tired I could faint, but then when David fell ill, suddenly I was treated with respect and with love by Henry.

So long ago. All that love and concern in his eyes.

The hospital staff couldn't do enough for me. Nobody likes to see a mother suffering along with her child; there is something in us as human beings that reaches out and tries to make it better.

"You look drugged up," Amber snaps. "Out of it."

I ignore her.

They operated on David and found the cause of his food reflux. From that point, he began to get better immediately. He kept his food down and began to thrive, and as he improved, the good feeling toward me changed. People stopped trying; Henry began staying out late again.

"I know it was you, Judi. Just tell me. Why did you do it? Make your own grandson ill like that?"

I found out that my little finger, pushed to the back of David's throat, brought his feed up beautifully again, just the same as before he'd had the op. I became very practiced at the maneuver—I told myself I wasn't really hurting him; he didn't even cry. Just in and out and up the milk would come. A doctor or nurse turning their back for a second or two was enough for me to have it happen virtually right in front of them.

It felt as if I was back in the sunshine for a while. Everyone fussing and worrying over David and me. All sorts of tests had to be done, we stayed over in hospital, and still they could find nothing.

Things somehow improved between Henry and me, and a few months later I fell pregnant with Ben and just sort of stopped doing it. David got better, and for a long time, everything was OK.

I sit down heavily on the kitchen chair as tears roll silently down my cheeks.

CHAPTER SEVENTY

Judi

"Judi. Judi!" Amber is shaking me. "For God's sake, what's wrong with you?"

She's swimming in front of my eyes, fading in and out of focus.

"I know your mother is alive," I whisper.

Her face pales. "My mother is dead."

"I saw her, Amber. I know about your family, your husband and children."

She slaps my face and I gasp, sitting up straighter. Suddenly everything is harsh and real again. "Don't say anything else. Don't you dare."

"Your sister . . . she died, too. Everyone dies around you."

"Same with you," she sneers, pressing her face so close I can smell stale coffee on her breath. "David died. After he met the girl at the cottage all those years ago, that is."

"How do you know about that?"

"Just tell me." She shrugs. "What happened?"

I hear myself start to speak. The words feel strange rolling over my tongue. They've wanted to be said for so long, and every time I've swallowed them down like sour clots of milk. Now, I can't seem to stop them.

"He was only fourteen years old and yet he became besotted with that girl. It was very odd." I look away from Amber's staring eyes and I'm back there. "A gangly, freckly thing she was, not at all pretty, in my opinion. Unflattering red hair and a bit of a tomboy. Playing football with the boys, climbing trees and scrabbling around in the dust with David, looking for stones on the clifftop, on the beach."

I glance back at her and see her eyes are burning with malevolence. I don't care. There's nothing she can do to hurt me now.

"Think what you like, but it wasn't what I had envisaged for my son. He started neglecting his studies, even his piano lessons. All he wanted to do was sit by the telephone talking to her each night, and then badger us senseless to go to the cottage far more frequently than we'd have ordinarily done."

Amber is quiet.

I stop talking and think back. Back to when we were at the cottage during spring bank holiday week in May. David wasn't interested in taking part in our family games on the beach, walks along the cliff or our shell-finding missions. His personality was changing. He began cheeking me back and making fun of me with his father. All the times I'd defended him against Henry's brutal punishments and it counted for nothing.

The girl was hateful. She laughed openly when I demanded David be back at a certain time or take part in a family activity. She started calling me a derogatory name behind my back. I heard her once or twice and ignored it. "The Moaning Mother," she'd say, which caught on immediately with both David and Ben, and then even Henry adopted it if I was in the least bit grouchy.

But it was David who hurt me the most. He was turning against me and I had to do something. I really had no choice in the matter.

CHAPTER
SEVENTY-ONE

Twenty-six years earlier

David

As soon as he opened his eyes, David knew that something bad had happened. Something very bad.

The darkness was so thick and heavy around him that for a moment he wasn't sure if his eyes were fully open yet, or if he had simply imagined it.

There was a strong, grazing ache in his legs and pelvis. Deep inside the bone.

An audio flashback echoed in his ears: people shouting, a girl screaming, rocks tumbling, a snapping sound, then... silence.

The ache in his legs spread, grew rapidly into a painful throbbing throughout the whole of his body. He tried to move his hand but nothing happened.

The darkness lay more heavily on his face, pressing him down into another place.

When hc opened his eyes again, it was light.

The gray clouds scudded across the sky overhead, masking

any trace of blue. David shivered and tried to move his head, grimacing against the shooting pains in his shoulder and neck.

He managed to turn it enough for his view to change. He gazed past the broken shape next to him, over toward Boulby Cliffs, where the Dinosaur Coast sat impassively, hard and cold and unmoved by his whimpering.

He squinted against the freezing wind that fanned hair on to his face.

And then he looked at her.

Long russet hair fanned across the slough of broken rocks, a couple of wisps caught in his own fingers. Her face was turned away from him. He knew her but he could not remember her name, nor why the two of them were here together.

She wore shorts, and her pale limbs lay splayed at unnatural angles.

He managed to make a strange noise in his throat. But she did not move.

A sound above him brought his eyes back to Cowbar Cliff, towering above. A figure stood halfway up, on a ledge. He saw slight movement and heard a sob, but he could not make out any useful details.

He put all his effort into raising a hand, but managed only a finger, lifted briefly from the fossil bed beneath him.

The figure shifted again, and a bundle of small rocks tumbled from the ledge, bouncing and rolling to a stop just a few feet away from where he lay.

David's throat gurgled. He was struggling to take in air.

He drifted in and out of consciousness. When he opened his eyes again, the figure was standing next to him. A blurred outline. A scuffling sound near his face.

The gulls screeched above the cliff and the rush of the sea answered them.

A hand and then a dark mass hovered above his face, descended quickly toward him; a soft stroke on his cheeks.

The sensation started to fade until he was only vaguely aware of the tears that fell on him from above.

As he took his last breath, he thought about the smooth stones in his trouser pocket, and his mother's face.

CHAPTER SEVENTY-TWO

Present day

Judi

"You killed them. The girl and your own son, the son you supposedly worshipped." Amber hesitates a second before speaking. "You pushed them off Cowbar Cliff. Both of them."

I shake my head vehemently. I pushed *her* off the cliff. But even in death she couldn't let him be. She grabbed him as she fell. She took my David with her.

My eyes fill up and Amber blurs in front of me. I see her move, hear a clatter and her snatching at something. I step forward and see that she is holding a knife from the block, the ones Henry keeps freshly sharpened.

"Judi, you framed me. You need to tell them it was a mistake, what you said about me hurting Noah. You need to tell them that you planted the bottle in my handbag."

"Why would I do that?" I laugh. "You could have made a friend of me, like dear Louise did before you. I just wanted to be part of my son's and grandsons' lives, that's all. Why couldn't you handle that?"

"You still don't get it." She shakes her head. "You've told

me the whole story and still it hasn't clicked, you're so wrapped up in your own problems."

I frown at her, trying to put the pieces together.

"I'll tell you my story now," she says. "Once upon a time there was a beautiful thirteen-year-old girl called Kathryn. She lived near the coast in a static caravan with her mum and sister. Their bastard father had long gone."

At last, too late, it seems I'm finally going to get the story of her family.

"The girls used to roam the beach and cliffs and one day Kathryn met a boy from Nottingham called David."

My face falls and she assumes an expression of satisfaction.

"No," I whisper.

"Yes," she hisses. "I found Kathryn's diary. All those years it lay in a storage box of her things that my mother never looked at. I found it three years ago when she went into the care home and the house was sold."

"You went in David's bedroom. I wasn't imagining it after all."

"I searched it. Trying to find something, anything he might've kept, notes he'd written to my sister."

"You took the necklace and then put it back, all to make me look like a crazy woman."

She frowns and laughs. "What are you talking about? You really *are* crazy."

"Don't bother trying to deny it, I know it was you. It could only have been you."

She waves my words away as if she's losing patience.

"For three years I've been planning how I could make you pay. Three long years. I couldn't go to the police because it wasn't evidence as such, but I knew my sister. I could read between the lines that she was afraid of what you'd do."

"Is that why you want to destroy this family? To get back at me?"

Amber shakes her head. "I came here because I wanted to hurt you, to make you pay. I wanted you to feel the same loss that's caused when someone else takes away the people you love. I don't deny that. I came looking for you and it took me a while to find you, but when I realized the situation—that Ben was now a widower with two small boys—it was like a gift. Everything fitted together so perfectly, I knew it was fate, that I'd have my family back again."

"Your family died, Amber...Ben, Noah, Josh—they're not your family to take."

As I stare at her, trying to weigh up just how crazy she is, her eyes cloud over and she smiles, as if she is watching a movie in her head.

CHAPTER SEVENTY-THREE

Six years earlier

Amber

The leaves are damp and cloying, like a mat of slime beneath her bare feet. The wind nips through her nightdress and it feels like a thousand screeching seagulls, each one pecking off a piece of her until she is swallowed and ceases to exist.

Still she runs, and when her ragged breaths can finally keep up no longer, she falls against the craggy tree trunk, sliding to her haunches and whimpering like a child.

"Amber. Amber?" The voice is kind and it rouses her from the edge of the abyss.

She opens her eyes and sees that it is Dr. Stevens.

"Let's get you back inside."

There are other people helping her up, but she keeps her bleary eyes on the doctor, for it is only she who truly understands.

Later, Dr. Stevens comes to her room. Amber takes the small white paper cup full of tablets and swallows them down with water.

"Why did you run?" the doctor says gently.

"The pictures," Amber whispers. "I was running from the pictures in my head."

"We talked about this. You can't run from the pictures; they just come with you."

"I know."

"Tell me about the pictures. Describe them exactly as you see them."

Amber closes her eyes and they flood her mind.

The twisted metal, the uniforms and bright lights. So much red. Everywhere. Like little Daisi's finger paints: thick red on the steel-gray asphalt.

"She was folded up like a rag doll under the front seat," she tells Dr. Stevens, smiling. "She always loved rag dolls, their floppy limbs, their tangled hair."

Tom's shoe in the road, just sitting there neatly, as if waiting for him to slip his little foot into it.

And Robbie. Her husband Robbie's head cracked like an egg over the steering wheel. He never wore his seat belt.

"And you drove past the accident on your way home?"

"I saw the registration plate. The car was unrecognizable, a twisted mess." Amber lies back on the white-sheeted bed in her clean white nightdress and stares at the ceiling. "I got out of my car and ran toward it. I broke through the cordon. I got to Robbie before they could stop me. I held him in my arms. I could smell his sandalwood aftershave mixed in with the smell of the blood."

She raises her hands, staring in horror at the blood and brains that remain there even though she washes herself a hundred times each day.

"One day the pictures will fade," Dr. Stevens tells her kindly. "And one day your hands will be clean again. Is that what you believe?"

Amber turns her head and smiles.

"I believe that one day I'll have my family back again."

CHAPTER SEVENTY-FOUR

Present day

Judi

Amber blinks and looks at me. She's still smiling, and I find it unnerving.

"You said your sister kept a diary." I glance at her handbag, wondering if she might have it with her. Evidence against me. "What did it say?"

"She talked about you and how you hated her. How she heard you telling Henry you wished she'd drop dead. In the later entries she talked about running away with David."

My face paled.

"You knew that," she said bluntly.

"I didn't know it exactly, but I knew she was poisoning my son. I used to listen when he sat on the stairs on the phone to her. I could only hear half of the conversation, but I could guess from his answers what she was saying to him."

"She said that the way you looked at her scared her."

"She used to call me vile names. She wasn't afraid of me."

"Kathryn lashed out when she was afraid. That's all it was." She smiles slowly and stares into space, remembering. "Kathryn had another boy too, you know. When David went home, there was a local boy called Archie she knocked around with."

Another boy?

"She would've grown out of the infatuation with David if only you'd given it time, instead of trying to control their lives. They were just kids, for God's sake." Amber's face twists. "You've never learned; you're just the same now with Ben and the boys. You're flawed."

"Shut up," I say quietly. "Just go. Leave my boys alone."

"You're forgetting, we're getting married. When I'm legally the boys' stepmother, I can stop you seeing them altogether. And when Ben hears what I have to tell him, he won't want you anywhere near them."

"He won't believe you above me."

"Really? He thinks you're overbearing. With him, with the boys. Even with the house furnishings, he's hated the control you've exerted."

It feels like something is lodged in my throat. A choking sensation.

"I have rights. I'm their grandmother," I say, coughing.

"You've no rights. Zero." She laughs. "When the chips are down, grandparents have no legal rights at all. Look it up."

I move toward her and she waves the knife at me.

"I'm not afraid to use it."

I lean against the side of the worktop and squeeze my eyes shut as she speaks.

"We had a document drawn up at the solicitor's," she says slowly. "It was my suggestion, but Ben was in full agreement. It gives me custody of both boys in the event that something happens to Ben."

"No!" My eyes spring open.

"I'm sorry to tell you it's true," she says, smiling. "The

boys will be mine. *Mine!* How does it feel to have your own flesh and blood taken away like you took Kathryn from us? I lost my entire family. You killed Kathryn, and a terrible accident robbed me of happiness with my husband and children."

She looks around the kitchen, gripping the knife in one hand and reaching for her phone with the other. In the split second that she looks down, I slide the largest, sharpest knife from the block.

She springs back and we face each other.

"Don't," she warns. "Don't do this, because you'll come off worse, I can guarantee it."

At that second her phone rings and she makes the fateful decision to glance at it. I take a stride forward and the knife slides into her torso like it's made of butter. I pull it out and she stands stock-still with a shocked expression, her mouth the perfect O shape.

She looks down at the red flower blooming on her blouse, and then she falls.

I hear the crack of her head on the floor tiles as she lands, and she lies there, very still.

CHAPTER SEVENTY-FIVE

Judi

I stand very still, holding the knife. My fingers press into the moist, sticky mess that covers the handle and thins to a trickle down my wrist.

The house is quiet and still, as if it's holding its breath. I can hear the ticking of the wall clock and a low rumble now and then as a large vehicle passes by on the road outside.

I stare down at Amber, crumpled on the floor before me. We have despised each other for so long, and toward the end there have been times when I simply could not bear to look at her. Now, I cannot tear her eyes away. I'm transfixed by the blossoming ruby-red halo that seeps from her head.

It couldn't continue, this silent war between us. One of us had to go.

I feel calmer inside, calmer than I have felt for a long, long time. How I have hated this woman. Hated her for so long, and yet now...now, I feel nothing.

The terrible things she forced me to do...Strips of raw chicken in Noah's Sunday lunch, which gave the poor mite food poisoning. Using Henry's medication and injecting him with insulin when she left him alone, sending him into a crashing hypo...contaminating his urine with glucose...I had to do all this to keep my boy safe from *her*.

Amber's eyes are closed, but there is still slight movement in her chest. Every few seconds there is a quick, desperate pulsing underneath the thin fabric of her soaked red breast. A blouse that used to be pure white.

Who killed Cock Robin?
I, said the Sparrow,
With my bow and arrow.
I killed Cock Robin.

I whisper the words of the nursery rhyme and smile as I remember how it was one of my own favorites as a child. The boys have a book at home with the rhyme in it, and sometimes I read it to little Josh.

My boys.

How happy they'll be that finally they are mine alone.

The one thing I have always been certain of is that the boys will be mine.

Alive or dead, they're always mine.

David, Ben, Noah and Josh. Nobody can ever take them away from me again.

A LETTER FROM
K. L. SLATER

Thank you so much for reading *Liar*, my third psychological thriller.

Readers often ask how I get my plot ideas, and I guess it all tends to start with something that piques my interest. That's what happened with *Liar*.

I've long been fascinated by the mother-in-law–daughter-in-law relationship. It's one that can be very rewarding; close and mutually supportive. But sometimes the connection can be fraught with negative emotions that bubble and simmer just under the surface—a power struggle that is often unseen and unnoticed by other family members.

Take a mother who can see no wrong in her darling son, add in a couple of perfect grandchildren and blend with a feisty young woman who is determined to run the show without interference . . . and suddenly you've got a whole load of trouble!

Most people fall into an amicable middle ground, of course, but *they* are not the relationships that interest me! I am attracted by the suspicion, the festering resentment and the point-scoring that can literally become a dangerous obsession.

The idea for *Liar* first began when I came across an article about estranged grandparents and the shameful fact that legally they have no rights in the UK to see their grandchildren. In researching further, I was shocked to find so many online groups and forums offering vital support and advice to heartbroken grandparents who are blocked, for one reason or another, from seeing their own grandchildren.

I thought about how my daughter, now a young woman, was very close to her granny as a child and enjoyed a special bond and the wonderful enrichment that most grandparents so selflessly give.

Then the usual thing happened for me: the psych thriller switch got flipped in my head and I began to wonder...if a new partner of an adult son or daughter entered a close family situation and all was not well, what lengths might a devoted grandparent go to protect her family? And how much power could a conniving and convincing stranger wield against her if she so wished?

We all know the difference between right and wrong, but when strong emotions come into play, would we be more concerned with our morals and integrity...or might our only priority be keeping our loved ones safe from a perceived threat?

In this book, I also took the opportunity of exploring the menopause through Judi's character, shining a spotlight on how women often suffer in silence and can feel embarrassed or even ashamed to ask for help in coping with this perfectly natural phase in life. Put up and shut up? I don't think so... Let's talk about it, girls!

The book is set in Nottinghamshire, where I was born and have lived all my life. Local readers should be aware that I sometimes take the liberty of changing street names or geographical details to suit the story.

Reviews are so massively important to authors. If you've enjoyed *Liar* and could spare just a few minutes to write a short review to say so, I would really appreciate that.

You can also connect with me via my website, on Facebook, Goodreads or Twitter. Please do sign up to my email list below to be sure of getting the very latest news, hot off the press!

www.bookouture.com/kl-slater

And just when I thought I had a short respite from the voices of wicked, scheming characters in my head after finishing *Liar*, a whole new cast has now arrived—not long to wait for my fourth psychological thriller!

Best wishes,
Kim x

ACKNOWLEDGMENTS

I am fortunate to have so many supportive and talented people around me.

Huge thanks must go to Jenny Geras at Bookouture, who came up with the fabulous title for this book and who has worked tirelessly with me on editing *Liar*, offering such useful suggestions and advice throughout. Also thanks to Lydia Vassar-Smith, who contributed to early ideas on the book before heading off on her maternity leave. Now the book has arrived and so has Lydia's beautiful new baby daughter, Mary, a sister to the gorgeous little Violet!

Thanks to ALL the Bookouture team for everything they do, especially to Lauren Finger and to Kim Nash, who is always there to support authors any time of the day and who, I am certain, must never sleep!

Thanks to my writing buddy, Angela Marsons. We've shared the ups and downs of our writing journeys from the very beginning and held hands on the crazy writing roller coaster...and now we share the same fabulous publisher!

Thanks, as always, to my agent, Camilla Bolton, who continues to give valuable support and advice in my writing career. Thanks also to the rest of the hard-working team at Darley Anderson Literary, TV and Film Agency, especially Mary Darby and Emma Winter, who work so hard to get my books out into the big wide world, and of course Kristina Egan and Rosanna Bellingham.

Massive thanks as always go to my husband, Mac, for his love and support and for taking care of everything so I have the time to write. To my family, especially my daughter, Francesca, and Mama, who are always there to support and encourage me in my writing. To Dad, who always asks how things are going.

Special thanks must also go to Henry Steadman, who has designed the most fantastic cover for *Liar*, which I loved on first sight!

Thank you to the bloggers and reviewers who have done so much to help make my first two thrillers a success. Thank you to everyone who has taken the time to post a positive review online or taken part in my blog tour. It is always noticed and much appreciated.

Last but not least, thank you SO much to my wonderful readers. I love receiving all the wonderful comments and messages, and I am truly grateful for the support of each and every one of you.

Three years ago, Toni's five-year-old daughter Evie disappeared after leaving school. The police have never been able to find her. There were no witnesses, no CCTV, no trace.
But Toni believes her daughter is alive.
She must find her.

Please turn the page for an
excerpt from *Blink*.
Available now.

CHAPTER 1

Present Day

Queen's Medical Centre, Nottingham

Tick tock, tick tock, goes the clock.

It sits neatly on the wall, just at the periphery of my vision.

At the other side of my bed there is a pool of light, a window. I can detect a soft, muted mass there. I think it might be the color green. It brushes gently against the glass, whispering, when everything else in this small, white room is still and silent.

There are voices, footsteps. I hear them just outside the door.

The two doctors step inside the room and I strain to catch their movements, a blur of white. They come every day at about this time, when the light is a little softer. This is how I know it is the afternoon.

My heart pulses faster. Will this be the time they notice I am still here behind the invisible, soundproof partition that now separates me from the real world?

To them, I am in a *vegetative state*, lying on the narrow bed, eyes wide open, frozen. Still as a corpse.

But inside my head I am standing tall, hammering my splayed fingers and flat palms against the nonexistent glass. Screaming to be let out.

Look at me, I yell. *Look at me!*

But they hardly ever do. Look at me, that is. They talk about me, observe me from a distance, but they don't touch me or look me in the eyes.

If they did, a doctor or a nurse might see the slightest flicker of an eyelash, an almost imperceptible tremor of a finger. Dear God, even the cleaner might spot a spark of life if she'd only *look* at me occasionally.

"It's the cruelest thing," the female doctor says softly, taking a step closer to my bed. "That she still looks so alive, I mean."

I am alive, I scream. *I AM alive.*

I summon every ounce of effort and determination I have in me and send it to the hand that lies motionless on top of the pale blue blanket. My left hand. The hand they can see because it is right in front of their unobservant faces.

All I have to do is move a finger, shift my palm. A millimeter of movement, a mere twitch would be enough. If they could only spot it.

Anything that can tell them I am very much still here. Frozen solid, but very much alive. A prisoner, buried inside my own flesh.

"There's nothing left of her. She's just a shell," the male doctor states quietly. "It's been that way since the day she had the stroke."

"I don't envy you," the woman sighs. "You'll have to speak to the family soon."

"There is no family," he replies. "We don't know who she is yet."

The door opens again, and then closes.

The footsteps walk away and the room falls quiet.

Now the only sound that fills the room is the raspy sigh of the ventilator that is keeping me alive. And in between each raspy sigh, there is silence.

I can't breathe without one machine. I can't swallow without another.

Breathe, I tell myself. *This can't be real. It can't be happening.*

But it is. It is happening.

And it's very, very real.

What I can still do is think. And I can remember. Somehow, I can remember the past with a clarity I didn't possess before.

Yet I know instinctively that if I remember too much, too soon, the pain will be too intense and I will close down completely. And then what will happen to my beautiful girl?

Everyone gave up on Evie some time ago. The official police line is that it continues to be an open case and any new information will be investigated, but I know they're not actively pursuing new leads, because they haven't got any.

No evidence, no sightings. Nothing.

For months after it happened, I slavishly read all of the comments people posted underneath the online news reports. They talked as if they had personal knowledge about Evie's "terrible, neglectful mother" and her "unhappy home."

Others openly discussed how Evie could possibly just disappear like that. Everyone an expert.

European pedophile rings, a child serial killer, Romany travelers passing through—all those terrible theories of how and why Evie had gone. I'd heard them all.

Eventually, and without exception, they all wrote Evie off.

Not me. I have chosen to believe that Evie is still alive, that somewhere out there, she is living and breathing. I have to hold on to that.

That's why I must not panic. Even though I cannot move a

muscle or utter a sound, there has to be a way for me to help them find her, save her, while I can still remember everything so clearly.

There is only one thing for it: I must think back, right to the very beginning.

Way back, to before it even happened.

ABOUT K.L. SLATER

For many years, Kim Slater sent her work out to literary agents and collected an impressive stack of rejection slips. At the age of forty, she went back to Nottingham Trent University and now has an MA in creative writing.

Before graduating in 2012, she received five offers of representation from London literary agents and a book deal which was, as Kim says, "a fairy tale...at the end of a very long road!"

Kim is a full-time writer, has one grown-up daughter, Francesca, and lives in Nottingham with her husband, Mac.

She also writes award-winning YA fiction for Macmillan Children's Books, writing as Kim Slater.

Learn more at:

www.KLSlaterAuthor.com
Twitter: @KimLSlater
Facebook: KL Slater Author